BLOODY JOE'S LAST DANCE

BLOODY JOE'S LAST DANCE

BLOODY JOE MANNION BOOK NINE

PETER BRANDVOLD

WOLFPACK PUBLISHING
— EST 2013 —

Bloody Joe's Last Dance
Paperback Edition
Copyright © 2024 Peter Brandvold

Wolfpack Publishing
701 S. Howard Ave. 106-324
Tampa, Florida 33609

wolfpackpublishing.com

Paperback ISBN 978-1-63977-377-0
Large Print Hardcover ISBN 978-1-63977-378-7
eBook ISBN 978-1-63977-376-3

BLOODY JOE'S LAST DANCE

CHAPTER 1

QUENTIN CAMPBELL GENTLY RAN HIS THUMB AND index finger over a clump of purple chokecherries and heard the soft, satisfying thuds of the small berries dropping into his tin pail.

Raw, the berries were bitter to the taste, but Ma would sugar them up and cook them until she had several jars' worth of the sweet, tangy elixir that tasted like nothing so much as the long, hot, dog days of summer itself with the prospect of the cool autumn ahead with its vibrant colors. It was the best topping for steaming hot pancakes God—with Ma's help, of course—ever created.

Beyond the screen of shrubs, a mule's bray cut through the afternoon's bucolic silence tempered by only a few birds piping in the cottonwoods and the rustling of the breeze fluttering the leaves in the chokecherry thicket and the sun-cured brown grass growing nearly up to twelve-year-old Quentin's knees clad in patched, faded blue overalls.

"Easy, Titan," Quentin called to his mule. "I have to fill one more bucket an' then we'll go home, and you'll have your oats an' plenty of water. Ma wants two full buckets, an' that's what she's gonna get, though I will admit that while I don't cotton overmuch to most chores, this one ain't half bad since I know how it's gonna end later tonight."

He chuckled as he deftly, gently nudged another diamond-shaped clump of berries off another thin stem, and they dropped into the bucket with a tinny rattle. He imagined the fresh, warm syrup poured over fresh whipped cream for dessert after tonight's supper of Ma's pot roast and all the sides, including garden potatoes, carrots, and wild asparagus.

Quentin's mouth watered.

Titan brayed again. Quentin heard the mule give his tail an agitated switch.

The boy frowned as he pulled another clump of berries from their delicate, dark-red stem, and they dropped into the bucket upon the others. The aroma wafting up from the bucket smelled like purple candy— the few times Quentin had had the opportunity to smell such a wonderous concoction, that was. "What's got a bur in your bonnet, Ti? I don't see no thunder clouds..."

Quentin let his voice trail off when he heard the distance-muffled drumming of hooves. The sound was coming from the north. As the seconds passed and the drumming grew louder, Quentin said, "Wonder who that could be. Sounds like quite a passel of riders comin' fast..."

Curiosity rising in him, Quentin turned away from the large, thick, berry-laden shrubs he'd been plundering for their bittersweet bounty, pushed through several branches, and stepped out into the clearing where he'd left Titan tied to a young aspen. The brindled mule was staring toward the trail a hundred feet beyond and which Quentin, turning his gaze to the north, saw angling down from a distant, sage-stippled rise.

It was the two-track wagon trail that led to the town of Lone Pine several miles beyond.

"Hmm," Quentin said again, his sun-bleached blond brows ridged with curiosity and a rising apprehension. "Could be a posse. Or maybe Mr. Wainwright is after stock thieves again."

Devlin Wainwright was the owner of the nearby Kitchen Sink Ranch which claimed most of the area around it, including the land near Hog Wallow Creek that Quentin was picking chokecherries on, and which the boy knew was open government range. He had as much right to be on it as did Wainwright's white-faced cattle—Herefords crossed with Texas longhorns.

Still, the boy's apprehension grew as the rataplan of the oncoming riders grew louder. Wainwright's men could get right notional especially after the boredom of pushing cattle all summer from one pasture to another gave one or two of them the thought of opening a bottle and passing it around to relieve the torpor. The thought had no sooner passed through Quentin's mind than he saw the riders top the distant rise and come galloping down, crouched low in their saddles, hat brims pasted against their foreheads by the wind.

Quentin frowned as he held the cheek strap of Ti's bridle and watched the riders approach through the screen of wild berry branches and willows. A growing apprehension tickled his spine. Those weren't Wainwright's Kitchen Sink riders. They weren't range riders at all. Most of the seven riders wore gold-buttoned, dark-blue uniform tunics and either yellow-striped, dark-blue Union cavalry trousers or buckskin breeches shoved into the tops of stovepipe, mule-eared cavalry boots. Most also wore the traditional cavalry kepi, though a few wore battered Stetsons while one wore a red bandanna knotted around his forehead, Apache style.

Just like an Apache, the man's long, black hair blew back behind him in the wind, and the dark-copper face beneath the bandanna was every bit as Apache as his hair.

Quickly, his apprehension growing heavy inside him, Quentin covered Ti's snout with his hand to keep the mule from braying again and giving him away. Standing close beside the mule, Quentin tightened his muscles, trying to make himself as small as possible, less easy to be seen by the riders who would pass his position in five... four...three...two...one second!

And then they blew past, none of the seven turning toward the boy but keeping the grim masks of their bearded or mustached faces. All except for the Apache riding in the middle of the group wore either a beard or a mustache or both. The lead rider had a long, craggy, sunburned face trimmed with a dark-brown mustache and goatee. A red feather jutted from the gilt braid encircling the high brim of his kepi, and a ring, worn on the outside of the man's gauntleted, butternut glove, winked in the New Mexico sunshine. A cavalry saber hung from his side. The twin bars of a captain adorned both shoulders of his tunic, also glinting.

The thunder of the running horses dwindled as the seven riders, faces set with grim purpose, galloped on past Quentin's chokecherry patch, heading south.

Removing his hand from Ti's snout, Quentin stared after the riders retreating ahead of the tan dust cloud dogging them, growing smaller and smaller until all Quentin could see was the dust of their passage before the dust, too, was gone.

"Wonder where they're goin' in such an almighty hurry," the boy said, scratching the back of his head with a purple-stained index finger.

Looking at them, he'd have sworn the War Between the States was still raging. He knew it wasn't. Lee had met Grant at Appomattox Court House back in '65, ten years ago. True, the war had spilled over into the mid- to late 60s, as some soldiers on both sides had refused to give up the fight, which Quentin had learned about in the one-room schoolhouse he attended in the winter when the warm weather chores didn't keep him on his family's small cattle and horse ranch. Still staring after the riders, Quentin had the uneasy feeling he'd somehow been transported back in time, to '64 or '65. That couldn't be possible. He'd been only two years old back then, and he was twelve now. Close to manhood—leastways, in his own eyes.

He'd either been transported back in time, or maybe the sun had gotten to him. Maybe it was making him see things he'd only dreamed about after one of his teacher's, Miss Olivia Markham's, afternoon lectures which, while most of the other boys in the class found so boring they had to fight off sleep, Quentin was often mesmerized by. It had nothing to do with the young teacher's beauty, either. Oh, maybe it did a little, but Quentin had still been transfixed by her lectures which were really stories bringing the times, places, and events in such tales to full, fascinating life.

He tried to obliterate the riders from his mind.

He gave Ti's wither an affectionate pat then picked up his bucket and started to push back through the branches to the shrub he'd been gleaning berries from a few minutes ago. He stopped when Ti brayed again, shook his head. The mule was staring southward, in the direction of Quentin's family's Circle C Bar Ranch.

The trail led past the ranch but surely that wasn't where the riders were heading. Quentin's family had come from a farm in Alabama five years ago, when Quentin was seven and his older sister, Danielle, "Danny" for short, was eleven. His parents had wanted to leave the South and start a new life out west, far from the memories of war and the dead child, a baby girl, Quentin's mother had delivered when Quentin was five.

But Quentin's father, Angus Campbell, had been dreaming of pulling up stakes and heading west ever since, as a boy, he'd accompanied his father and uncle to a crossroads store/tavern in Culvin's Hollow to find an old western frontiersman holding court while smoking a corncob pipe, telling thrilling stories of life in the Rocky Mountains. Quentin's baby sister's death had cemented Angus Campbell's plans. They'd sold their cotton farm, bought a Conestoga wagon, and headed west via wagon train comprised of eight other Southern families who'd had similar ideas.

Angus Campbell had stopped in Socorro, in the New Mexico Territory, and filed a claim in the shadow of the San Francisco Mountains. And here, five years later, they still were, struggling to make it from year to year in such a remote, arid country still occasionally plagued by reservation-jumping Indians as well as rustlers. Still, they pushed on, too stubborn to quit or, as Quentin's mother, Murron, often put it, "Too Scot to quit."

Quentin stared across the sage and creosote and greasewood toward the Circle C Bar Ranch.

Yes, his family was from the South. But Quentin's father hadn't fought in the war due to a hand he'd mangled in a cotton picker. Of course, his father and mother had championed the cause of the South to remain a free and independent nation, but they'd never had much taste for slavery. They had never owned slaves, though plenty of their more prosperous neighbors had.

They were Southerners, and proud, but they had not seen themselves as Confederates.

No, those Union soldiers or whoever they were...still possibly a hallucination caused by a waking fever dream... had not been headed for the Campbell ranch. Quentin had no idea where they were headed, but his mind refused to accept the possibility they were heading for the Circle C Bar intending to do harm. The thought was too staggering for serious consideration. Besides, there were plenty of other places the riders could be heading, as several ranches and hay farms lay south of here, along the Rio Grande and, thirty miles from Circle C Bar lay the ranching and mining supply town of Socorro, though the Campbell family usually did business in the nearer, smaller town of Lone Pine.

Quentin went back to picking.

He had trouble concentrating on his work.

He soon found himself working too quickly and automatically and losing to the grass at his feet as many berries as he picked.

Again, Titan brayed, louder this time. The mule stomped, shook his head.

Quentin turned with a frustrated sigh. "Oh, come on, Ti. There's nothin' to..."

He let his voice trail off because he'd just heard the crackle of gunfire in the direction of the Circle C Bar.

He whipped his head around with a gasp.

Men's distant muffled shouts and loud, raucous whoops mixed with the crackle of the gunfire, set Quentin's heart to racing. He dropped the bucket and ran through the branches to where Ti stood, staring back in the direction of the Campbell ranch, blowing and shaking his head, obviously agitated. Some said mules were not smart, but Quentin knew that wasn't true. Ti was as smart as they came, and he knew trouble had come to the Campbell family's home.

Silently castigating himself for not listening to the mount, who was obviously smarter—leastways, more willing to look reality in the eye even when he didn't want to—than Quentin was, the boy tightened the mule's saddle cinch, shoved Ti's bit into his mouth, and hopped up onto a rock and then onto Ti's back.

He reined the mule through the brush and onto the two-track trail then wildly batted his heels against Ti's flanks. The mule brayed and lurched into a rocking lope, putting his head down, flattening his ears back against his head, and fairly flying up the trail. As he did, the shooting, shouting, and whooping and hollering—all sounds out of a distant decade and from farther east and south, not way out here in western New Mexico Territory—grew louder.

Suddenly, a girl's shrill scream lofted above the gunfire and the men's shouting.

Quentin's heart leaped into his throat.

The girl screamed again.

Quentin's sister, Danny...

CHAPTER 2

QUENTIN'S HEART WAS IN HIS THROAT AS HE GALLOPED up the trail toward the Campbell ranch headquarters. It leaped higher when he saw the plume of black smoke rising from behind the screen of cottonwoods and mesquites lining the creek that ran along the headquarters' near side.

The trail that branched off from the main one to the ranch yard lay ahead another hundred yards. Quentin reined Titan off the trail's right side and into the sage and bunchgrass, approaching the ranch from behind the barn, where he hoped he wouldn't be seen by the Union marauders whose gunfire had dwindled and become sporadic before stopping altogether, leaving a menacing silence as well as that thick, terrifying plume of black smoke rising from beyond the barn, which meant the cabin, Quentin's home for most of his young life, was on fire.

The shouting and Danny's screams had stopped, as well.

Quentin put the mule through the screening trees and shrubs, across the creek that ran through a shallow, sandy cut along the edge of the ranch yard, on its northeast side, and into the yard itself. The bull in the barn's rear fenced paddock stood frozen in a corner of the corral, pointing its big head with the long sweep of curved horns in the direction of the main part of the ranch yard, which it couldn't see because the barn was in the way.

Quentin dismounted, tied the mule to a rail of the fence enclosing the paddock, and made his way along the fence to the rear of the barn, one door of which was partway open. Fresh hay was in the bull's manger, at the front of the paddock, which told Quentin his father or sister may have been feeding the bull, whom Quentin had named Agamemnon after an especially riveting school lecture by the pretty and beguiling Miss Olivia Markham.

Quentin slowed his pace as he closed the gap between himself and the barn. He edged a look around the partially open door and stared up the barn's dark alley toward the front. Both front doors stood open. A wooden wheelbarrow filled with hay and manure from which a three-tined fork poked up sat near the front of the barn. Beyond the open doors, men obscured by the smoke milled, talking and smoking, joking and laughing, adjusting their hats on their heads or removing them altogether and smoothing their hair before donning them again.

Fifty yards beyond the barn lay the long, low, brush-roofed cabin. The roof was on fire and orange flames licked up through the three front windows—from the large one in the kitchen area near the cabin's far right end and from the two windows on either side of the door.

The door was open. A body lay on the ground in front of it. A rifle lay on the ground to the right of the body, which was not simply a "body" to Quentin. He could tell by tawny hair and the checked day dress and the apron she wore, both of which had been pulled up to expose the rounded twin mounds of her pale, tender bottom, that it was Danny who lay out there.

She was moving a little, turning her head from side to side, feebly reaching behind her with one hand, trying to lower the dress and her apron, to cover herself while also trying to push up on her hands and knees. To Danny's right, ten feet away, lay a bloody, furry mound—their dog, Juno.

Quentin slipped into the barn and stole quickly to the left side of the barn alley. He moved up along the stalls, only one of which was occupied—by a lineback dun with a bad hoof Quentin and his father were doctoring. Black, fetid smoke from the cabin pushed into the barn. The horse was whickering uneasily, occasionally knocking against the stall partitions and the rear door, making the steel latch rattle.

Most of the marauders stood around the stone tank at the base of the windmill between the barn and the cabin, to the right of where Danny and Juno lay. As Quentin approached the open doors displaying the horror that had come to the Campbell ranch in stark relief against a broad bowl of arching blue sky save the black smoke unfurling into it, he stopped suddenly. Two hearts now hammered in his throat; his knees turned to mud, threatening to buckle.

Another, larger body lay near the stock tank at the base of the windmill.

A bearded man in wool shirt and dungarees, one suspender hanging down against his side. Angus Campbell's black, leather-billed immigrant hat lay on the ground to his right; his Spencer repeating rifle lay on the ground to his left. Pa lay on his side, his head resting on an arm. Quentin gasped when he saw the man's chest bibbed with dark-red blood, and that his cobalt blue eyes, "the blue of the Scottish sky on winter mornings," their mother always said, were wide open and staring with cold, mute accusing toward his killers.

"Oh, god." The words bubbled up out of Quentin's throat in a sob. "Oh, god—Pa!"

He pressed his shoulder against the wall to the left of the open barn doors. For a minute he thought he would faint. And then he thought he would vomit. His mind was aswirl.

Then he heard, "Get ready to mount up, fellas. Our work here is done. Oh, just one last thing."

"What's that, Cap?"

Quentin edged a look around the side of the open doors, gazing out toward the men gathered in a loose group around the stock tank at the base of the windmill, drinking water and whiskey from tin cups. They were passing a bottle while two men held the horses at the edge of the yard, away from the fire. One of the men separated from the pack by the windmill, walked over to the burning cabin and, wincing against the flames lapping up out of the windows and open door, straddled Danny from behind and slid a long-bladed knife from a sheath on his shell belt.

Quentin stared in horror. Oh, god, no! Don't you... *dare*!

Quentin couldn't make out the man's face because of the smoke and the deep shadows of the late afternoon sliding across the yard. All he could see was the kepi, the red feather jutting up from the band, and the twin bars on his shoulders—marking him as the lead rider Quentin had seen on the trail—as the man leaned down, pulled

Danny's head up by her hair, and ran the Bowie knife across her throat.

Danny screamed.

Blood welled.

Her killer released her hair and her head dropped into the bloody dirt. Her body quivered as she died.

Instinctively, Quentin stepped out from the edge of the barn door, wanting to rush to his sister's aid. Just as he did, he saw her killer, wiping the blade of the knife off on Danny's apron, suddenly lift his head. His face was obscured by the smoke and shadows, but Quentin saw his eyes beneath the hat brim. They stared straight toward Quentin.

The boy gasped and jerked back behind the barn wall.

Quentin was breathing hard, heart racing. Cold sweat pasted his shirt to his back.

He drew a breath, trying to calm himself so he could think.

The shotgun!

He moved into the shadows on his left, made his way through the barn's dusky interior to wooden rungs climbing the wall to the hayloft. His father had stowed a shotgun up there in case of just such an occurrence as the horrific one here this afternoon, though Angus Campbell had worried more about reservation-jumping Indians and Wainwright's men than he had about Union cavalry riders galloping out of the past, hungry for Confederate blood. He as well as his son had thought those days were long since over.

Quentin quickly climbed the rungs and shoved his head and shoulders up through the three-by-three-foot square hole that gave access to the loft. He used his hands and arms to hoist his legs up through the hole and rolled away from it quickly. He'd just heard a spur trill as someone approached the barn.

Gritting his teeth, sweat bathing him, Quentin made his way over to where the shotgun was secured behind slats nailed across two studs in the barn's sloping loft wall. Carefully, quietly, he used both sweating hands to pull the shotgun up from behind the slats. He didn't bother breaking open the old Richards coach gun Angus Campbell had likely taken in trade or barter or had perhaps bought for cheap secondhand in Lone Pine. His father wouldn't have stowed the greener there empty; there was nothing more useless than an empty gun, he would have said.

Pa...

The image of his father lying dead in the yard amid the wafting smoke from the burning cabin flickered to life in his memory, chilling his bones. Quentin returned to the hole in the loft floor. He dropped to his knees then slid his feet out behind him and settled belly down on the hay-strewn floor.

He slid a look around the edge of the floor, peering into the barn's dense shadows relieved only a little by the open barn doors. As he did, he saw a tall man standing between the open doors, holding a rifle up high across his chest. Quentin couldn't see the man's face save a faint glittering in his eyes beneath the brim of his Union kepi adorned with that single feather. Quentin saw the ring worn on the man's right little finger, on the outside of his gauntleted glove.

He turned his head toward Quentin.

He was staring straight at him!

Now he began to swing the barrel of his rifle out away from him, loudly jacking a round into the Winchester's action.

With an inexplicable calm, Quentin kept his head right where it was—at the edge of the hole in the loft floor. He rolled onto his left shoulder, shoved the shotgun's barrel down through the hole, and ratcheted back each of the double-bore's two hammers. Holding the twelve-gauge in both hands, he aimed the gut-shredder down through the hole at an angle, centering the double barrels on the man's chest.

The man froze with the Winchester only half turned toward Quentin.

The ring on his pinky finger glinted in a stray, wan shaft of firelight angling into the barn over the man's left shoulder and which he was silhouetted against. The ring was dark-red or orange and square in shape, set in gold. Two gold letters, U.S., were set into it.

That was the only clear detail Quentin could see of the man.

The rest of him, save his eyes reflecting the same light, was murky and dark.

His eyes bore into Quentin's. They widened slightly. Fearfully.

He was afraid.

Was his life flashing before his eyes, as Quentin's had been? Did his heart lurch with the possibility he might be dead within seconds, or at least down and howling with his guts pierced by two barrels of twelve-gauge buckshot?

Quentin held his right index finger taut against the shotgun's right, steel, eyelash trigger. He wanted to squeeze that trigger. He wanted to kill this blue-clad son of Satan in the worst way possible, but he held fire. Doing so would be suicide. He'd likely die, anyway, but...something told him to wait. That he might not be quite as doomed as he thought he'd been only a few seconds ago, when he'd imagined shooting the leader of the marauding gang and then being overcome by the others.

But what did he really have to live for, anyway?

His family was dead. Father, sister. His mother had likely burned up in the cabin.

His dog...

The gang leader stared back at him for a few more stretched seconds.

One of the others spoke behind him. "See somethin', Cap?"

When the captain did not reply, another man said, "Hey, Dalton—see somethin'?"

Dalton held his apprehensive gaze on Quentin, who somehow managed to hold the double-bore steady in his sweating hands, aiming at the gang leader's chest and belly, at the gold buttons running up the front of the bib-front tunic.

"Nah." The man stepped back and, lowering the Winchester, turned, and said, "Nothin'. Thought I did. Nothin' in there." He walked away from the barn, spurs jangling. "Let's ride out, boys. Be dark soon."

Quentin waited, sure it was a trick.

But now, as he kept the barn blaster aimed at the barn's large, darkening open doorway, he heard the squawk of tack as the gang members mounted their horses.

Heard the thuds of their horses' hooves as they galloped out of the yard.

The thudding dwindled until all Quentin could hear was his own pounding heart and the snapping and crackling of the burning cabin.

He frowned, puzzled. Then he realized what had happened.

The man—the gang's fearless leader—had been afraid.

Afraid of a twelve-year-old kid aiming an ancient shotgun at him. Humiliated in his fear, he'd elected to walk away rather than let the others know he'd been afraid, frozen in place by a boy.

His hands suddenly shaking again, sorrow moved into Quentin, replacing the momentary resolve he'd felt, the resignation at his imminent demise. He pulled the shotgun out of the hole, depressed the hammers, and moved heavily back down the wall rungs to the barn's main floor. He turned to the front door, steeled himself for what awaited him outside, and walked out through the open doors and into a whole new and different world from the one he'd awakened to earlier that morning.

This was a bleak, dark, wretched one in which he suddenly found himself alone.

Alone but somehow buoyed by the half-formed notion that he would one day find the gang, especially the man who led it—the man with the U.S. ring on his little finger—and exact his revenge.

Like a true Confederate, not a chicken-livered bluebelly.

CHAPTER 3

"Bloody" Joe Mannion, town marshal of Del Norte in the south-central Colorado Territory, sat upright in bed with a horrified yell, finding himself wide awake and bathed in sweat.

"Joe!" his wife Jane said, also sitting up, placing one hand on his heaving chest, the other on his shoulder. "Oh, honey—it was just a dream." She caressed his shoulder.

The forty-seven-year-old former Kansas-to-Texas town tamer was breathing as though he'd run a long way uphill and bucking a Panhandle wind.

"Lordy," Joe said, shaking his head. "I'll be..."

"What was it, Joe? What made you scream like that?"

Mannion turned to her, scowling his incredulity at his pretty, red-headed wife, her hair exotically mussed from sleep. Jane was in her early forties, but her hair did not betray her age with a single strand of silver. "Darlin', Bloody Joe Mannion don't scream." His scowl deepened the lines cut across his ruddy forehead. "I didn't really scream, did I? You think the neighbors heard?"

He looked at the wall behind him and then at the wall

just beyond Jane's side of the bed. Beyond that wall lay the hall. They were in Jane's suite of rooms in the hurdy-gurdy house, the San Juan Hotel & Saloon, which Jane had owned long before she and Joe were married and where they overnighted during the week, since they both worked in town and their own house lay outside of town —farther for them both to travel in case of trouble, which was in no short supply in the ever-growing Del Norte to which the damnable iron horse had come nigh on two years ago—the glistening silver rails laid right down the heart of the town's broad, main drag, San Juan Avenue.

The train had done nothing to stem the trouble but had only increased it, what with the con men, cardsharps, gunslingers, and curly wolves of every stripe it brought to town, many of whom, finding the pickings ripe in the caldron of roiling, unwashed humanity, stayed. Some lay in unmarked graves on Boot Hill. The others likely had unmarked graves on Boot Hill in their futures.

Jane snickered. "I don't think anyone heard. Anyway, it wasn't really a scream."

Mannion shook his head, ran his big hands through his longish, salt-and-pepper hair, still thick even now in his middle age just as his belly was relatively flat, shoulders broad, wolfish gray eyes clear and as keen, or nearly as keen as when he had fought Apaches in the frontier cavalry. "When I was in that box, I was sure screamin'!"

"I heard you groaning."

"That was me tryin' to, uh...scream. Or demand to be let out, more like."

"Let out of what, Joe?"

Mannion turned to her, his heart still beating abnormally fast as the nightmare was slow as camp smoke took to clear on a still morning. "I dreamed I was in a pine coffin. The lid was nailed down. Somehow, that coffin got thrown into a river. I even know what river it was. The Arkansas. Don't ask me how I know that, but I do. I think one of the outlaws who knocked me out, tossed me into the coffin and then nailed the lid down, told me. Just before they all had 'em a good laugh as they threw me an' that damn coffin into the water!"

"Joe," Jane said, concern in her amber eyes. "Whatever made you dream such a thing?"

"I got no idea."

"Have you dreamed it before?"

"Never."

"Do you have a fear of such a thing—of being locked in a coffin and thrown into a river?"

"Not till now!" Mannion gave a droll laugh and scrubbed his scalp with the knuckles of his right hand, making his hair stand up in spikes. "Damnedest thing..."

"Joe," Jane said. "That's a death dream."

"A what?"

"A death dream."

"Hmm."

She stared at him, her worried gaze unwavering.

"What's it mean when you have a death dream?" Mannion wanted to know.

She held his gaze with the worried one of her own for several stretched seconds before she shook her head quickly, turned away, drew her knees up beneath the bedcovers, and rested her arms over them. "Never mind."

"Never mind what?"

"Never mind, Joe."

"How can I 'never mind, Joe.' Honey, what does it mean to have a death dream?"

"Joe, please—I shouldn't have said anything. Let's let it go." Jane glanced at the window in the wall near Joe's side of the bed. Dawn light shone around the edges of the drawn drapes. "It's morning. I'll go down and fetch us up a pot of coffee and some rolls."

Mannion reached across himself and closed his left hand around her upper right arm, holding her where she was. "Does havin' a death dream mean...I'm gonna *die*? Is that it?"

Jane shook her head. "No. Of course not. Not all death dreams mean you're going to die. I've had them before myself. You know the one—you step off a cliff and you're screaming and yelling for help though you can't really speak in your sleep but just groan like some animal. And just as your body plunges into the ground at the bottom of the cliff, you wake up. Screaming and sweating."

"You said I didn't scream."

"Oh, Joe!"

"No, no. Hold on, honey. My dream meant more than your fall-from-the-cliff one did."

"Or so you believe. How? In what way? Joe, couldn't we just let this go, please? I'm craving coffee."

Mannion released his beloved's arm with a sigh. "All right, all right." He bequeathed her a crooked grin, slid her curly red hair away from her neck to nuzzle the tender, freckled skin below her ear. "My lovely, sweet-smellin', superstitious redhead."

Jane chuckled, planted a kiss on his broad nose, then tossed the covers back and rose from the bed. "Ohh," she said, shivering, holding herself and stamping her bare feet. "It's cold in here!"

"I'll get a fire goin' in the stove," Mannion said. "It is only May, after all."

"Late May!"

Mannion threw his own covers back and rose to his

full six feet four, stretching his tall, lean, still-muscular body clad in his wash worn, red longhandles. His aging joints crackled and popped. "Below...around Denver and Colorado Springs...it's June. Up here, at seven-thousand feet, it's still May. *Early* May."

"Yes," Jane said, shrugging into her green plaid robe that set off the red in her hair and stepping into wool-lined, buckskin slippers, "but it's a woman's prerogative to complain about any ol' thing she wants." She gave her husband a saucy smile and opened the bedroom door. "Be back in a minute."

She walked out into the parlor area of the suite and left the rooms via the door to the hall, which Mannion heard her close and latch behind her. He smiled. God, how he loved that woman. *I must*, he thought. *I married her twice.*

He ran his hands through his hair again, chuckling as he strode over to the small charcoal brazier in the large, wooden-floored room's rear corner, near a zinc tub and a room divider with colored glass running along the top of the folding panels. When he got a small coal fire burning, he poured water from a stone pitcher into the basin sitting atop the marble-topped washbasin and set about taking a quick sponge bath.

His mind was on Jane.

Yes, he and the former Jane Ford, one of the most prominent business leaders—man or woman—in Del Norte had divorced once and married again. Hell, the San Juan Hotel & Saloon was one of the most popular such establishments in the entire southern part of the territory, rivaling even some of the toniest places in Leadville, one of the most hopping towns—small city, really—in the territory. There was a lot of pressure involved in running such an establishment, and Jane had needed Joe's support and distracting company in her off hours.

The trouble was, Joe had been as married to his job as he had been to Jane.

Often, even the few times when he was present in her life, his mind was elsewhere.

As often happened with two successful, strong-headed people, they'd fought.

And Jane had left for a time.

During that time, Mannion and Jane had both realized they couldn't live without each other. So, they'd married in a double ceremony with Joe's daughter, Evangeline, "Vangie," for short, and her young, Harvard-educated doctor, Benjamin Ellison, in a double ceremony.

When Jane was badly wounded by the raging, drunken bounty hunter Ulysses Xavier Lodge, who had taken umbrage with Jane's having had the man thrown out of the San Juan because he'd been attacking one of the girls he'd had the mistaken notion he was going to marry, he'd returned to the saloon and drilled three .44-caliber rounds into Jane's chest. While Dr. Ellison had tended Jane, somehow saving her life even with three bullets in her chest, Mannion had hunted Lodge down high in the Sawatch Mountains north of Del Norte, and, like the wild, lunatic human bruin the bounty hunter was, sent him back to the demon that had spawned him.

"What're you thinking about?"

Shaving in the mirror above the washstand, he saw Jane come into the room and set a tray with a silver coffee server and cups and two small plates adorned with cinnamon rolls on the small table against the wall near the bedroom door, by a large oak armoire and a cabinet clock woodenly clicking away the minutes. The clock reminded Mannion he needed to get over to the jailhouse and relieve his night deputy, Cletus Booker. Having only three deputies in the growing Del Norte, he was badly shorthanded. He needed to keep the men he did have fresh.

"Me?" Joe said, plowing up a snowy mound of thick, white soap flecked with silver-brown beard stubble. "I don't think."

In fact, as Jane sat in a brocade-padded armchair and filled a china cup with piping hot black coffee from the server, he regarded his pretty, smart, ambitious, and hard-working wife tenderly, a little anxiously. For they both knew that while Ellison had done a miraculous job in saving Jane's life, there was one bullet he hadn't he been able to extract from her chest because it had been too close to her heart.

It still was.

It was sort of like a bomb in her chest. One that if nudged too close to her heart, would explode. Would, in fact, steal her away from Mannion, Vangie, Ellison, and all the rest of the folks in and around Del Norte who loved her.

Like the dream of floating downstream in a nailed-shut casket, the prospect was nettling, a thought that plucked like a burr in your boot, was as hard to fade as camp smoke on a still mountain morning.

"You think too much is your problem," Jane said, kicking the leg she'd crossed over her other knee and taking a large bite of the cinnamon roll slathered in white frosting and melting butter. "Looking at you, it's hard to imagine I married a thinking man."

Mannion chuckled.

That was Jane.

She knew what he'd been thinking. She likely knew quite well the cast in his gaze when such thoughts of his beloved's mortality came creeping up on him like a red-eyed specter in the night. She'd filed the beast's fangs down, distracted Mannion, made him laugh.

"Mrs. Jane Mannion?" he said, scrubbing the remaining soap from his cheeks with a towel. He'd left the salt-and-pepper mustache he wore over his broad mouth, dragoon style. "I do admire to have you as my wife, though I sorely do not deserve you."

"Well, you're stuck with me." Chewing, shaking her leg over her knee, Jane smiled saucily. "Now get over here and dig into this roll and coffee before they both get cold. Mr. Anderson really outdid himself in the kitchen this morning!"

She tore hungrily into the roll once more.

Joe's mouth watered.

———

MANNION LEFT THE TONY, SPRAWLING, THREE-STORY building a half hour later, sated by the roll and the coffee, which would last him till noon. It had to. He didn't have time for a real breakfast. That much was evident by the hustling and bustling along both sides of San Juan Avenue and by the ranch wagons and ore and lumber drays lifting dust as well as a sometimes near-deafening din from the street itself, on both sides of the damnable tracks of the Colorado Springs & San Juan Line.

The sun hadn't yet cleared the eastern ridges of the Sangre de Cristo Mountains rising in the east, so the deep shadows clinging to the busy street made crossing even more dangerous than usual. Mannion took extra care when he stepped off the boardwalk on the street's east side and stopped several times lest he, obscured by the dust fog of those passing wagons, got smashed as flat as a dinner plate. Several poor fellas and even a few women—usually drunk—had met such unceremonious fates to join the battalions of other unfortunates pushing up makeshift wooden crosses at the heads of stone-mounded graves on Boot Hill.

"Mornin', Joe!" he heard from several quarters, giving a weak smile and a nod, pinching his hat brim at ladies strolling along the boardwalk on the street's west side.

Even at this early hour, not all the ladies were "ladies." Quite a few working girls, usually the independent ones, not affiliated with any particular hurdy-gurdy or parlor house, strolled the boardwalks trolling for customers who'd been up all night drinking and gambling and who might find themselves in need of a sleep tonic of sorts.

As he strode north, in the direction of the jailhouse, locally known with more than some amusement as "Hotel de Mannion" in ironic contrast to its proprietor's, Bloody Joe's, bloody reputation, Joe kept his eyes skinned for trouble. Sometimes those customers just washing out through batwings and into the light of a new day got into skirmishes instigated by previous gambling losses or perceived slights inflicted on their tender egos hours before. Miners were most notorious for going at it right out on the main drag with pickaxes and shovels, both of which could leave lasting marks when the injured weren't killed outright.

Mortimer Bellringer, Del Norte's main undertaker, was a wealthy man. He took his prim and proper not to mention high-headed wife to Denver by train just for wining and dining and hotel stays every couple of months. Bellringer had built himself a large, flower-enshrouded brick and stone house on a low hill on the town's southwest side and which everyone around called, with typical western jocularity, the Mausoleum.

All appeared relatively peaceful, however—busy but peaceful—on San Juan Avenue this early in the day.

Until Mannion passed the batwings and large, front, plate glass window of the Black Cat Saloon, that was, and stopped at the building's far side. Before starting across the street on that side of the saloon, Mannion glanced to his right, toward the rear of the building, in time to see a man quickly pull his hatted head back behind the building's rear corner.

Hmmm, Joe thought. Frowning.

Wonder what's happening behind the Black Cat, which was often open all night long. It was open now, though, when Joe had glanced through the front window, he'd spied only a few men and a scantily clad, weary-looking doxie standing at the bar.

Gazing down along the saloon's adobe brick north wall, Mannion unsnapped the keeper thong from over the hammer of his big, silver-chased Russian .44 holstered for the cross-draw on his left hip. He stepped off the boardwalk and walked down the side of the building toward the rear from where he heard someone say in an urgent but hushed voice, "Let's go—Bloody Joe's comin'!"

Holding the Russian barrel up at his right shoulder, Mannion clicked the hammer back.

"Ah," he muttered to himself. "The start of a brand-new day in Del Norte!"

CHAPTER 4

"HOLD ON," ANOTHER VOICE ROSE FROM BEHIND THE saloon. "I almost got this fella's—"

Mannion moved quickly around the Black Cat's rear corner, extending the cocked Russian straight out in front of him.

"Hold it! Got you dead to rights!"

Two men were running toward three horses tied to a gnarled cedar behind a grocery store—between the store and a large keeper shed overgrown with sage and buck-brush. They froze and turned toward Mannion. Ten feet from Joe, another man was struggling to remove a silver ring from the ring finger of a man who lay unconscious on the ground before him.

The unconscious man was dressed in the tony attire —smart-looking three-piece suit, a crisp black Stetson on the ground nearby—of a gambler. Another man dressed similarly lay in front of the open door of the two-hole privy, his own Stetson with smashed crown on the ground behind him. A swift survey of the scene told Mannion all he needed to know.

The man standing frozen holding the hand of the

man whose ring he was trying to steal, and the other two, also standing frozen in place, staring toward Mannion, had jumped the gamblers on their way out of the privy, knocked them out with a pair of two-by-fours, also lying nearby, and were trying to plunder the two men's gambling winnings won over the course of the night in the Black Cat.

The three robbers weren't really men, though. They were vermin—bottom-feeding, penny-ante criminals, the kind who followed the consarned railroad. All three were clad in ragged, mismatched duds with patched knees, torn pockets, and soiled undershirts behind wool or sack cloth coats. The man staring up at Mannion had a sunburned, craggy face carpeted in three- or four-days' worth of brown beard stubble, and a badly weathered, funnel-brimmed hat.

All three wore old model Colts in low-slung holsters.

The man still frozen in the act of trying to remove the gambler's silver ring stared up at Bloody Joe. "Um... uh...fellas..."

"Down on your knees—all three of you!" Mannion ordered.

The two farthest away from Joe looked at each other, then wheeled hard left and ran into the brush on the far side of the alley from the Black Cat.

The man trying to plunder the gambler's ring yelled, "Hey, fellas, you can't leave me—"

He cut himself off abruptly as he dropped the unconscious gambler's hand, straightened, and slapped leather. Mannion sighed and shot him before he had his old Colt, its handle held together with baling wire, through the dead center of his chest. The man hadn't hit the ground before Mannion ran around him and took off running after the other two.

"Stop or I'll shoot!" he bellowed, seeing the other two running around a large trash heap and continuing toward a dry wash angling around that side of the town.

One of the two—the man on the left—stopped suddenly. He whipped around, and, grimacing, brought up the Colt in his right hand.

Mannion dropped him with a single bullet without slowing his pace.

He leaped the robber's quivering body and continued after the other thieving devil, who just then pushed through the willows screening the wash and into the wash itself, disappearing from Joe's view.

Mannion slowed his pace as he approached the willows. He heard running footsteps and labored breaths. The last of the thieves was running along the arroyo to his right. Joe pushed through the willows, leaped into the wash, and took off running. He saw his quarry running around a sharp leftward curve in the wash, and followed him, squeezing his cross-draw Russian in his gloved, right hand. His second, matching Russian was secure in the holster tied down on Mannion's right thigh.

He had a hideout gun in his boot—a two-shot, over-and-under derringer he always hoped he wouldn't have to use because if he did, he was in a dire situation. His large Bowie knife with a deer antler handle jutted from its buckskin sheath on his left hip.

He ran around the bend in the wash, past a large boulder on the bank to his left, then slowed his pace. He stopped altogether.

He could see a good distance up the willow- and cedar-sheathed wash, but he could not see his quarry.

He waited, looking around, listening, wary of an ambush.

The slight crunch of sand and gravel sounded behind him.

"Freeze, lawdog!"

The voice had come from behind Joe as did a girlish cackle.

"Got *you* dead to rights, Mannion. Lower the hogleg and turn around slow."

Mannion lowered the Russian in his right hand. He turned slowly until he could see his quarry standing before him now, fifteen feet away. A short, stocky man with a paunch bulging out his sack shirt. A round face, unshaven, with a badly sunburned, peeling nose. A ragged bowler hat sat an angle atop his head, long, greasy hair hanging down from it to nearly his shoulders.

He was grinning devilishly, delightedly, showing a crooked, rotting front tooth.

For some reason, Mannion hadn't recognized him when he'd seen him before, trying to remove the gambler's pinky ring. But then, the man's face was fleshier, more bloated from drink, and his hair hung longer and was turning gray.

"Teddy Wiley," Joe said with a wry chuff. "Now, didn't I kick you out of Del Norte for life over a year ago?"

Wiley snickered.

Then his expression grew hard, flat brown eyes narrowing with anger. "That was right embarrassin', Bloody Joe. The way you kicked me out of the Cat... threw me into the street like I was just some...some..."

"Drunken grub line rider?" Joe said. "That's what you are, Teddy. You blackened a girl's eye that night, shot a horn off a mounted elk head, and refused to pay for the bottle you'd bought."

"I was just honin' my aim an' the previous bottle had a diamondback rattle at the bottom of it!"

"Which you discovered only *after* you'd finished the whiskey."

"Damn near swallowed the wretched thing!"

"Put the gun down." Mannion raised the Russian, aimed it back at Teddy Wiley staring down the barrel of his old Colt conversion revolver at him. "I'm takin' you in."

"Told you to lower the hogleg, Mannion!" Wiley said, nervous now, scared, shifting his weight from one worn stovepipe boot to the other. "You lower it, or I'll shoot... I'll kill the great Bloody Joe!"

His voice was hoarse and high-pitched, desperate, pleading.

Calmly, keeping his voice level, steady, Mannion said, "Lower it, Teddy."

"You'll...you'll put me away!"

"You deserve to be put away." Mannion narrowed one eye threateningly and drew his index finger back taut against the trigger. "Better to be put away for a time than to die. You get out—hell, you could start a new life."

"Dang it, Bloody Joe!"

"Drop it, Teddy."

Sweat had popped out on the man's forehead. It ran down his cheeks cutting runnels through the dirt and trail grime. His gun hand was shaking. Mannion heard a ticking sound and looked down to see the man was making water on his right boot from down the inside of his checked pants.

"Ah, hell!" Teddy lowered the old Colt suddenly.

Just as suddenly, screaming, he whipped it back up.

Before he could draw his finger back against the Colt's trigger, Mannion's Russian roared. The .44-caliber round punched a puckered blue hole in the middle of Teddy's forehead. Teddy's eyes widened in shock. His right hand dropped down against his side, the fingers opening, the Colt dropping into the sand and gravel of the arroyo's floor.

Teddy dropped straight back down to the ground, not breaking his fall, dead before he struck. He lay flat on his back, dead eyes staring straight up at nothing.

To Mannion's right, crows lighted from a pine bough and winged off, cawing peevishly.

Mannion frowned. He stared at his hand. It was shaking. Just a little, but shaking, just the same.

Running footsteps sounded behind him.

He swung around to stare back along the wash. As he did, his junior-most deputy, Henry McCallister, who until recently had gone, albeit reluctantly, by the moniker "Stringbean." Henry formerly "Stringbean," formerly a horse breaker, had been tall and thin but over the past couple of years he'd filled out, gained some muscle to go with his broad shoulders. Also, he'd matured, drifted close to his midtwenties, and his several successes as a deputy lawman had caused everyone to naturally drop the boyish handle.

Behind Henry, huffing and puffing, came Bloody Joe's senior-most deputy, the middle-aged Rio Waite, formerly cowpuncher, ranch foreman, jehu, and shotgun rider. Every year of the frontier seasoning as well as the long hours in the sun shone on his craggy, fleshy face; a few too many go-rounds in Del Norte's eateries and his love for beer shone in his paunch, which turned the buckle of his cartridge belt nearly flat to the ground and made a lesson in futility attempting to button the first shirt button above his baggy denim trousers.

The faded red of his longhandle top shone through the gap.

"Heard the shootin', Marshal!" young Henry McCallister said now as he slowed his pace, his clean-shaven face flushed with exertion but mainly concern.

"Picked up your tracks behind the Black Cat," Rio put in, running up to stand beside Henry now. His own, deeply lined features were sunset red and swollen. Rio leaned forward, hands on his knees, raking deep drafts of air in and out of his lungs. He looked down at the dead man behind Mannion, who had turned to face his deputies. "Who's the fresh beef? Those gamblers were comin' out of their stupors an' said they was robbed. He one of the robbers?"

"I didn't shoot him for whistlin' Dixie," Joe said, finding himself in a foul mood of a sudden. Killing men who deserved killing didn't usually do that to him. But then, killing men who deserved killing didn't usually make his hand shake, either.

"No, I reckon you didn't." Rio, who knew Mannion as well or better than almost everyone, save Jane, looked up at him, having caught the sharp tone of his voice as well as his sarcasm. "That the last of 'em?"

Mannion turned back to stare down at Teddy Wiley still staring skyward through sightless eyes. In the sky above the wash, buzzards were already turning slow circles, waiting for a chance to dine. Coyotes were likely hunkered in the brush nearby, waiting, as well. "He's the last."

"Saw the other two," Henry said. "Want I should fetch Bellringer?"

"Yeah."

"You got it."

Henry turned to start walking back the way he and Rio had come. He stopped and glanced back at Mannion, frowning. "You all right, Marshal?"

"What? Yeah, yeah, I'm fine. Fetch Bellringer before

those carrion eaters cheat him out of a payday. Been a lucrative morning for the old devil so far."

"Got it."

Henry jogged off.

Rio regarded the younger deputy peevishly, flared a nostril of his broad, pitted nose. "He just loves to show how fast he can run. Ain't even any purty girls around for him to impress with his runnin'!"

Mannion dropped to a knee and started going through Wiley's pockets, rising a minute later with a good hundred dollars in greenbacks in one hand, a gold ring, and a pearl-gripped pocket pistol in the other. Shoving the loot in a pocket of his corduroy jacket, he said, "Let's see what the other two have."

CHAPTER 5

As he strode back along the arroyo, Rio, who was nearly a head shorter than Mannion, quickened his pace to keep up with his boss, the mule ears of his low-heeled cavalry boots dancing around his calves, his rusty spurs jangling raucously.

When Joe had taken the gamblers' winnings off the body of the man who hadn't made it to the arroyo, he and Rio headed back to the privy flanking the Black Cat. One of the gamblers was up, standing near the first robber Mannion had shot. His partner sat up against the privy, being tended to by Mannion's tall, dark, and handsome son-in-law, Ben Ellison. Mannion did not begrudge the man his Harvard education. The medico was a good husband for Joe's daughter, Vangie. Like Jane, the rugged, uncompromising former town tamer and Del Norte head lawman, loved her more than life itself.

"Mannion, what kind of a town are you running here?" the conscious gambler wanted to know. He looked a little bleary-eyed beneath the brim of his black Stetson, which still had a small dent in it and dirt on it, but otherwise seemed fit enough.

Ignoring the man's rhetorical question, Mannion turned to his son-in-law, who was down on one knee, gently parting the thin, sandy hair of the other gambler, examining a cut on the top of the man's head. "How's he look, Doc?"

Ellison glanced at him. He wore a brown suit with a blood-red four-in-hand tie and a brown bowler hat with a silk band. He had his suits tailor-made in Denver. When Joe had first learned, after Ellison had already married Vangie, that the medico had his suits tailor-made in Denver—"the Paris of the Plains" some called it, though they'd likely never been to either city—Mannion had considered looking into divorce proceedings, possibly an annulment. However, Jane's cooler head had prevailed. He'd decided that many a father-in-law had to overlook much more serious transgressions than those of Dr. Ellison and his tailor.

"He'll live," Ellison said. "Going to need a few sutures, though."

"Where's our money?" groused the man the doctor was working on.

Mannion shoved his entire gleanings into the hands of the man's angry partner wearing the black Stetson which needed brushing as well as shaping.

The black-hatted gambler, taller than the other one, cursed as Mannion shoved the money and other paraphernalia including the pocket pistol at him. Then, ignoring both men's angry comments about the uncivilized nature of Del Norte—Mannion knew he didn't have much of an argument, though he and his deputies did their best—Joe and Rio continued their trek back in the direction of Hotel de Mannion, where they found Joe's newest deputy, Cletus Booker, leaning back in Mannion's

Windsor chair, both his size fourteen boots hiked atop Mannion's cluttered desk.

Also on the desk were two large breakfast platters so well cleaned it looked as though a pair of hungry dogs had scoured them both. Booker was a big man. Even bigger than Joe. He was somewhere in his early thirties and when he ordered a meal, he usually ordered two. He wasn't much of a conversationalist, but Mannion hadn't deputized him for his gift for gab. The man had been known as a head-breaking deputy in a lawless mountain mining town high in the Sawatch, and when his former employer had let him go for breaking the wrong man's head, Mannion had hired him.

He figured that for every wrong head the undis-cerning Booker broke, he'd likely broken ten or fifteen heads that had needed it. Any gambler worth his bejew-eled rings and gold watches would tell anyone those were good odds.

Booker dropped his feet to the floor and rose with a grunt as Mannion and Rio entered the office. "How'd it go last night, Cletus?" Joe asked the big man, pegging his hat on the wall by the door.

"Two downstairs. Drunk and disorderly."

Booker glanced at the stout, oak door that led to the basement's stone-walled, stone-floored cellblock that contained eight iron-banded cages, four on each side of a narrow corridor lit by hanging coal oil lamps. There were four, ground-level windows with iron bars and steel mesh over the bars so no one could drop a gun or a file down to the prisoners. When Mannion had first become the marshal of Del Norte, he'd had the basement dug and stone-lined and the small brick office built over it. The office and jail replaced a small, adobe, two-cell, earthen-floored cooler manned by only a part-time constable. It had mostly been used by the locals for storing milk and eggs.

Back in those early days, Mannion's jail had filled those eight cages nearly every night. Now, however, after having gotten the town on a leash of varying lengths, he and his deputies usually had only a couple of so-called guests at Hotel de Mannion on weeknights, maybe four or five on the weekends. Most prisoners spent a night or two on the city council's dime, paid a fine set by Mannion himself—usually an arbitrary call he deemed fair—and were released on their own recognizance or to brow-beating wives and employers.

Those accused of murder had to wait for the circuit court judge. Mannion usually had a gallows built in antici-pation of a hanging.

The current circuit-riding judge, Herman "Hemp-Stretchin'" Glenhaven, didn't trifle with killers, meaning he didn't waste time on sending for the U.S. Marshal's jail wagon to haul the convicted off to the territorial pen. Usually, the echoes of his gavel hadn't died before the accused and convicted were led in chains out to the gallows where a crowd of citizens, gathered to enjoy the carnival-like festivities, partook of sandwiches, meat sticks, caramel apples, and tacos from wheelbarrows manned by boys and barking dogs, awaited the condemned, who were promptly hanged by the neck until they stopped twitching.

Then a four-piece band would start blowing their horns and strumming their guitars, fiddles, and banjos, and dancing would break out on San Juan Avenue, closing down traffic for a good two or three hours or until the revelers retreated from the oncoming night's gathering shadows and repaired to the town's countless saloons and hurdy-gurdy houses or to a barn dance on the town's perimeter.

Not even a Fourth of July rodeo could compete with a good, old-fashioned hanging.

"I'll tend the drunk and disorderly later." Mannion filled a stone mug at the range. "Go on back to your rooming house, Cletus. See you at ten this evening."

Booker grunted as he stomped across the room to the front door, which he had to duck low to get through, and left.

Rio's cat, Buster, meowed plaintively from his small wicker chicken cage padded with straw on a shelf above the table used as a desk by Mannion's deputies. With his black-and-white coat and furry black bow tie, Buster always appeared gaudied up for a governor's banquet and speech. He liked the shelf for its proximity to the stove, which warmed the jail office in the mornings and evenings, both of which were cool even in the summer. This late-spring morning the cat would call it downright cold. Mannion had seen his own breath frosting the air when he'd left the San Juan and his beloved Jane still enjoying her coffee while she had a couple of the young women working for her heat water for a bath.

Answering the cat's plea, Rio fetched a bottle of cream from under a floorboard, where he'd dug a small hole to keep the cream cool and fresh. He filled a small muffin tin with the cream and set the tin on the shelf before the cage.

Buster trilled eagerly, purred and, rising and stretching, curled his tail. He poked his head out of the cage, hunkered down, and went to work, lapping the cream and purring. At least the cat was pleased by the day's start.

Mannion slid Booker's platters aside, set his cup on

his desk, and sagged into his chair. He leaned back and ran his hands back through his hair with a weary groan. When he'd returned Buster's cream to the hole in the floor and replaced the floorboard over it, Rio poured himself a cup of coffee and leaned a shoulder against the wall across from his boss and said, "What is it, Joe? You look a little off your feed."

"Ah, hell." Mannion blew on his coffee and sipped it. "I reckon I'm just gettin' old. Startin' to reflect on things I don't like reflectin' on." He found himself gazing through the window above his desk, remembering the dream—or nightmare, rather—he'd had earlier.

"Don't do that," Rio said after he'd taken a sip of his own hot mud. "That's a bad way to go." He gave a rueful chuckle. Not a year ago he'd endured a nervous time, a time in which he'd come to think he didn't have the spine to do his job anymore. "Don't I know," he added, and took another sip of the coffee.

"Had a dream," Joe felt like confessing, though he didn't like getting personal with anyone but Jane. It had taken him a long time to feel comfortable enough with even her, which was one of the reasons she'd left him their first time around the maypole, so to speak. If there was anyone else he didn't mind airing his spleen to, however, that person would be Rio, the best of his few friends.

"Had a dream I was locked in a coffin and dropped in a river."

Rio regarded him keenly, gray-brown brows stitched over his suety eye sockets.

"Yessir," Mannion said, setting his cross-draw Russian on the desk beside his coffee cup. He broke open the top-break piece and added, "The lid on the coffin was nailed shut. Pitch black. Blacker than a banker's heart...the inside of a glove...the bottom of a well..."

Rio whistled.

"Could hardly breathe as that coffin twisted and turned and pitched and rocked. And there I was, shut up tight inside it, hot but cold sweating, my heart banging away like a drum on a parade ground."

Rio stared at him.

"What is it?" Mannion asked.

"Joe, uh..." Rio hesitated, staring at his boss with grave concern in his eyes. "That was a death dream, Joe!"

Before Mannion could respond, footsteps sounded on the stoop.

Finished with his cream, Buster sat just inside the open door of his chicken cage and regarded the front door warily. He meowed as though in warning. Mannion had seen the cat's reaction. Now he closed his hand over the Russian still open on his desk, though he had not replaced the spent shells in the wheel with fresh ones from his cartridge belt.

The doorknob turned and the door opened suddenly.

Mannion closed the Russian and started to raise the gun, his thumb on the hammer. He forestalled the motion when Jane strode into the office and stopped, casting her own concerned gaze from Rio to her husband.

"Joe!"

Mannion was relieved it was Jane. Buster had reacted as he had because for some reason the tomcat didn't like women in the jailhouse. Apparently, he saw Hotel de Mannion as a domain for the males only of both species —humans and cats.

Mannion set the Russian back down on his desk and rose from his chair. "Jane? What's wrong, honey?"

"What's wrong? That's what I came to ask you." Jane glanced at the deputy Mannion's senior by ten years, and said, "Or Rio...if you weren't able..."

"Why wouldn't I be able?"

"I heard about the shooting. Someone said you were involved. Not surprising, of course, but given the..." Jane let her voice trail off. Standing in front of the door, her hand on the knob, she stood staring at her husband, the bodice of her low-cut dress rising and falling sharply as she breathed.

Rio looked at her. "You heard about it, Miss Jane?"

"About *what*?" Mannion said in disgust.

Jane turned to Rio, and the deputy said, "His dream...?"

Jane nodded.

"My *death* dream?" Mannion said, hooking an ironic smile beneath his brushy mustache.

There sounded a *ping!* followed by a *thump!*

Mannion looked at the window. There was a fresh hole in it spoked with cracks.

He looked down.

Two inches to the left of his Russian was a hole in one of the several wanted dodgers littering his desk. The circulars had been blown aside to reveal the hole in Mannion's wooden desk.

A bullet hole.

Now the whip crack of the rifle that had fired the slug reached Mannion's ears.

"Shooter!" Mannion bellowed. "Down, honey!"

CHAPTER 6

Jane stared at Mannion in shock, her hand still on the outside knob of the open door.

Buster gave a loud, frightened meow.

Mannion snapped his Russian closed and ran over to the door just as Rio grabbed Jane, led her away from the door, and shoved her down to the floor in front of the deputies' desk and Buster's cage. Mannion kicked the door closed and, cocking the Russian he held in his right hand, edged a look around the window, between the frame and the fresh hole in the pane.

He caught a brief glimpse of a man just then running up and over the peak of the tonsorial parlor on the other side of the street. All Mannion saw was the man's cream Stetson and the rifle in the man's hand as well as the back of a buckskin coat just before the man disappeared down the peak's opposite side.

"I see him!" Joe said. "Rio, keep her here and keep low!"

"Joe!" both Rio and Jane yelled.

But then Mannion was outside, pulling the door closed behind him, and quickly but carefully negotiating his way across the busy main street roiling with dust from a passing sawyer's dray heaped with long, unpeeled pine logs likely from the higher reaches of the Sawatch. When the dust cleared on the opposite side of the street, he saw that the barber, John Dunham, was out on his front boardwalk clad in his customary green eyeshade and sleeve garters, a soapy straight razor in one hand. He was twisted around, trying to get a look up at his roof.

When the barber saw Mannion leap up onto the boardwalk to his left, he said, "Thought it must be thunder. Then I came outside and seen there wasn't a cloud in sight!"

"Wasn't that kinda thunder!"

Mannion ran down the break between the barber shop and a potion shop. When he reached the far end, he stopped and looked to both his right and left along the trash-strewn alley.

No sign of the shooter.

Joe cursed.

He whipped around, raising the Russian, when he heard running footsteps behind him. He drew his horns in when he saw his junior deputy, Henry McCallister, running toward him, his Colt in his hand.

"Heard another shot, Marshal! Seen you crossin' the street!"

"Another shooter," Mannion said. "Got away. Could be anywhere by now. Probably mixing with the crowd on the main drag."

"That bullet meant for you, too?"

"Aren't they all?"

Henry had stopped near Mannion. Joe felt a little of Rio's previous pique. Henry was only a little out of breath, though he'd come running at a good clip and probably from a good distance away. There was nothing that rankled older men more than younger ones. Especially when said younger ones seemed so oblivious of being young and in better shape.

"You get a look at him?" Henry asked.

"Just his hat. It's cream. He had a rifle. Wore a buckskin coat. Didn't get much of a look beyond that. Damn the luck!" Fury burned in Mannion as he saw in his mind's eye that hole in the window only a few inches from where Jane had stood in the open doorway, as well as the hole in his desk. The hole in the desk didn't bother him as much as the hole in the window did because it had been closer to Jane.

She might have taken a bullet meant for him.

Of course, it had been meant for him. Men were trying to kill him all the time. It was the neatly wrapped package, ribbon and all, that came with being a lawman for as long as Mannion had. Well over twenty years. A man, especially one with Bloody Joe's uncompromising temperament, made a lot of enemies. The bastard with the cream hat and the rifle could have been any of a good hundred men with chips on their shoulders.

Henry looked puzzled. He nudged his tan Stetson up on his head from behind to scratch the back of it. "You think this is related to earlier? Maybe a friend of the fellas you turned toe down?"

"Nah. Men like that don't have friends. Leastways, not any that would be loyal enough to go seeking revenge for their demises."

"I reckon you're right."

"Walk around—will ya, Henry? Make your usual rounds but keep an eye out for a fella, medium tall and wearing a cream hat."

"You got it, Marshal."

Mannion gave a wry chuff. He knew he'd sent Henry

on an impossible mission. If his junior deputy reported all the medium tall men in cream hats and wielding nondescript rifles, he was liable to see within the next half hour alone, he'd have a suspect list as long as Mannion's arm.

Joe again took his life in his hands just by crossing San Juan Avenue. As he stepped up onto the porch of Hotel de Mannion, the office door opened before him.

"See him?" Rio had his double-bore, twelve-gauge shotgun in his hands.

"Joe!" Jane said. "Are you all right, Joe?"

Mannion held up his hands, palms out, as he stepped into the jail office. To Rio, he said, "No, I didn't get another look at him." To his wife, he said, "I'm fine, honey."

Mannion kissed Jane's cheek then drew her close to him, hugging her. He didn't normally cotton to public displays of affection, but he couldn't help himself. He was deeply worried about Jane. She'd come within inches of taking a bullet meant for him. If he had another killer on his trail, she was in danger. Anyone close to Mannion was in danger. He had to stay as clear of Jane and Vangie as possible.

Damn this crazy job! It had been one thing when he'd been relatively alone in it. But now he had Jane and Vangie, who'd moved to town to live with her husband in their own house, to worry about.

Pushing Jane back away from him, he kissed her forehead and said, "You'd best head back to the San Juan. I'm going to start bunking here until I can wrangle that devil with the long gun."

"No, why?" Jane said, frowning, causing a forked vein to bulge just above the bridge of her freckled nose.

Mannion glanced at the bullet hole in the window.

"Oh, Joe," Jane said. "Don't worry about me. It's you the shooter was after."

Ignoring her, Mannion turned to Rio. "Escort her back to the San Juan—will you, Rio? Stay with her until she's safely inside." He gave his wife a commanding look. "You stay there, now, hear?"

"Joe, I want to talk to you about something."

Jane retrieved his coffee cup from his desk. At the stove, she added more coffee to it then filled another one. She gave Mannion his cup and then leaned back against his desk, holding her own cup down low against her belly in both hands. She glanced at Rio, who hiked a shoulder and sipped his own coffee.

"What's this about?" Mannion gave a dry chuckle. "Feel like I'm bein' taken to the woodshed."

"The dream you had, Joe," Jane blurted out. "It was a warning."

"The dream I had was a warning." It wasn't a question. He was merely repeating her words to try to make sense of them himself. "Is that what you were trying to tell me earlier?"

"It's a well-known thing, Joe," Rio said, his own voice grave, concerned. "Bein' locked in a coffin...set downstream..."

Mannion chuckled. He couldn't believe what he was hearing. "You two can't be serious." He shuttled his gaze between them both, grinning his incredulity.

They stared at him.

"You are!"

"I had an aunt," Jane said. "She read tarot cards...could see into a person's future by looking into their eyes...the lines in their hands. She told me once that over the years people had come to her with stories about dreams they'd had. One in particular, and the one they all had in common, was the same one you had last night. Being in a nailed-shut coffin, dropped into a river. The darkness, the lack of air, the fear. They'd all experienced the same thing. They'd all died...or been killed...within the month."

Mannion stared at his pretty wife in shock. He'd known she was superstitious. He'd found that to be one of the many charming things about her. But up till now, he'd had no idea just how superstitious she *really* was.

He turned to his senior deputy still looking at him gravely, tapping his big, brown thumb against the side of his steaming coffee mug. "You believe that nonsense, too, Rio?"

Rio hiked a shoulder. "It's a well-known thing, Joe. Bein' locked in a coffin...the water...the panic. Heck, ever'body knows that!"

Mannion looked in astonishment from Rio to Jane then back again. He leaned back against the wall by the door. "Why, I've never heard the like. Two reasonable, normally level-headed people believing in voodoo!"

Just then foot thuds sounded on the porch fronting the jail office. Mannion slapped his hand to the silver-chased Russian holstered on his right thigh. Rio quickly set his cup down on the table beside him, turned to the door, and raised the double-bore in both hands, his right thumb on one of the rabbit ear hammers, ready to rock it back.

The door opened and Henry McCallister stepped inside then stepped back, raising both his gloved hands shoulder-high, palms out. "Whoa! Whoa! Whoa! Sorry I didn't knock, but...just came back for my rifle."

Rio sighed in relief and lowered the double-bore.

Mannion returned his Russian to its holster.

"Henry," Joe said. "You ever have a dream you were locked in a coffin and dropped in a river?"

The young deputy's face scrunched up and he stepped back against the open door behind him. "Oh, heck no! And I don't wanna have one, neither. Why, that's a death dream, Marshal!"

"Oh, no—you, too?"

"Why, everybody knows that!" Henry stared at Mannion. "Did you have a dream like that?"

"He had that very dream," Jane said.

Mannion decided to go along with the nonsense but maybe try a little subtle reasoning, as well, though he knew from experience that superstitions were slippery, stubborn things to try to quell. He looked at Jane, and said, "You say it's a warning. What's a fella to do with such a warning?"

"Take some time off," Rio said. "Let me an' Hank handle Del Norte for a while. Us an ol' Cletus an' his axe handle." He chuckled.

Booker made his nightly rounds with a shotgun and an axe handle, and he didn't hesitate to use either one. Just seeing the big man coming, thus armed, had made many a drunken miner lay down his pick and his shovel and shuffle off to a pile of hay, as passive as an orphan kitten.

"Yeah, go up to your fishin' shack," Henry suggested. "Catch some of them mountain trout in the Sawatch. Nice an' cool up there this time o' the year. Gonna be gettin' hotter'n hot down here soon."

"In more ways than one," Rio muttered into his mug, then sipped his coffee.

Mannion was exasperated. "You expect me to run"— he jerked his chin to indicate the roof of John Dunham's Tonsorial Parlor—"from that catamount with the rifle?"

"You wouldn't be running, Joe," Jane said. "You'd merely be taking a badly needed vacation. How long has it been since you've had one of those? Why, we never even took a honeymoon because you're so wedded to your job!"

"Ah, hell, honey—let's not start this again. Besides, if I go on your so-called vacation now, on the heels of having some drunk miner or some equally drunk cowpoke trying to make good on a bet, it won't take long before my reputation takes a running leap into the nearest privy, an' every gunslinger in the territory comes to Del Norte thinking I've turned coward. Then all bets *will be* off!"

Pulling her mouth corners down in frustration, Jane looked at Rio. Rio shrugged. Jane turned to Joe. "You've been shot at twice today," she said softly, coolly. "And it's not even noon."

"Mere coincidence," Mannion said. "I've dodged bullets before."

"But not after a dream like the one you had last night," Rio said, his own voice soft but laced with dark portent. "Sooner or later, it's gonna catch up with you, Joe."

"What is?"

"Fate," Jane answered for Rio.

She took the last sip of her coffee, set her cup on the table beside Rio, and walked over to Mannion. "I know it all sounds like crazy blather to your practical ears, my love. I also know we've said about all we can on the subject—me and Rio and Henry." She rose onto the tiptoes of her side button shoes and gave Mannion a quick but affectionate kiss on the lips. She looked up at him from beneath her copper brows, pleading in her amber-eyed gaze. "Let's run off to Denver together. We'll take the honeymoon we still have coming. One *without* bullets. You think on it. You'll know where to find me."

Jane stepped between Mannion and Henry and left.

Mannion looked at Rio, who finished his own coffee and set his cup down.

"Don't worry—I'll see to her!"

He hurried out of the office after Jane.

CHAPTER 7

MANNION MADE TWO THOROUGH ROUNDS ABOUT THE town armed with his two Russians and his prized 1873 Winchester "Yellowboy" repeater in the event he found himself needing to take a long shot at the devil who'd come close to cleaning his clock earlier that morning.

He had to make his usual rounds.

He couldn't let anyone in town think he was laying low because he was afraid of getting back shot. Laying low, cowering like a yellow-livered cur, was not how lawdogging worked. Just as an old wolf could show no fear, and tried like hell not to show his age, Mannion knew he had to do the same lest the younger wolves take advantage of that weakness, of his age, and converge on him, ripping and tearing, howling like banshees, leaving his old bones strewn around some arroyo.

Humans were not all that different from wolves. All it took was age and experience to realize that.

He made his rounds, but he had to admit to a nagging apprehension tickling his spine, making him feel as though he had a target drawn on his back. But he made them, all right—two thorough rounds about the entire town, even the most peripheral backstreets, keeping his eyes skinned on the nooks, crannies, alley mouths, and rooftops around him.

He couldn't help feeling relieved when he'd finished the last of those two rounds. It was early afternoon, a little after one if his old, bullet-nicked railroad turnip was keeping the right time—hell, it was pret' near as old as Joe himself was, a gift from his mountain man father when he'd turned thirteen and had taken down his first bear all by himself with an old Hawken rifle. He went into the Three-Legged Dog on San Juan Avenue, bellied up to the bar, set his rifle on top of the mahogany, his hat atop that, ran a hand through his sweat-damp hair, and ordered a beer.

"Crack an egg in it for me—will you, Charlie?" he asked the burly bartender, a former mule skinner named Charlie Thurman. "Didn't have much for breakfast and I skipped lunch, don't ya know."

"What do you mean?" Thurman said, drawing the beer and scraping the foam off with a flat stick. "This is lunch." He cracked an egg and let it slide down out of the broken shell and into the rich, golden ale, the yolk glowing the deep orange of a Colorado sunset as it dropped slowly to the bottom of the glass and lolled there, tiny bubbles rising from it to join the inch of creamy froth at the top of the mug.

"Ahh."

"Enjoy," the barman said, expertly sliding the mug down and across the bar to the lawman. "Never know when it's gonna be your last."

The apron gave a wry chuckle then moseyed down the bar to fill the order of a cowpuncher in town on a supply run.

Mannion growled and glanced into the backbar

mirror, keeping an eye on the room behind him. Young Harmon Haufenthistle, the twelve-year-old odd-job boy and errand runner, was just then walking down the stairs at the back of the room, bouncing one hand along the rail beside him, humming. The boy was Viking blond and blue-eyed, his naturally fair skin nearly as dark as an Apache's from all the time he spent in the Del Norte outdoors, hustling from one job to another, jiggling the coins in his pocket.

When he saw Mannion in the mirror, he said, "Heard they tried to trim your wick again, Joe, and you turned 'em all toe down!"

Young Haufenthistle always lumped Mannion's would-be killers together under the collective pronoun "they," as though there were a whole pack of human wolves lying in wait for him, with the sole intention of planting Del Norte's town marshal six feet under. And that their single-minded ambition made them a collective one. The notion always made Bloody Joe wince inwardly.

He often wondered what it would be like for a man to go his whole life without having someone gunning for him. He'd heard there were such men.

The boy leaped from the third step to the bottom of the stairs and straightened the pair of burlap sacks connected by a short rope slung over his right shoulder. He'd probably delivered a new pair of shoes or a dress to one of the working girls upstairs, ordered from a wish book at Wilfred Drake's Mercantile. Or maybe he was headed out to place such an order. One never knew. Harmon was one of the most industrious, hardworking, fast-hustling males in town, young or old.

Mannion met the boy's eyes in the backbar mirror and raised his glass to him.

Young Harmon headed for the batwings, tugging the

brim of his black wool immigrant cap down lower on his forehead. "I'll keep an eye skinned for suspicious-looking characters, Joe. I can spot one right off. Only problem is the town's so dang full of 'em!"

He chuckled as he pushed through the batwings and strode off along the boardwalk, whistling.

"That boy is already lobbying for a deputy position, Joe," said Charlie Thurman, drawing another beer.

"Harmon doesn't aim that low," Joe quipped, raising his mug to his mouth once more. "He's out for *my* job!"

Several men and one doxie sitting around the room behind him or standing at the bar to his right, laughed.

Mannion took another sip of the beer and in the corner of his right eye spied movement out front of the saloon. He turned his head quickly, one hand ready to reach for the Yellowboy. He kept his hand at the ready, trigger finger twitching. A man in a cream hat and with a rifle jutting from a scabbard strapped to the right side of his saddle was just then putting his brown-and-white pinto pony up to one of the hitchracks fronting the Three-Legged Dog.

Hmmm, Mannion thought. *Cream hat, rifle. No buckskin coat, but it's warmed up some over the past couple of hours.*

Never mind there were likely at least a hundred other men wearing cream hats and armed with rifles in Del Norte at that very moment, a little bird whispered in Mannion's ear as he kept his eyes on the newcomer, who swung down from the pinto's back and tied the reins at the rack. As he did, he lifted his head to glance through the Three-Legged Dog's plate glass window, locking eyes briefly with Mannion.

He was neither young nor old—maybe late twenties. Dark blond hair hung down from beneath his hat to nearly brush his shoulders. A good-looking man with intelligent, dark-blue eyes, even features that bordered on "chiseled," with broad, high cheekbones that bespoke more than a little Nordic or Celtic blood.

He had broad shoulders and the good strong legs of a man accustomed to the saddle. When he straightened after tying the reins at the rack, Mannion noted he was of average height, which he'd also noted about the man who'd tried to snuff his wick, as young Harmon Haufenthistle had so aptly put it, from the roof of Dunham's Tonsorial Parlor.

The young man loosened the pinto's saddle cinch and slipped the bit from the horse's mouth. He removed his weathered cream hat, slapped it against his denim-clad legs, making dust billow, then donned the hat again and headed for the batwings.

As he did, Mannion leaned forward on the bar, took another sip of his beer.

He considered the newcomer. The man and the horse had obviously ridden a long way. Both were dusty and the horse had trail lather on his withers. That didn't take the young man out of the running as Mannion's would-be assassin. He could have taken the horse into the country outside Del Norte and run him hard to make them both look like they'd come a long way.

This wasn't Mannion's first rodeo. He'd keep his guard up, though not obviously so.

He kept his eyes on the mirror and watched the man saunter toward him, angling toward a place at the bar to his right. A Colt revolver was strapped low on his right leg. When he gained the bar, he glanced in the backbar mirror, eyes flicking toward the badge pinned to Mannion's dark-red corduroy shirt. He nodded affably.

"Mornin', Marshal. Or...is it afternoon? I plum lost track."

"Afternoon," Mannion said, lifting his beer to his lips.

"That's what happens when you travel as much as I do, I reckon. You lose track of time—days, nights, minutes, seconds..."

"Been on the trail awhile, have you?" Joe asked the newcomer as Charlie Thurman drew the man a beer.

"Awhile."

"Lookin' for work?"

The newcomer sighed. "I'm always lookin' for work, seems like."

"Cowpuncher?"

The man tossed a nickel onto the bar. "Yessir."

"Don't stay long on any one spread, eh?"

The younger man smiled into his beer as he raised the mug to his lips. "Me—I get itchy feet. I'm one o' them grass is always greener fellas." He chuckled then sipped his beer.

"Got a handle?"

The newcomer man set the beer down on the bar, turned to Mannion, and extended his hand. "Quentin Ferguson..."

He let his voice trail off as Mannion shook Ferguson's hand then saw the strange cast that came to the young man's blue eyes when another man pushed through the batwings to enter the Three-Legged Dog and saunter toward Mannion's place at the bar.

"Hello there, Joe!" said the tall, lean grocer, Norman Davis, who strode toward the bar in his brown three-piece suit and natty bowler hat, his small, round, steel-framed spectacles glinting in the light angling through the plate glass window.

"Hello, Norm," Mannion said. "How's the grocery business?"

"Ah...you know. Say, I heard Ol' Scratch reached up to tickle your toes again this morning!"

Davis laughed and shook his head. He turned to include young Quentin Ferguson in his mirth but just then a strange cast, even stranger than a few seconds earlier, darkened the younger man's eyes. Ferguson turned abruptly away, sipping his beer as though to cover the stiff expression on his face, and strode over to a near table and sat down, facing Mannion and the affable grocer, who ordered a beer just like the one Mannion was having.

"That looks might good," said Davis, setting his hat on the bar. He canted his head toward Ferguson and lowered his voice as he said to Mannion, "Hope I didn't interrupt anything, Joe." He grabbed the handle of his beer schooner with his right hand, the square garnet pinky ring with the gold U.S. monogram set into it glinting in the sunlight from the window.

———

QUENTIN CAMPBELL, ALIAS QUENTIN FERGUSON, USING his mother's maiden name, felt his heartbeat increase and heat rise along his spine and move down into his knees.

He stared toward Mannion and the grocer, who faced each other, one elbow on the bar, chatting, smiling, making small talk.

Quentin hoped he hadn't appeared too suspicious nor his reaction to seeing the man again too obvious. Yes, he was certain the grocer in the three-piece suit was, indeed, the captain who'd led the Union-sympathizing marauders in the raid on Quentin's family's ranch, the Circle C Bar, fifteen years ago. Over that long stretch of time, he'd hunted the seven men who'd murdered his family and raped his sister, Danny.

By hook and by crook, just dumb chance, he'd found four. One had been a ranch foreman he'd found bucking the tiger in Hayes, Kansas, late one winter night. He'd lain in wait in the shadows outside the saloon, and when the man had finished playing faro, Quentin had slipped up behind him, knocked him out, dragged him into an alley, and cut his throat but not before explaining to the man why he'd been about to die.

He had the faces of most of the raiders stamped on his brain, but even though he'd been nearest the leader, all he could remember about the man was the flat, evil cast to the man's brown-eyed gaze and the garnet ring with the U.S. monogram on his right pinky finger. Finding the man here, now, so unexpectedly, had been a shock Quentin had thought he'd steeled himself for.

He'd wanted to be prepared.

He'd lain awake many nights in some lonesome, back-country camp, beside a near-dead fire, staring up at the stars and imagining what seeing the gang leader who'd cut his sister's throat again would be like. Imagining seeing him again at long last, Quentin pulling his .44 Colt from the holster thonged low on his right thigh and drilling several rounds into the man's belly.

Yeah, two or three pills he couldn't digest!

Then, while the man lay there on the ground or on some sawdusted floor of some smoky hole-in-the-wall saloon like the very one he was in now, he'd remind him of that bloody, nightmarish afternoon at the Circle C Bar headquarters. He'd remind the man of his cowardice, being turned away by a shotgun wielded by a twelve-year-old boy.

He'd laugh in his face and tell him how long he'd been hunting him and the others, working on one ranch or in one saloon after another but meanwhile appraising the face of every man he met on every ranch and on every range and around every watering hole...in every town...every saloon... every feedstore...every café...every mercantile he visited.

But now at long last he'd found him, and in his mind, he was killing the killer slowly.

"There—how do you like that, you son of a bitch!" Quentin would spat in his face.

He'd had another fantasy, one in which he tortured out of the gang leader the names and whereabouts of the last two men who'd ridden with him that bloody, horrible afternoon—the Indian and a red-haired man with pale blue eyes. He doubted that would come to pass, however. He doubted he'd be able to restrain himself, not kill the man outright. He'd carried a killing fury inside him for too long.

He'd have to settle with exacting his revenge on the leader. Then, after the leader was dead, he could start looking for the last two. He wouldn't give up until all seven of those brutal killers were dead. He'd continue his journey of revenge and bloody, howling death, haunted endlessly by the look of horror in his sister's face when the gang leader had walked up behind her, lifted her head by her hair, and ran the blade of his Bowie knife across her throat.

He thought Danny had seen Quentin peering around the barn doors. Briefly. Just for a second before the blood geysered from her throat and tender neck. He wondered if seeing him had comforted her at all. Even just a little would be enough.

Of course, he'd never know.

The only thing that comforted him was avenging Danny and his parents' murders.

Now he stared at the seemingly affable, bespectacled grocer standing with the town marshal at the bar. He tried to maintain an even, impassive expression. But he found himself grinding his molars and squeezing the handle of his beer mug in his gloved right hand. He squeezed it so hard the glass shook. Quentin hadn't taken a sip yet, and the foam at the top of the glass threatened to spill down the sides.

He leaned forward and, leaving the mug on the table —his hand was shaking too severely to pick it up and not make a spectacle of himself—slurped the beer down to a half inch below the rim. He looked up to see the town marshal glance at him briefly, skeptically. Then the tall, mustached, salt-and-pepper haired star-toter returned his wolfish gray eyes to the grocer, who was telling Mannion a story about one of the market hunters who worked for him and had become entangled with a rancher who hadn't wanted him shooting game on his land.

The rancher had wanted a fifty-fifty split of the bear the hunter had shot. Somehow, the story must have turned out all right, had ended humorously, at least for the hunter, because the grocer slapped the bar with his beringed right hand.

He and Mannion laughed.

Quentin reached under the table and unsnapped the keeper thong from over the hammer of his holstered Colt.

CHAPTER 8

No sooner had Quentin released the keeper thong, he snapped it back into place.

What do you think you're gonna do? Shoot the man down while he's standing at the bar palavering with the lawman? You wanna get yourself hung?

He had to admit he'd harbored a death wish ever since witnessing the horror the bluebelly sympathizers and rogue Union agents had perpetrated on his family. He couldn't get the horror of that afternoon out of his head. Many nights he didn't sleep but tossed and turned, those images flashing through his mind, keeping him from slumber, keeping his heart pounding, cold sweat oozing from his pores.

He was in his late twenties, but he hadn't been able to start a life for himself.

His need for revenge had robbed him of the past fifteen years.

But revenge he had taken, and he wasn't finished yet. Not by a long shot.

As he'd done in the past, he had to go about exacting revenge in a sensible manner. He couldn't get himself killed in the process. He still had three men to hunt down and kill. He might have just found one of them— the most important one.

He drew a deep, calming breath, let it out slow.

He had to wait and make sure the grocer in the three-piece suit standing with the local lawman was really the leader of the gang that had killed his family. All he had to go on so far was the ring on his little finger. And the look in his brown eyes. Yeah, Quentin had seen the flatness, the quiet, subtle malevolence stirring around behind the man's smile, behind his little, round spectacles. He was the sort of man who could smile and laugh at your jokes while at the same time imagining putting a pitchfork through your heart.

That was the man Quentin had seen in the barn that day.

He'd seen that look in the man's eyes, behind his smile, as he'd sauntered up to the bar, craggy, timeworn cheeks on either side of his brown-mustached mouth dimpling. Now as Quentin watched, the man glanced into the mirror and patted down his short, brown hair, pomaded and parted on one side. Quentin met the man's gaze in the mirror and looked away suddenly.

The man's eyes had met his.

Had he recognized Quentin?

How good of a look had the man gotten of Quentin that smoky, shadowy afternoon, as the boy had stared down the twin barrels of his father's twelve-gauge shotgun?

Quentin stared down at his beer. As he lifted the mug carefully in both hands, trying not to shake, he glanced into the mirror again. In the upper periphery of his vision, he saw the grocer turn back to the lawman. He was listening to what the lawman was saying. He was smiling, clean-shaven cheeks dimpling, nodding.

"Now, that I would have to see to believe, Joe!" he said, and slapped a hand down on the bar.

The lawman, Joe, chuckled, raised his beer glass, and drank the last of the beer including the yolk that had been lolling and glowing orange at the bottom of the glass. As he pulled the mug away from his mouth, he turned his head slightly to his left, casting another curious, sidelong glance toward Quentin, who had taken several swallows of his own beer and, using both hands, carefully set the dimpled schooner down on the table beside his trail-dusted, cream Stetson.

The grocer, whom the lawman had called Norm, finished his own beer and the egg at the bottom, set his glass down, donned his bowler, and turned to the marshal. "Well, I gotta go, Joe. If I'm away from the shop too long, Iris gets the wild idea I've gone somewhere other than just the post office!"

Both men laughed. The grocer wheeled on his brown brogans and strode across the room and out the door before turning to his left and disappearing in the busy town's hustle and bustle. As he did, an unseen man yelled, "Have a good day, Mr. Davis. I'll be over in a bit for some o' them pork ribs!"

Davis...

Quentin began to rise, to get after the man, to see where his store was. He wanted to learn more about him, to make sure he was the man he'd been hunting. The leader of the other six. But then he saw the lawman giving him the woolly eyeball in the backbar mirror, and, feeling his ears warm with chagrin, sat back down in his chair.

Take it easy, you fool. You've waited too long for this to muck it up now! The lawman is suspicious. Now, you have to do every-thing you can to ease those suspicions.

He sipped his beer, though he was so enervated he couldn't taste it. He turned to face the window, one boot hiked on the opposite knee, feigning a casual air, slowly turning his beer schooner with his right thumb and index finger, round and round in the ring of water from the glass itself.

Mannion paid for his and the grocer's beers, bid the barman good day. The barman told him to keep his nose out of trouble. The lawman, Joe, turned to Quentin, smiled, pinched his hat brim in parting, and said, "Good luck looking for work, young man. Plenty of jobs to be had in these parts for a straight shooter."

He nodded, pushed through the batwings, and turned to his right. Quentin watched him walk past the large, plate glass window then disappear just as another male voice rose above the street racket, "Hey, Bloody Joe—heard they tried to plant ya again. How many lives you *got*, anyway?"

Ribald laughter.

Quentin picked up his beer, sipped it. His hand shook only a little. Good.

He knew other eyes were on him. Leastways, he had to assume so, anyway. He'd looked suspicious. Now he had to waylay those suspicions. He'd just sit here, a youngish man passing through town, looking for work, taking a break, just sitting here nursing a beer and watching the crowd trundle past the large windows on both sides of the batwing doors.

Slowly, wanting to spring up from the chair and run after the man called Davis...Norman Davis...he sipped his beer. He didn't taste a single drop. He took the last sip from what he judged would be the last one. He hummed to himself, slowly turned the dimpled schooner around in the circle of its own condensation then, imagining every eye in the room was on him, casually lifted the glass and drank the rest.

He set the schooner back onto the table. He rose, stretched, making a good show of it, then peered into the backbar mirror as he adjusted the angle of his hat. He smiled and nodded at the several other saloon patrons then sauntered on out of the Three-Legged Dog, grabbed his reins off the hitchrack, and swung into the saddle of his pinto.

He waited for a lull in the traffic then turned the gelding out into the street and spurred him south, the same direction in which the man calling himself Norman Davis had headed. He rode along the street, turning his head left to right and back again, looking for the name Davis on any of the business signs either stretched across false facades or poking out into the street, tacked across two long pine posts, some peeled, some unpeeled.

He came to the south edge of town then swung back north. At the north edge of town, he swung the pinto back around, shoved his Stetson up onto his forehead, and scratched the back of his head, scowling his frustration. Del Norte was larger than he'd thought. If the name Davis graced any sign in town, it must be on some sign on one of the several side streets.

Searching could take him all day. And he'd be drawing attention to himself. Best to just go ahead and...

"Say there, sonny," he said, booting the horse over to the street's right side, to where a young man maybe eleven or twelve years old, tan, blond, and blue-eyed and wearing faded overalls and a black immigrant cap was walking north along the boardwalk, stooped under the weight of the burlap bags he was carrying over his right shoulder. "Can you tell me where I might find Davis's Grocery Store here in this fine, hoppin' town?"

In this fine, hoppin' town? That was wayy overdoing it!

You're nervous and acting the fool just like you almost *did in the Three-Legged Dog!*

The boy didn't hesitate, though he looked a little miffed at being waylaid. He half turned, jerked his chin to indicate behind him, and said curtly, a little impatiently, "Next right. Second block down on the right. The Davis family own South-Central Colorado Fresh Meats & Dry Goods."

Quentin smiled. "Ah, thankee...thank..."

He let his voice trail off as his young benefactor hiked bulging bags a little higher on his shoulder and stepped into the post office, nearly knocking the well-dressed and coifed elderly lady off her feet just exiting the place.

"Oh, Harmon—do please look where you're going!" the matron chirped.

Quentin swung the pinto back into the street, between an ore dray and a covered prairie schooner driven by a bearded man in homespun pilgrim garb; sitting beside him on the driver's seat was a tired-looking young woman in a dusty white sunbonnet and holding a fussing, blanketed baby in her arms.

Ah, the wash of humanity, Quentin thought. It had just been sheer luck he'd run into the man his fellow marauders had called "Captain" and "Dalton" on the day they'd raided the Campbell ranch.

Captain Dalton. That was the only other thing, besides the man's eyes and the ring, Quentin had to go on...

Dalton had changed his name to Davis. Not very imaginative. A dead giveaway.

Still, Quentin had to be sure.

He took a right on the next side street to the north

and saw the sign stretched across the top of a high, halved-log false facade on the street's right side. SOUTH-CENTRAL COLORADO FRESH MEATS & DRY GOODS. A smaller sign beneath it read simply: LAURA'S CAFÉ. The building itself was a large, two-story log cabin with two large windows in the front wall, to either side of the halved-log door, which was propped open with a brick. A tin chimney pipe poked up out of the roof on the near end of the cabin as Quentin approached; he could see several men sitting around a table behind the window on the cabin's near end, as well.

LAURA'S CAFÉ was stenciled in gold-leaf lettering on the window, forming an arc. From the open door issued the smell of coffee, soup, and sweet pastries.

Quentin put the gelding up to one of the two hitchracks fronting the place. A small, black, leather-seated buggy was parked before the building and two saddled horses lazed at one of the hitchracks. Quentin tied his pinto and stared up at the large sign stretched across the facade.

Having his name as well as the names of several others in his gang on that fateful day, he'd visited several other ranches in New Mexico and Arizona that the gang had struck, following one rumor after another, tidbits of information acquired in towns near the sacked ranches, which was next to nothing. Some said the marauders, who usually struck at night, were former Southwestern ranchers who'd been driven out of business by drought and low stock prices, which they blamed on the new railroads hauling a glut of cattle up from the South. No one could figure out the Indian riding with them. Needing an enemy to pin their hard times on, the marauders took up arms against former Confederates who'd gone west after the war.

They rarely left alive anyone who could identify them. When they struck, they struck hard and fast and left bodies and buildings burning in their wake. No one seemed to know who they were, though Quentin had sensed that a few of those he'd talked to did know or thought they knew who some were but were too afraid to share the information lest their homes be burned, families murdered, their daughters raped, throats cut.

Quentin couldn't blame them.

He'd witnessed firsthand the horrors of the raiders' wrath—complete annihilation of those they'd deemed their enemies. They'd raided for two or three weeks back in the mid-'70s, and then they'd stopped. They hadn't been heard from since. Quentin assumed they'd split up and gone back to more quiet lives, maybe waiting for their trails to cool before another bout of bad luck sent them on the warpath once more, conjuring enemies where there were none, but nursing their deaf, dumb, and blind killing fury just the same.

Some men were crazy.

Some were just plain stupid.

And angry, perpetually in need of enemies to blame for their unsuccessful endeavors.

When you put all those traits together, you had men like those who comprised the gang of marauders led by Captain Dalton riding under the guise of the Union cause, though it had long since been decided that the Union had won the war, and that America would remain one country.

"Oh, hello..."

The distinctly female voice had seemingly come from nowhere to nudge Quentin out of his reverie. He looked around at the broad boardwalk fronting the store, crowded with display barrels, wooden crates, and addi-

tional pieces of merchandise including a few field imple-
ments, and finally picked out of the midmorning shadows
a girl—a young woman, rather—standing in the open
doorway in a cream-and-brown print day dress and
apron.

In the apron she held potatoes, in the cradle of her
pale, slender arms. As Quentin's eyes went to her and
stayed there, she blushed a little, color rising in her oval-
shaped face as she walked over to one of the several
display barrels on the boardwalk and dumped her load of
potatoes into it.

She was a small girl—slender but womanly. Maybe
eighteen or nineteen years old. Her eyes were lilac, her
hair long and flaxen blond. Some of that lovely hair was
loosely braided and wrapped around the top of her head
like that worn by a pretty, fresh-faced young damsel at a
May Day fair. It was tied in back so that a short, slender,
queue hung down the back of her head. The skirt of her
dress was long, but Quentin could see that she wore red
felt slippers on her feet.

Straightening after dumping the potatoes, she
brushed dirt from her apron, scowled down at the
garment, and said, "I just washed this only yesterday.
Now look at it." She sighed and let it drop back down
against the front of her dress. "A long wash day doesn't
last long around here."

Quentin leaned forward against his saddle horn,
favoring the pretty girl with his gentle gaze. He hadn't
had the time for pretty, young women. He'd grown up
fast after having been orphaned at twelve years old. He'd
lit out on his own, made a man's way long before he was
a man.

He'd missed out on much.

Now, unable to keep from staring at the pretty, flaxen-haired girl before him, sadness touched him for all the lost years, missed opportunities. He had only the gang of Union-sympathizing marauders to blame. They'd given him no choice but to spend the remainder of his childhood and then the first years of his manhood trying to track them down with the intention of killing every one. He'd kill every one. He had three left, including the Indian riding with them.

"Can I help you find something?" the girl asked, brows arched above those gray-blue, sweet, intelligent eyes.

"What's your name?" Quentin blurted out the query only half-consciously, making him painfully aware that he needed to learn more subtle ways of male-female communication. You didn't just ask a girl her name without preamble in the form of bemused small talk, indirect flirtation. He'd heard such banter during his travels, but he obviously had not acquired the art himself.

"Laura," the girl said. "Laura Davis."

CHAPTER 9

Miss Davis looked Quentin over skeptically.

He cowered a little under her scrutiny. He'd moved too fast in asking her name. Now his tongue felt twice its normal size and he was having trouble forming his next words.

"Well?" she said with a chuckle. "What's yours?"

Quentin fumbled his hat from his head, held it down against his thigh. "Quentin," he said, too quickly. "Quentin Camp...er, I mean...Ferguson. Quentin Ferguson."

Again, she laughed. "Well, which is it? Campbell or Ferguson?"

His ears warmed with chagrin. What was the point in using an alias if after you meet a pretty girl—one of very few over the past fifteen years—you get bashful and get it confused with your own name? Some man hunter.

Pushing thirty, he'd had very little experience with the opposite sex.

He'd spent too much time honing his killing prowess with the .45 thonged to his thigh and the Winchester in his saddle boot. Both were secondhand, but they'd still cost him a pretty penny he'd made punching cattle here and there and now and then. The .45 was a pretty gun with perfect bluing and staghorn grips. He knew it and the handsome repeater likely attracted attention, but he hadn't been able to resist either. He'd saved the money for both when he'd first struck the stalking trail, after spending two months working for a tony saloon in Leadville. Afterward, he'd been eager to hit the trail, fully armed.

When he'd first started out on his stalking trail, he'd had only an old, brass-framed, Confederate-made Griswold & Gunnison cap-and-ball revolver he'd found among the ruins of the cabin, not far from where he'd found the charred thing that had been his mother lying before the burnt ruins of their kitchen table.

Yeah. He'd spent too much time alone, working on his skills as a shooter, filing down the firing pin on the .45 until it had a hair trigger. Too little time among people, especially those of the opposite sex. Now he knew that ancient male attraction to such a lovely creature standing before him, but little of the subtleties of effective communication.

He was a killer, an avenger, not yet fully a man...

He looked at Laura, his face warming.

She was waiting, head canted to one side, brows arched over those lilac-leaning-toward-frosty-gray orbs that stood out to beautifully compliment the rich flaxen of her long, straight hair.

Quentin's mind raced. He forced it back onto its leash. He'd made a mistake, but he could fix it. He looked around as though worried someone might by spying on him then turned to the girl, chuckled nervously—that part was genuine!—and said, "It's Ferguson. You mind forgetting about...you know..."

"The surname that nearly escaped your mouth?" Laura Davis smiled, showing perfect, white teeth. Or nearly perfect. Her right eyetooth was a tad crooked, and it made her speak with a very slight, intoxicating lisp. "Sure." Again, she frowned. "You on the dodge, Quentin, um...Ferguson?"

"Well, if I was, I reckon I'd be a fool sayin' so, now, wouldn't I?"

"Ahh." Laura chewed her thumbnail, scrutinizing him once more, her expression telling Quentin she liked what she saw. "A man of mystery, eh? How...mysterious." She lowered her hand to her side and gave her head a pretty toss, shaking her hair back away from her face. "What can I help you with, Mr. Ferguson? Need a grub sack for the trail?"

Again, Quentin's mind whirled.

Again, he slowed it down.

"Uh...no, no. I just came over to get some licorice, if you have any, and...an apple."

Again, that skeptical look in those pretty, vaguely ironic eyes. "Licorice and an apple..."

He leaned forward, rested an elbow on his saddle horn. "Got any?"

"Oh, I think so. Do you want to climb on down from that handsome horse of yours, or do you want me to fetch you the, uh...licorice and apple?"

Quentin glanced at the building behind her. He'd been so taken by the pretty girl that he'd almost forgotten what had brought him here in the first place.

This girl's father.

But if Davis was the Captain Dalton who'd led the raid on Quentin's family's ranch, how could such a man have spawned such a lovely, obviously cultured and intel-

ligent young woman as the young woman standing before
Quentin now?

All questions he'd find answers to in due course.

He couldn't rush it and thus draw suspicion on
himself.

He fumbled his hat back onto his head, swung down
from the saddle, and tossed his reins around the
hitchrack with aplomb, unable to not to show off a little
for the girl. He knew guns and horses. Not pretty, young
women—aside from the occasional doxie, of course. He
had a man's needs. Laura smiled bemusedly then turned
and started back through the open door behind her.

"Right this way, Mr. Ferguson."

He really wished he hadn't screwed up his name. He
might be close...as close as he might ever get to the killer
of his family—the lead rider, anyway—and he might have
royally messed it up. Any mistake could be fatal. He just
had to hope the girl didn't mention the name Campbell
to Davis. Especially not if he was who Quentin thought
he was...

Quentin removed his hat while he followed her into
the grocery store side of the building, which was to the
left of the door. It was a large, cavernous place—row after
row of dry goods displays, with hams and sausages and
cheese wheels hanging from the ceiling. Clothing
including hats, boots, shoes, and denim jeans occupied
several aisles. To the right of the door was the little
coffee shop and café in which two cowboys sat around a
flour keg, sipping coffee and talking. When Quentin had
entered, one of them, the man facing him, stopped
talking suddenly and frowned at him with a mixture of
curiosity and defensiveness.

His partner hipped around on his chair to also study
Quentin.

Laura showed him to the candy section, reached into a barrel near the counter, and handed him an apple. She moved farther down the counter and, with her small, open hand gestured to two large blue jars, one bristling with red licorice, the other bristling with black licorice.

"As you can see, we're well supplied in the licorice department, Mr. Ferguson."

He wished she would stop emphasizing his last name, not subtly mocking him for his ill attempt at subterfuge.

Quentin glanced around at the large but well-stocked store. There was hardly room in any aisle for turning full around. "Looks like you're well stocked in *every* department," he said.

When he turned back to the young woman, his eyes strayed to the bodice of her conservative but tight, well-filled day dress. He hadn't realized he'd done it until he'd done it.

He became very aware of it, however, when he lifted his gaze and saw a look of incredulity in her large eyes, another flush rising in her cheeks and reaching up into her ears, as well, her long hair tucked behind each.

"Oh!" Quentin said. "That's not...that's not what I meant!"

Before she could reply, one of the cowboys yelled from the café part of the store, "Laura, Dave and I could use a refill!"

Laura looked past Quentin, annoyance in her features. "Coming, Lars!"

Shuttling her gaze back to Quentin, she quirked her mouth corners in a smile of sorts. "I know that wasn't what you meant." A curious frown dug deep lines across her otherwise smooth, pale forehead. "You certainly are a strange one. Half-wild, aren't you? And lonely. Tell me, are you one of those children who was found living with wolves up in the mountains?"

She jerked her pretty, dimpled chin to indicate the San Juan Mountains rising west of Del Norte.

Quentin laughed and looked down at his hat, which he held against his chest. "Well, you're close, Miss Laura. Very close, but—"

"Laura!" Lars yelled again. "Pronto! We need the mud to wash down the last of these buns of your'n. They're a little dry if you don't mind me sayin', hon!"

"Laura." A man's peeved voice sounded down a hallway behind Laura and on her left. Footsteps sounded. The man who emerged from the shadowy mouth of the hall opening off the end of the business counter, was none other than Norman Davis himself. He scowled down at his daughter. "Didn't you hear the man?" he said quietly. He glanced at Quentin briefly, a vague reproof and annoyance showing in his face and flat, brown eyes, before returning his admonishing gaze to his daughter. "Old Olaf's men do a big business here. Please don't keep them waiting."

Olaf Gunderson was Lar's cranky, old father.

"Yes, Pa." The girl glanced once more at Quentin before wheeling, the hem of her skirt and her dirty apron billowing out around her and hurried into the restaurant part of the shop.

As she did, Davis scrutinized Quentin more carefully behind his spectacles. "Weren't you in the saloon...the Three-Legged Dog...earlier? Yes, you were talking with Mannion."

Quentin took one look into the man's eyes—he didn't need another look at the ring on his little finger—to know this was the man he was looking for. His mouth was dry. His heart hammered the backside of his breastbone. He shook off the nerves...or tried to. Again, his tongue felt swollen to twice its normal size.

"Y-yeah, just pulled into town. Seems a right nice enough feller." *Now, don't spread the ah, shucks, out-of-work ranch hand and current grub line rider too thick.* "Just swung through town for supplies."

He grinned sheepishly and held up the licorice and the apple. "This oughta do me for now."

"You out of money?"

Again, the aww shucks, poor ol' broke but proud me look. "I reckon I might have a dime or two to rub together, but otherwise I don't jingle much when I walk. Say, uh...Mr. Davis, I take it?"

"Yep, that's me. If you're looking for work...and you're a good, hard worker...you have the shoulders for it, looks like...I can pay you a dollar a day to unload supplies when the freight wagons pull in. I'll also need you to unload supplies from the trains at the depot station twice a week, and to off-load them in the supply shed out back. Think you can do that? Good, hard work, but it'll keep you out of trouble. I sense by the wild look in your eyes and that pretty pistol on your hip you might just get into your fair share—am I right?"

The man smiled. Quentin was a little put off by the smile. It caused that feral, flat quality in his gaze to soften. Maybe even to disappear.

Davis *was* the fella he was looking for, wasn't he?

Quentin couldn't believe his luck. He didn't have to turn himself into any stage actor from New York City, for the part he played now was genuine. He drew a deep, relieved breath and shook his head. "Boy, I sure could use the work. Most of the ranches in these parts ain't... aren't...hiring until the fall gather."

"No, they won't," Davis said. "Most of the hands are

looking for other work. But I'm particular. I won't hire just anyone. I don't trust just any young man around here, and I'm sure you can understand why."

Davis cast his gaze past Quentin into the café part of the store, where Laura was chatting with the two ranch hands.

"Yessir, Mr. Davis. I can understand that. Pretty girl."

"If you can respect her...and her mother and me—Iris works upstairs, keeping the books—we have an apartment up there—then the job is yours."

"I'd like that mighty fine, Mr. Davis. When do I start?"

"Since you just rode into town, you'd best find accommodations for both yourself and your horse. For you, I recommend Ma Branch's Rooming House." He hooked his thumb to indicate west along the side street the grocery shop was on. "It's on the end of the block. Big, three-story house. Mannion's deputy, Henry McCallister rooms there. Mavis Branch is good at making sure the young men she boards toe the line, however—I warn you."

Davis gave Quentin a mock severe, admonishing look, a smile quirking a corner of his mustached mouth. Quentin saw that while he was likely around Mannion's age, pushing fifty, he was still muscular with lean, broad shoulders, corded forearms, and large, work-toughened hands. He had a somewhat bulbous forehead and heavy brows, and they added to the severity of the man's countenance. Quentin knew he was not a man who would brook any nonsense.

Especially not where his daughter was concerned.

He could understand that. He'd just met her, but he suspected you didn't have to know Laura Davis long to conclude that she was a special young lady. If only she wasn't the daughter of the man who had, most likely, led the killers against his family.

He couldn't let Laura complicate matters. He had to remain single-minded. He had to find out for sure that Davis was the man Quentin thought he was, and then he'd kill him...despite his daughter.

"All right, sir," Quentin said, finding it harder than blazes to call such a man, likely a murderer, "sir," but he must keep up the appearance of a respectful, hard-working man. "Mrs. Branch's rooming house it is."

Davis pulled a pencil down from behind his ear, scribbled a note on a pad on the counter, ripped off the leaf, and gave it to Quentin. "Here. This is to let her know I'll vouch for you and that you have a job with me. I'm sure she'll extend you credit for the first week. There's a reputable livery barn not far from her house."

"Thank you, sir," Quentin said, folding the penciled note and stuffing it into the breast pocket of his shirt.

In fact, he'd saved money from previous jobs, and had a nice wad of greenbacks in his boot. But Davis didn't need to know that.

"I appreciate it...sir."

"Until bright and early tomorrow morning, then."

"Bright and early, sir." Quentin reached into his denim pocket for a dime. "Here's for the licorice and the app—"

"Keep it."

Quentin shook the man's hand, taking a moment to look deep into Davis's eyes. That flatness, that malevolent darkness was not there now. Had Quentin only imagined it? Still, the ring was there on the man's right little finger.

Stuffing the licorice into his denim pocket, Quentin crossed to the door. Laura was no longer talking to Lars and Dave in the café part of the grocery. Two more customers were sitting in the café's small dining room—an elderly couple. Laura had probably gone into the kitchen to cook for them. As Quentin turned to step out onto the boardwalk, he noticed the man he took to be Lars—tall and lean, yellow-haired and with cold, angry eyes—glaring at him from beneath heavy, ridged brows, leaning a little out from his chair to look around Dave at Quentin.

Quentin saw no little warning in the man's eyes.

She's mine, those eyes were saying. Stay away.

Quentin smiled at him, pinched his hat brim to him, and left.

He'd just swung up onto his pinto's back when Laura appeared in the open doorway. Her hands on the frame, she leaned forward, vaguely coquettishly, smiling. "Leaving town?"

Quentin smiled back at her. "What if I wasn't?"

"Well...I don't know." She toed a knot in the boards with one velvet slipper. "I might say you could stop by again...if you wanted to."

"I reckon we're both in luck."

She frowned, curious.

"Your pa gave me a job off-loading freight."

Laura's eyes snapped wide in surprise and what Quentin hoped was delight. "Oh...he did?"

Quentin pinched his hat brim to her, reining the pinto back in the direction of the heart of town. "See you bright an' early in the mornin', Miss Laura."

She smiled.

Quentin took a bite of the apple and booted the pinto into a trot, too preoccupied to see Lars's big, angry face glaring at him through the window on the café side of the building.

As he chewed the apple, Quentin was smiling but there was a disconcerting mix of emotions inside him.

"You have to stay single-minded," he told himself. "You know what you have to do. You know what *needs* to be done."

CHAPTER 10

MANNION STOOD ON THE PORCH OF HIS JAIL OFFICE, leaning against a ceiling support post, nursing a cup of coffee and staring into the street where the itinerant ranch hand he'd met only an hour before, Quentin Ferguson, rode past on his pinto.

The man turned to Mannion, offered a too-friendly smile and a wave to which Mannion responded with a nod, and sipped his coffee. The young man turned his own head forward and trotted the pinto off to the south along San Juan Avenue. When Ferguson was a half a block away, he jerked a quick look over his left shoulder at Mannion. Seeing Joe still staring after him, the man jerked his head forward again, fooled with his hat, feigning a casual air, and turned down a side street to the north.

Likely heading for a livery barn.

"What is it, Joe?" Rio Waite stepped out of the open jail office door, holding a half-eaten fried chicken leg in one hand, wiping the greasy fingers of his other hand on the red-and-white checked bib hanging down over his shirt and vest. "What's piqued your interest?

You think that rifle-wielding son of Satan is fixin' to take another shot at you? I sure wish you'd try to stay out of sight as much as you can. You make me nervous, standing out here, making yourself an easy target like this!"

Rio chomped into the chicken leg, tore off a large chunk of meat, and chewed. He'd brought a platter over from the locally popular café appropriately if unimaginatively named Ida's Good Food and had been working on it for the past half hour, feeding Buster morsels from his plate. Rio usually took his meals over at Ida's, but today Mannion's senior deputy wanted to keep a close eye on his boss, though he didn't say as much.

The lumpy, middle-aged Rio was a good deputy, but he was more than that. He was a good, loyal friend. Being who he was, a roughhewn badge-toter from the wild old days of the wide-open cow towns from Kansas to the Texas Panhandle, Mannion had few friends. Plenty of enemies. But few friends.

Rio was at the top of that short list.

"If I cower under my desk," Mannion said, a bit distracted, thinking more about young Ferguson than his would-be assassin, "I'll just be delaying the inevitable. I want to see the varmint coming."

He took another sip of his mud. "Blow his lamp out before he can blow out mine." Staring south along the same side of the street the jailhouse was on, he frowned. "Hmmm...there he is again."

"There who is again?" Rio asked, throwing the chicken leg into the street where one of the town's many homeless curs would quickly find and devour it. If not them, the coyotes would make fast work of it; the "brush wolves," as many called them, paraded through town after dark, panting, feet thumping, the pack breaking up to hunt the trash heaps, howl back and forth at each other, bragging about the spoils they'd found.

"That kid I met earlier over at the Three-Legged Dog."

Mannion watched the young man walk out from the cross street and onto San Juan Avenue, heading in the opposite direction of the jailhouse. He held a rifle in one hand, the barrel resting across his right shoulder; his saddlebags were slung over the opposite shoulder. As he strode away, young Ferguson cast another, quick, down-right suspiciously furtive look back over his right shoulder toward the jailhouse before jerking his head forward again, adjusting the set of his hat, and quick-ening his pace along the boardwalk fronting a haber-dashery and a lady's dress shop up on the other side.

"Newcomer," Mannion said. "Saddle tramp."

"He look to be trouble, Joe? I see he's wearin' a cream hat. That's a rifle on his shoulder, too."

The frown lines across Mannion's broad forehead, beneath the brim of his high-crowned Stetson, deepened as his brows formed a bulging ridge over his wolfish gray eyes. "I don't know. Maybe. He tried awful hard to put me at ease, to make me believe he was just another grub line rider looking for a stake. Tried awful hard. Too hard. Then, when Norm Davis came into the saloon, he looked like someone had just stepped over his grave, and saun-tered away. He sat down but kept staring at me and Norm in the backbar mirror."

"Maybe you put his daddy away in jail, or..."

"Or worse," Mannion silently mused. "Or some other kin...a fellow gang member, say. Take your pick." Mannion paused as the young man disappeared down the next side street to the south. "You just never know who has bone to pick. But this kid..." Ferguson was no kid, but to Mannion, anyone not yet forty was a kid. Joe shook his head, puzzled. "I don't know. I don't think he has one with me..."

"Davis, maybe?"

"If so, awful coincidental for Norman to enter the saloon right then."

"Maybe their stars lined up. Why, I was talking to Madame Hanover just the other day, an' she said..."

"Oh, please, Rio. Not more superstition! I've heard plum enough of those for one day!" Madame Hanover was a traveling gypsy fortune-teller who also sold a vast array of elixirs to cure everything from poor circulation to a sluggish liver and foggy thinker box, though she called it "Clarity of the mind, eyes, and soul..."

The dream about the coffin floating down the river had not left Mannion. Nor had Jane's and Rio's interpretations of it.

"All right, Joe. Have it your way. Just tryin' to help."

"Have a feeling he might be heading for Ma Branch's Rooming House. He has a look about him, like he's fixin' to stay awhile."

"Want me to go over an' give him the usual?"

The "usual" was Mannion and Rio's practice of grilling newcomers about where they'd come from and where they were heading—especially those who came in on the train. The consarned train brought in one misfit after another including confidence men and more than a few women of the same ilk to fleece the miners and wood cutters out of their hard-won pay. Mannion and his deputies did their best to "encourage" such bottom-feeders to move on up the rails, let some other underpaid, understaffed, and overworked lawdog tend them.

However, Ferguson had ridden into town on his horse; he hadn't taken the train.

Mannion scratched his neck, pensive. "Nah. I just want to keep an eye on him. I don't think he's the shooter. Not sure why I say that, but I just don't think he is. I think he might have something else up his sleeve."

"What're you two starin' at? Ain't you never seen a well-set-up pleasure girl before?" said a boy's voice. Er... the voice of a boy on the edge of jaded, old manhood.

Mannion turned to see Harmon Haufenthistle approach the jailhouse with two bulging leather burlap mail pouches slung over his right shoulder. The morning train had come and gone a half hour previously, setting up a near riot of unwashed humanity swarming around the depot station's platform at the south end of town, under the suffocating, nauseating clouds of coal smoke issued by the Baldwin locomotive's big, diamond-shaped stack. That was where Harmon had acquired the mail—he worked twice a week for the head postal clerk in Del Norte. One of his many occupations.

"We weren't lookin' at no pleasure girl," Rio groused.

"Oh, I thought you was starin' holes through that well put-together blonde with the red parasol crossin' the street yonder a few minutes ago. Here's your mail, Marshal."

Mannion accepted the large manila envelope likely stuffed with a fresh batch of wanted circulars.

"Thanks, Harmon."

"Well, I *seen* her, of course," Rio said, absently patting Buster who had come out of the jailhouse to lounge on the porch rail before his master. "But that wasn't who Joe and I were lookin' at," he added, a little defensively. "Harmon, you're a sprout. You're the one who shouldn't be lookin'!"

"Ha!" Harmon said, shifting the mail pouches on his shoulder. "You should see what I see. The girls don't pay me no mind because I'm just a kid. That blonde up there, I've seen her gettin' ready for a bath over at the Come One, Come All, and let me tell you, fellas—"

"That's enough, Harmon!" Joe admonished the boy. "You shouldn't be seein' such things nor thinkin' such thoughts!"

"Neither should you, Bloody Joe. You're married!"

Harmon chuckled and continued along the busy street, doling out the mail, but stopped when Rio said, again defensively, "We was starin' at that young newcomer. Me an' the marshal been wondering what he's about."

"Oh, I know who you mean," Harmon said. "That blond fella on the brown-an'-white pinto. I can tell you one thing he's about. That's the Davises."

Mannion jerked a surprised look at the boy, though he knew he should know better than to be surprised by any of the observant young Haufenthistle's observations. "Why do you say that?"

"He asked me where he'd find Davis's *grocery store*. Everyone knows they call it South-Central Colorado Fresh Meats & Dry Goods." Harmon shrugged a shoulder. "That told me the stranger was lookin' for one of the Davises, not just the store."

"Harmon, you're a caution—you know that?" Mannion said.

Harmon grinned. "Just the curious type, Marshal." He continued down the street to the south. "Just the curious type's all..."

Rio said, "That boy's gonna be mayor of this town one day, Joe. You know that?"

"Yes, I know," Mannion quipped. "And we're gonna be the first two city employees he gives the axe!"

He and Rio chuckled.

Mannion set his cup on the porch rail and started down the steps.

"Where you goin'?" Rio asked.

"Gonna go on over to the Davis' place. That young stranger has me, like Harmon, right curious. Mind the store while I'm gone."

"You got it, Joe. Watch your back!"

Ten minutes later, Mannion mounted the boardwalk cluttered with display bins and barrels and entered the South-Central Colorado Fresh Meats & Dry Goods.

"Howdy, Marshal," greeted Laura Davis, having just taken a lunch order in the café end of the building and heading for the door behind the counter to the kitchen.

"Howdy, Laura," Mannion said, removing his hat. "Your pa in?"

"Should be in the back room filling out orders, Marshal."

"Obliged!" Mannion called to the young woman, who appeared prettier and prettier each time he saw her.

Not so absently he wondered if young Ferguson had seen or met her, and what effect the girl had had on him. When Mannion and Rio had last seen him, likely heading for Ma Branch's Rooming House, the youngster had definitely had a certain spring in his step despite the paranoid looks he cast over his shoulder at Mannion and his senior deputy.

"I'm here, Joe," Norman Davis said from the rear of the store, hidden by several aisles of tall display shelves and racks—men's shirts and women's dresses, boots, shoes, overalls and, nearer the back counter, barrels and crates of foodstuffs including peaches, apples, and bananas, some of it dried, some fresh. The turkeys, hams, and venison and elk sausages that the hardworking Davis smoked himself and that hung from the ceiling added a delightful aroma.

Mannion moved down a wider central aisle until he saw Davis standing at his counter, leaned forward and going over an open, clothbound ledger with a sharp pencil. Straightening, the grocer tucked the pencil into the crease running down the middle of the big book, arched his brows, and smiled. "What can I do you for?"

Mannion thought his response over quickly, and said, "Oh...just stopped for an apple. I was making the rounds and just found myself with a hankerin'." He plucked an apple out of a barrel, rubbed it off on the sleeve of his shirt, and took a bite. "What do I owe you?"

"Since you bought my beer earlier, it's on the house."

"Ah, thank you, thank you."

"That's the second free apple I've given away today."

It was Mannion's turn to arch a curious brow. "Oh?"

Absently, the grocer ran his beringed right hand through his neatly barbered, thinning hair. "You know that young fella who was talkin' to you over to the Three-Legged Dog when I walked in?"

"I do remember, yes." Mannion felt lucky. He hadn't had to open the topic of the young newcomer and risk giving his suspicions away. He saw no reason for anyone else to be suspicious about Ferguson until Joe learned if there was anything that needed being suspicious about.

"He was just here...for an apple and licorice." The grocer gave a foxy smile. "Although he seemed just a tad more interested in Laura than the licorice or the apple."

Mannion chuckled. "Well, that girl's a head-turner—that's for sure."

"You know how protective I am about her, but after getting to know him a little," Davis said, "I found myself offering the boy a job." He winced and, placing his hand on his hips, flexed his back. "I am getting so tired of back-and-bellying the stock from the freight wagons into our warehouse, I've been thinking for quite some time I needed an extra hand. Well, I'm thinking I might have found one. The Ferguson kid seems strong enough. And he was ready and willin'. Don't seem lazy. All in all, seems like a pretty nice fella. I can't hold his interest in my daughter against him."

He grinned and winked. "If I did that—"

"Oh, I know," Mannion said with wry chuff, "you'd be shuffling that freight around all by your lonesome till the cows came home!"

They both had another laugh on the subject of Davis's fetching daughter.

When their laughter died, Mannion said, "Well, I'd best get back to it." He took another bite of the apple and started to walk away.

"Joe?"

He stopped and turned back around. The grocer was leaning forward, fists on the counter, one eye narrowed shrewdly behind his glasses. "You didn't really stop for an apple, did you?"

Mannion started to feign innocence then skipped it. Davis was right. He'd had some concerns about young Ferguson...concerns especially where Davis himself was concerned. He'd be remiss in not giving voice to them. Especially since his daughter was working in the store, as well.

Joe swallowed the bite of apple he was chewing and said, "Right you are, Norm. I don't think I'd let down my guard around him. I'm probably just getting owly in my old age, extra cautious about folks, but when you walked into the Three-Legged Dog earlier this morning..."

"He made a quick exit from the bar, didn't he? Young Ferguson."

"You noticed, too. I remember."

"I thought I'd interrupted something important."

"No, nothing important at all." Mannion tossed what was left of his apple into a waste bucket and, grimacing, ran his hand across the back of his neck. "It almost seemed that when he saw you...well..."

"It almost seemed that he knew me," Davis said, frowning, equally as puzzled as Mannion.

"It did seem that way."

"I noticed it, too. My memory isn't as good as it once was—I'll be the first to admit that—but I don't recollect ever seeing him before. He didn't look one bit familiar."

"What about Laura?"

Davis shrugged. "She didn't mention anything. If he'd been around before or if she knew him from elsewhere, she didn't say. No reason she wouldn't."

"Right."

"He did look a little, well, sheepish—didn't he, Joe? When he first saw me in the Three-Legged Dog."

"Looking back on it," Mannion said, "yeah. That's a good way to describe him. Sheepish. Or...surprised. Like he had seen you before and was startled out of his boots to see you again."

Davis shook his head, chuckled dryly. "It is peculiar. Maybe he just *thought* he knew me. I'll bring it up with him tomorrow. He's starting work bright an' early."

"Good idea," Mannion said. "Might as well get your concerns right out in the open. Especially with..."

"Laura being here." The grocer smiled. "I guess you know my concerns, Joe. We share them—don't we? Both of us having good-looking daughters known to attract many a young man's eye."

"That we do, that we do," Mannion said. "I'm just glad mine's married off so she's the good doctor's worry now!"

"Yeah, but we'll never get over worrying about them —will we?"

"No, I reckon not. More's the pity. Anyway, I'm glad you brought it up. I wasn't sure I should mention it. Like I said, it's probably nothing. Just an aging lawman's overly busy mind at work here, most like."

"Thanks for stopping, Joe."

"Thanks for the apple!" Mannion threw up an arm in a parting wave as he headed for the door.

"Anytime, but you don't need an apple to pay a call on us here!"

Chuckling, Mannion stepped out onto the boardwalk fronting the grocery store. He was still thinking about young Ferguson when he spied quick, furtive movement out the corner of his right eye. He whipped his head around in time to see a man step into a juniper and cedar thicket surrounding a pale boulder on the lip of a wash.

The man had been closer this time, but all Joe had glimpsed was a cream Stetson and a rifle again.

Then the man was gone, the cedar and juniper branches jostling back into place behind him.

"That tears it," the lawman bit out between gritted teeth.

He released the keeper thong from over the hammer of his cross-draw Russian, slid the piece from its holster, and clicked the hammer back.

He moved out into the street and headed—where?

Possibly into the jaws of death. He'd been there before. Like most times before, he'd be ready for his current stalker, by god!

CHAPTER 11

MANNION STRODE TOWARD THE BOULDER AND THE brush growing up around it.

He kept the boulder between himself and the wash, which he knew lay on the other side of it, concealed by the junipers, cedars, and willows. He unholstered his second Russian, the one he wore thonged low on his right thigh and clicked the hammer back.

Slowly, he moved around the boulder and shoved several branches out of his way until he could see into the sandy, gravelly wash. Fresh bootprints led across the wash, up the slight rise on the other side, and into the pines and cedars growing around the ragged western edge of Del Norte.

Here, ancient and mostly abandoned cabins, stock pens, privies, and stables were positioned willy-nilly in the brush and trees. These were the shacks of Del Norte's first settlers, gold-seekers who every spring, during the mountain snowmelt's runoff, had panned this wash and the countless others that lay in and around Del Norte. Until the growing population had run them out.

Joe knew the feeling.

Like those old, hardworking salts likely pushing up daisies by now, he didn't necessarily mind people. He just liked them a whole lot better when they weren't around.

He walked down into the wash and, sweeping the area with his gaze, followed the meandering course his stalker had taken through the pines. The man had tried to disguise his trail by walking on the balls of his feet, but Mannion caught glimpses of enough obscure, partial prints to be able to follow the would-be assassin's trail.

He walked steadily forward, keeping both cocked Russians aimed straight out from his shoulders, tracking them from left to right and back again.

A soft thud sounded behind him.

He wheeled. A fallen pinecone rolled down a small hummock to pile up against a sage shrub.

Mannion wheeled back forward in time see a rifle aimed at him from around the side of a tall pine whose branches began thirty feet up from the ground. Mannion fired his right-hand pistol first, then the left. Between the two shots, the stalker's rifle lapped flames and smoke. The bullet screeched wide of Mannion to spang off a rock behind him.

The shooter pulled his cream-hatted head and the rifle back behind the tree. For a moment, Joe couldn't see him. Then he saw him running straight out away from the tree, away from Joe. Mannion stepped wide of the tree and sent two more rounds caroming toward the man just as he swung behind a large cottonwood then ran up a steep rise ahead and to Mannion's right.

Mannion fired two more rounds, gritting his teeth in fury. Each round merely plumed dead leaves and pine needles ahead of the fleeing would-be assassin. A third shot plunked into a pine branch.

Cursing, Mannion heaved himself to his feet and took

off running up the hill. He ran hard, scissoring his arms and legs, suppressing the rake he felt in his lungs, the tar and nicotine from his hand-rolled quirleys congealing his throat. He hacked it up, spat, and continued running. He saw his quarry gain the top of the ridge; the man stopped and glanced back behind him.

The man gave a foxy grin beneath the brim of his cream hat.

He was ruddy-skinned, and a thick, black mustache mantled his broad mouth. He swung full around, loudly levering a round into his Winchester's action, and fired from the hip once...twice...three times. Mannion took two more running, lunging strides ahead and up the rise and dove behind a large rock on his right. One of the shooter's rounds smashed into the face of the rock with an ear-rattling bark and prolonged, reverberating whine.

Mannion edged a look around the rock.

At the top of the hill was nothing but sky and distant, vaulting stone formations. The shooter had taken off down the ridge's opposite side.

Mannion rose, wheezing. A sharp pain pierced his chest. He grew dizzy, staggered from his right to his left, trying desperately to keep his feet beneath him.

"What the hell...?"

He clawed as his shirt collar and neckerchief, loosening both.

The pain in his chest relented a little. But just a little.

Cursing, he continued running.

He gulped air but his lungs felt too small to accept it.

He was sweating, the icy beads running down from the band inside his hat.

He gained the top of the ridge and stopped suddenly, crouching, lungs and knees about to burst. Twenty feet down the ridge, the duster-clad shooter stood aiming down the barrel of his Henry repeater at Mannion, mustached upper lip stretched back to show the jagged, white line of his teeth.

Mannion grunted with a start and from somewhere found the strength to throw himself to one side, striking the ground, rolling, as two slugs howled through the air where he'd been standing a second before. He rolled onto his belly, extended both cocked Russians straight out before him and, just as the man swung the Henry to track him, punched two rounds through the shooter's chest.

The whip-cracking report of the Henry rose above the ringing in Mannion's ears as the shooter fired skyward. He screamed, dark eyes wide in sudden fear and exasperation, and stumbled backward, down the slope, trying desperately to get his feet set beneath him.

Mannion punched another round into him, high in his left breast. The slug knocked him off his feet. The Henry dropped. The man fell backward, struck the downslope, and rolled wildly, the flaps of his duster winging out around him, two filled holsters on his thighs gleaming with the cold steel of two smart-looking revolvers.

He piled up against a large rock and lay breathing hard, chest rising and falling sharply.

Slowly, wheezing, feeling as though a crab had a claw around his ticker, squeezing, Joe gained his feet. He moved heavily down the slope, knees popping, ankles aching. He stood over the man, whose chest and belly were a mass of bright-red blood glinting in the after-noon sunshine through the crowns of several near ponderosas.

The man had short, dark-brown hair and a week's worth of dark-brown beard stubble on his dark-brown cheeks. He glared up at Mannion, muttering softly but angrily in Spanish, wincing at the pain racking him.

"Who sent you?" Joe asked the Mexican, bent forward, hands holding pistols resting on his knees, trying to catch his breath.

The Mexican killer croaked a jeering laugh. "You'll know soon enough!"

Then his body spasmed. His head turned to one side, the eyes remaining open but acquiring that far-away death look. His muscles slackened; he lay still.

Mannion staggered over to a pine, sat down, leaned back against it, one knee raised. He holstered both smoking Russians then reached up to loosen his shirt and neckerchief a little more.

Running footsteps sounded on the other side of the ridge.

He knew who was coming even before he recognized the raking breaths. He quirked a grim smile as Henry McCallister gained the top of the ridge, looked around, found Mannion, then the dead Mexican. He turned back to Mannion and said, "Oh, for mercy sakes, Marshal!" He ran down the slope and dropped to a knee beside his boss. "Where you hit?"

Joe shook his head. He was still trying to catch his breath. The crab in his chest was still squeezing his heart. "Not hit. Just tired's all. That run up the ridge took the... took the wind out of my sails." He glowered at young McCallister. "I'm with Rio. You're annoying."

Henry chuckled then frowned again and said, "You don't look so good, Marshal. You're awful pale. We'd best get you—"

He cut himself off when distant hoof thuds sounded.

A young woman's voice loudly urged the mount she was riding, and the hoof thuds grew louder.

Henry looked down the slope bristling with firs, pines, and aspens. "It's Vangie!"

He rose and waved his arm broadly.

The girl said, "There, Cochise—let's go!"

"Ah, hell," Mannion complained. "I don't want her to see me like this." He raised a gloved hand to his young deputy. "Help me up."

Henry dropped to a knee again beside Mannion, placed a hand on his chest. "You best stay right there. You don't look too good. Where's it hurt?"

"Nowhere. I'm fine. Dammit, now—!"

Just then the hoof thuds stopped. A horse snorted nearby. Another thud as Vangie leaped down from the blue roan stallion Mannion and Henry had captured for her, running wild with its harem and colts in the mountains and causing trouble for area ranchers, who'd been going to shoot it.

Mannion and Henry had brought it back to the Mannion's small horse ranch at the edge of town, and Vangie had put in long hours, day after day, gentling the handsome beast that stood blowing now, pawing the ground with a front hoof and shaking its head, its black mane buffeting beautifully, glinting in the sunshine.

Truly a beautiful beast that smelled of horse and leather and wind and the tang of pine and sage.

Vangie had not tamed all the wild out of Cochise; she wanted him to remain as wild as his namesake. She liked that part of him that still yearned to run unfettered in the mountains, like she did herself. For the girl—woman now, of course, nearly twenty-one—would always be half-wild herself, which made her marrying a Harvard-educated medico somewhat puzzling and ironic to her father, though he knew deep down she'd wanted in a husband the opposite of Joe himself.

Someone who didn't give her so much trouble and worry her every time he left the house. She'd had a tumultuous childhood because of her wild-assed father, and he felt bad about that while knowing it could never have been another way.

"Yep, I heard shooting while I was out running some stable green out of Cochise and I said"—she placed a finger to her lips—"hmmm, wonder who that could be. Shooting in the middle of the day. Could that be my father? No, certainly not!"

She stepped forward and dropped to both knees beside Mannion. "Where you hit, you big idiot?"

Mannion glanced at Henry kneeling on his other side. "See what happens when you spare the rod an' spoil the child? They talk like that to you. Let that be a lesson to you, Henry, my boy!"

"Where you *hit*, Pa?"

"He's not hit," Henry said.

"No, I'm not hit." Mannion drew a deep breath, doffed his hat, ran a hand through his sweaty hair. "Didn't take a bullet. Just feelin' a little off my feed's all."

"You don't look good, Pa."

"I'll be all right in a minute. Just havin' trouble catchin' my breath." Mannion looked at his deputy. "Son, will you walk back to town, saddle Red, and bring him to me? You know where I stable him."

"You can ride the roan, Pa," Vangie said.

"I'll ride my own horse to town, if you don't mind."

"I know where you stable him, Marshal." Henry fairly leaped to his feet. "Same place I stable Banjo. Be back in a minute!"

He turned and began running up the ridge.

"Walk, don't run!" the weary lawman called after him.

Henry didn't slow his pace. He just threw up an arm, crested the ridge, and disappeared down the other side.

"Show off!" Mannion groused.

Vangie put a hand on his chest. "Lay back, Pa. Take it easy. We'll get you into town, have Ben check you out."

"Oh, hell, no! I just need some lunch. I haven't eaten since early this morning!"

Vangie leaned toward him, gazed into his gray eyes with her brown ones, eyes that always reminded Joe so much of his dead wife, Sarah, the mother whom Vangie never knew, that it often wrenched his heart and brought a tear to his eye. Sarah had committed suicide by hanging herself from a tree in their backyard in Kansas when Vangie had been only a few weeks old.

"Listen to me, you stubborn, stubborn man." Vangie flared a nostril of her straight and resolute nose, hardening her jaws, a flush rising into her face, darkening her suntanned cheeks. "You will see Dr. Ben Ellison. Do you hear me? That was not a question. That was an order. If you won't go with me, you'll go with me *and* Jane!"

"Oh, now don't go bringing her into this!"

Vangie laughed with only a little mirth. The concern in her eyes was grave. "That not so little threat rocked you back on your heels—didn't it, Bloody Joe?"

"You're a caution. Purely. I didn't raise you right."

"You did what you could with what little I gave you."

It was Mannion's turned to laugh. It kicked up the pain in his chest. He pressed the end of a fist against it and coughed.

"It's your heart—isn't it?"

"Nah, just my lungs. That run up the hill..."

"That must've been some trick after all the cigarettes you've smoked."

"I could use one now." Mannion reached into his shirt

for the makins sack that hung from a thong around his neck.

Vangie closed her hand over his. "The hell you do!"

"Stop badgering me! And don't swear. It ain't ladylike. I'm your father, dammit. Show some respect!"

Vangie thrust herself against him, wrapped her arms around his back, hugged him tightly, ferociously, and planted a hard, prolonged kiss on his forehead. She pulled her head back and stared at her father pointedly, her nose an inch from his.

Her eyes crossed a little and glinted angrily as she said, "If you go and die on me, I will piss on your grave, Bloody Joe!"

Mannion stared at her in astonishment. He'd rarely heard his daughter swear. If ever. Maybe when the bronc grazing contentedly behind her had thrown her in the breaking corral one too many times one afternoon. But never at her father.

"Evangeline!"

"I know, I know. It's not ladylike!"

"How you dress isn't, either. Look at you. Wearing a wool shirt and denim jeans and scuffed boots. You look more like a thirty-a-month-and-found cow nurse than the wife of the town doctor!"

Vangie looked off, pursed her lips, shrugged a shoulder. "You married me off, anyway. You've been trying to do that for a few years now."

"Thought you needed more than a cranky old reprobate of a broken-down father and wild horses in your life."

"I sure did!" Vangie sat up straight and crossed her arms on her chest. "Don't try to give me another dress for Christmas."

"Oh, hell—I know you won't wear it, anyway. You'll

just take it back to the ladies' dress shop like you did with the last one I tried to give you."

"Exactly."

Mannion hooked a crooked smile at her. "You're just stubborn, like me. You'll come around. When you're good and ready. Just like you did with the doc."

Vangie thumbed herself in the chest and crossed her eyes again. "When I'm ready!"

Mannion laughed, winced, coughed again. "I'm old before my time and I'm staring at the reason right now."

Vangie drew a deep breath as though trying to quell the emotion rising in her. She dropped her chin and sobbed. Arms crossed on her chest, she cried, her head bobbing, shoulders jerking.

"Ah, honey." Mannion caressed her arm through her shirtsleeve. I didn't mean it. You ain't the reason—"

"Oh, hell—I know that!" Vangie jerked her head up, eyes angry and afraid. "I raised *you*. You didn't raise *me*. All you ever really did was keep the boys off the porch until you realized I didn't want them there anymore than you did."

"No." Mannion wagged his head. "You always loved your horses more than any other living soul." He smiled. "Except me."

"Except you." Vangie sniffed, wiped tears from her cheeks with the backs of her hands. "Leave it to me to love the two wildest men in Colorado." She jerked her chin to indicate the roan cropping grass and switching his tail behind her.

"You got your Harvard-educated doctor."

"Thank God for him!"

Mannion found himself trying to memorize every detail of her face, her hair, her shoulders, her arms... hands. The gold buckle of the wide brown belt she wore.

Her denims...her boots. He wanted to take her all in, like drawing the scent of a rare and beautiful flower deep into his lungs...into his being...so deep into his soul from which it could never escape. So he could remember at a time when they were no longer together, and that day would come, though the very thought of not having his dear Evangeline seemed as unthinkable and horrific as the thought of the sun going out and the world going cold and black.

He wanted her to say something so he could memorize her voice. To tuck it away and protect it inside him forever.

And then she did. Lifting her chin sharply, having heard something, she turned to glance toward the crest of the ridge behind her.

"That'll be Henry. Let's get you up, Pa. Get you checked out by Ben!"

CHAPTER 12

VANGIE ELLISON AND DEPUTY HENRY MCCALLISTER sat in Dr. Ben Ellison's office, which until recently the young doctor had shared with Doc Bohannon, a longtime medico here in Del Norte. After working with Bohannon for a year, who'd helped Ben get started in his practice, Bohannon retired and went to live with his son's family in Albuquerque.

Ellison had a large comfortable office in a new, neat brick building, with two examination rooms and three hospital rooms. Deputy McCallister had heard that the town council along with a church here in town had made grumblings about building a hospital; a town the size of Del Norte needed one desperately. But for now, Ellison's three rooms were the only hospital the town had. When the doctor needed more, Jane Mannion, formerly Jane Ford, made rooms available over at the San Juan Hotel & Saloon.

Yeah, the doc's office was comfortable, with a half dozen comfortable chairs for folks to wait in. Henry and Vangie were sitting in two of them now. But Henry wasn't comfortable. He was worried about his boss. He hadn't

realized it before, but he'd come to see ol' Bloody Joe as a
father of sorts. Or maybe a grumpy uncle.

Despite his unease, he smiled at that thought as he
leaned forward in his chair, elbows on his knees, staring
at the floor between his feet. He absently lifted the toe of
one boot and set it back down on the floor. Then he
lifted the toe of the other boot, set it back down on the
floor.

At least the marshal had taken down the man who'd
been out to kill him. The young deputy hadn't discussed
the shooter with his boss. Mannion's health was at the
forefront of both men's minds. They'd talk about it in
due time. On his way into town, Henry had sent the
undertaker out to fetch the body back to his shop. If
Mannion didn't recognize the would-be assassin, Henry
and Rio would go over the several stacks of wanted circulars they had in the office, try to match the man's descrip-
tion with one of those.

In due time...

Sitting in the straight-backed, leather-padded chair to
his right, Vangie reached over and placed her hand on
both of Henry's, which he had entwined between his
knees, lifting his fingers, lowering them, fidgeting.

He looked at her. Vangie gave a wan half smile.
"Worried?"

"Me? Nah," Henry said. "Bloody Joe's tough. Whang
tough. A little shortness of breath won't bring him down.
Not if that fella with the Henry rifle can't."

Vangie removed her hand from his. "Who was he? Do
you know?"

"No. Maybe the marshal does."

Vangie's voice darkened. "If there one, there
might be more." She shook her head slowly, staring at the
thick rug on the floor of the waiting room. "The life that

man has led. I reckon you really"—she drew a deep breath as though bracing herself against the thought haunting her—"can't expect him to live to a ripe old age."

Her voice cracked a little at the end.

Henry drew a deep breath, steeling himself against that thought, as well. He couldn't bear the notion of Mannion dying. He couldn't imagine Del Norte without the big, famous as well as *infamous*, uncompromising old lawman with the two big, silver-chased Russian pistols he always carried and his prized Yellowboy repeater.

Walking down the street, even when he knew men were gunning for him, like he owned the whole town. Hell, like he owned the whole damn West! Confident, surly, grumpy, often overbearing.

Immortal.

That was Joe Mannion.

Footsteps sounded on the small stoop fronting the doctor's office. A familiar face peered through the glass pane.

A heart-shaped, gray-eyed face of a pretty young woman just under twenty years old. A gentle-eyed face creased with concern.

The face of the girl Henry had once loved until life and all its complications—he and Molly Hurdstrom had known more than a few of those—had come between them. As had the pretty young schoolteacher who had taught Henry how to read and whom he'd ended up stepping out with, though he'd tried his best to see her as only a friend.

Grace Hastings, however, had turned out not to be the person he'd thought she was; she'd merely been using him for protection against the gang of cutthroats her brother had once ridden with and who'd shown up in Del Norte looking for the same cache of stolen gold she'd been looking for. Grace's brother had hidden the loot when he'd pulled a double cross on the rest of the gang.

That stolen money and Grace's greed had gotten her killed in the end.

Molly had warned Henry about her. He hadn't listened.

Yes, so many things had come between them.

Molly was alone now, however, having estranged herself from her parents who had threatened to send her away to a school for wayward girls if she didn't marry the young man they'd wanted her to marry—a young man from a wealthy family. She'd killed Adam McClarksville, a common albeit rich thug from a military academy, when Adam had nearly beaten Henry to death in a fit of jealous rage...

So many things. So much water under the bridge.

Too much.

Vangie looked at Molly then turned to Henry. "Well...?"

Henry rose from his chair. He'd just started toward the door when Molly opened it, closing her blue parasol, and poked her head through the door.

"Are you all right?" she asked, a concerned frown wrinkling the skin above the bridge of her nose. "I heard there was trouble, and you were over with the doctor..."

"I'm fine." Henry moved to the door, opened it wider, and followed Molly out onto the stoop. He closed the door behind him and said, "It's the marshal. Doc's with him now."

"Oh," Molly said, sliding a lock of her brown hair back behind her left ear with her right hand on which she wore a long, white glove. "I'm sorry about the marshal." Her eyes bore into Henry's. "I was worried...about you."

She looked down, smoothed the skirt of her dress

against her thighs. The pleated frock was spruce green; it made the gray in her eyes stand out. She had a little hat trimmed with faux flowers pinned to her hair, which was piled in a loose bun. She was taller than Henry remembered. For the last year or more, he'd seen her only from a distance. They hadn't been on speaking terms.

Had that changed? He vaguely wondered.

No. Too much water.

When Henry didn't respond to her last statement, about her being worried about him, she shot him an accusing look and said, "I can still be worried about you, you know. Even though...even though..."

"We're not seeing each other anymore," he finished for her.

She looked at him, frowning again, a vague question in her eyes. She didn't seem sure if what he'd said had been a statement or a question. He wasn't sure himself.

"Yes," she said finally.

"How've you been?"

She shrugged a shoulder. "Busy. The town is growing, the shop's been getting more and more business. Funny how people with money are moving to town...the women shopping for nice dresses."

She worked in one of the two or three ladies' dress shops in town. Thus, her own stylish attire. Which looked good on her, Henry had to admit. He remembered her a girl. But the Molly Hurdstrom standing before him now was a young woman. She'd grown taller and her body was shapely, supple.

He heard voices in the office behind him and turned to see that Dr. Ben Ellison had come into the waiting room and was talking with Vangie.

"Looks like the doc has some news," Henry said. "I better get back inside."

"All right." Molly opened the parasol. "Like I said, I was...I was worried. Thought I'd check on you."

She smiled briefly then turned away. Henry opened the door and started to step into the office but stopped and turned back to Molly.

"Molly?"

She turned back to him, one brow arched.

"Maybe...if you're not seein' anyone...I don't want to intrude...but maybe we could...I don't know...take a walk sometime. Along the creek or...anywhere." Henry shrugged. "Just for old time's sake."

She scrutinized him closely with her clear-eyed, woman's gaze. She smiled, nodded. "I'd like that. Just for old time's sake."

"All right, then. You're still at the rooming house?"

Again, she smiled. "Yes. Under Mrs. Bjornson's watchful eye." Mrs. Bjornson's was a female-only rooming house.

She continued down the steps and then up the side street the doctor's office was on, heading toward San Juan Avenue. Henry went into the office where Vangie and the doctor—a tall, dark, handsome man but with medical skills that were far from typical, at least for these parts—were still talking, the doctor with a hip hiked on the antique liquor cabinet Doc Bohannon, a known tippler, had left behind.

They stopped talking and turned to Henry.

"Ben thinks Pa had a heart attack." All the color had drained out of Vangie's face, but her eyes were dry. She was making a good attempt at sucking back her emotions. A definite chip off the ol' Bloody Joe block.

Dread touched Henry. Most of his family was dead, including his parents, but he felt as though he'd just been given the news about his own father.

He moved slowly forward. "Is he..." He winced, glanced at Vangie, who turned to her husband.

"Is he *what*?" came a lion-like roar behind the door leading to the office's examining and hospital rooms.

Henry could feel the reverberations of the stentorian bellow in the floor beneath his boots. Loud footsteps. The door opened and Bloody Joe Mannion emerged from the shadowy hall, setting his big Stetson on his head and hiking his cartridge belt up higher on his hips.

"Is *he* gonna get back to *work*?" he bellowed, stomping toward the front door. "*He* sure as hell *is*! Thanks for the pills, Doc!"

"Pa!" Vangie yelled.

Ellison said, "Take those pills only when needed, and do not mix them with whiskey!"

Mannion pulled the door open, cast a wolfish grin back to the young sawbones, and said, "Don't worry, Doc —I always take my whiskey *straight*!"

Then he was gone, leaving the door standing open behind him. Hooves thudded as the lawman and his prized bay, Red, galloped off toward Hotel de Mannion, the rataplan dwindling quickly.

Mentally cowering from the human hurricane that was Bloody Joe Mannion, Henry rubbed his sweaty hands nervously on his denims and shuttled his gaze from the doctor to Vangie, saying, "Should I...should I...go *after* him?"

"There's nothing to do for him!" Vangie said, bitterly. "If he wants to dance, raving like a madman, into his grave, let him. I told him what I was going to do if he did, and I will!"

She kissed her husband quickly then marched across the room and out the front door.

Gone.

Hooves thudded loudly, dwindling quickly.

Rocked back on his heels by the two Mannion hurricanes, Henry turned to Doc Ellison. The young doctor gave his head a single shake. "Like father, like daughter..."

He sighed.

CHAPTER 13

IF YOU RECUGNIZE THIS FELLA SEE BLOODY JOE.

"THAT ISN'T HOW YOU SPELL 'RECOGNIZE,'" SAID Deputy Henry McCallister.

The town's undertaker, Mortimer Bellringer, who had become a wealthy man since Joe Mannion had come to town a little over five years ago to put Del Norte on its leash, was just then putting the finishing touches on the sign the undertaker had hung around the neck of the mustached Mex who'd tried to snuff the marshal's wick. Bellringer had laid the long, tall, would-be assassin out in a simple, pine coffin in front of his store and propped the coffin up against the storefront, between the big, front, casket-display window and the door, for all to see.

Holding a can of red paint in one hand and a paint-brush in the other hand, Bellringer straightened with an annoyed chuff and turned to the deputy, frowning in annoyance behind his small, round, steel-framed spectacles. "Young man, are you telling *me* how to *spell?*"

Once a poor man, Bellringer's newfound wealth with

which he'd built his large house locally, jokingly known as the Mausoleum, had caused the undertaker to become prideful and self-important. To put on airs. The man's always immaculately attired and coifed wife had, as well.

Henry guessed he shouldn't talk. Since Grace Hastings had taught him how to read...as well as a few other things no gentleman would mention, though such "other" things sure were sweet and damned hard to keep to himself...he'd put on some airs of his own, occasionally correcting Rio's and Cletus Booker's conversational grammar, say, though he'd never corrected the marshal in fear of getting a pistol whipping for his egotism. He just couldn't help himself, though, when such mistakes, like the undertaker's now, were so obvious.

Especially when the man himself had become so arrogant though he'd been a simple, failed farmer from Dakota before coming to Del Norte in a simple box wagon with a burr-laden mutt following close behind, tongue hanging, both him and his wife skinny as scarecrows.

"And it's 'fellow,' not 'fella.'"

Bellringer blinked. "*What?*"

"And you need a comma after 'fellow.'" Henry pointed out the mistake with the barrel of the rifle he'd been carrying around town as he'd made his rounds—several hours' worth. It was now getting late in the afternoon, shadows growing long across San Juan Avenue, though the traffic hadn't let up any. "I mean, if you want to be proper."

"Why, if you don't have some gall!" Bellringer scowled behind his glasses. "I think most folks around here will get the point...if they can read any of the words on this board at all, that is. The marshal asked me to put a sign on the Mex, and I'm putting a sign on him. If you think you can do better, Deputy"—he shoved the paint and brush toward Henry—"be my guest!"

Henry stepped back, throwing his rifle and free hand out to both sides. "No, no, no. I reckon that'll do the job. I do apologize, Mr. Bellringer. I didn't mean to put a burr under your saddle."

The undertaker nudged his glasses up higher on his nose with the hand holding the brush. "Well, that you definitely have done! So, if you don't mind, I'll just finish up here under my own counsel. In other words—good day, Deputy!"

"Just tryin' to help," Henry said, setting his rifle on his shoulder and turning to walk up the street in the direction of Hotel de Mannion. "Just tryin' to help," he repeated. "Didn't mean to ruffle your feathers..."

Though he should have known he would, and he felt genuinely sheepish about it.

He remembered having been condescended to when he'd been an ignorant, lanky lad known as "Stringbean." As he walked along the boardwalks toward the jailhouse, he remembered Grace teaching him phrases from the Bible, though her own bitter end made such teachings— what was the word? Ironic. Yeah, that was it. "Pride goes before destruction," they'd read together one afternoon in her tiny cabin flanking the schoolhouse. "A haughty spirit before a fall."

Henry winced at the memory. Not just the lesson but all of it—Grace, her use of him to fulfill her duplicitous intentions, and her bloody end. His ears warmed at his own arrogance, and he cautioned himself to remember the lesson if nothing else, most of which he wished very much to forget. It was so dang easy, he realized now, for a fellow to get all high and mighty...

"Marshal, what are you doing here?" he said now as he

entered the jailhouse to find Bloody Joe at his desk, writing out what appeared a tax summons on a form pad, pen in one hand, a tightly rolled cigarette in the other. His high-crowned Stetson was on the desk before him, as was a bottle of his preferred unlabeled hooch as well as a half-filled shot glass.

The big man was hunched over his cluttered desk, scowling down at the paperwork, which had always been his least favorite aspect of the job of bringing law and order to the frontier west. Though the deputy had always secretly opined Bloody Joe would have been sorely lost if he'd ever accomplished that seemingly impossible task, for what would be left afterward? Only paperwork, most likely.

No, Bloody Joe was more at home running down crooked gamblers and con artists and rustlers and bank robbers than sitting here in his office, filling out incident reports and tax summons and fines and writing letters to the county sheriff and the federal marshal in Denver and to the circuit court judges. He felt more comfortable with a gun in his hand than a pen with an ink-soaked nib.

"What do you mean what am I doing here?" the marshal growled, pausing to take a deep drag off the quirley and blowing the smoke disdainfully down at the pad before him. "I work here. Remember? I'm Bloody Joe Mannion, town marshal of Del Norte, or has something changed in the past few hours?"

Scowling, he resumed scribbling. The note appeared a summons to tax court to one of the local ranchers who had neglected to pay his yearly taxes and Bloody Joe was calling the man to town to explain himself, likely with an attorney or two in tow. No matter how big or important the rancher or town businessman, the marshal let him get away with nothing. Not under his watch.

Henry rubbed his left, free hand on the thigh of his denims and nervously shifted his weight from one foot to the other. Sitting near the floorboard beneath which Rio stowed his cream, the cat meowed testily, as though sensing the decidedly dour mood in the room and regarding the deputy with his big, green eyes as though in warning.

"Well, uh...no. But I just figured..."

Henry let his voice trail off. He'd been going to say he'd figured that the marshal would have gone over to the San Juan for a nap like most men might have done after they'd been told they'd had a heart stroke. But he'd realized, thank God, before the words had escaped his lips, what a mistake that would have been. He might as well have gone ahead and spoken his mind, however, because Mannion turned to him suddenly, frowning, those big, gray eyes of his hard and drawn up at the corners, like those of a wolf standing at the edge of a defenseless sojourner's firelight, anticipating the taste of fresh blood on his fangs.

"We won't speak of this," he said. "Not again."

Henry glanced at the whiskey glass and the quirley smoldering in his boss's fingers, and winced. He couldn't help but say, "I don't th-think Doc Ellison would approve of you drinkin' and smokin', though, M-Marshal. If you don't mind me sayin' so..."

He'd known his boss was defiant, but holy smokes!

Again, Buster meowed.

Mannion took a deep drag off the quirley and, exhaling the smoke toward his deputy, said, "God love that sissified dandy from Harvard for saving my daughter from a solitary life in a horse barn, but he's overeducated. More book smart than reasonable. I just got a little short of breath. Hadn't had a proper breakfast. I'm fine. Just fine." He patted the pocket of his dark-red corduroy shirt. "He gave me these here pills, and with a few slugs of Who-Hit-John, they make me feel just fine."

"What are the pills?"

"I don't know. Same thing they make dynamite out of or some such." Mannion chuckled deep in his chest, shoulders jerking, genuinely amused. "They clear the phlegm out of my lungs. So, now, like I said..."

Mannion stopped when the door opened, and Rio Waite stepped into the office behind Henry. The older deputy in the battered hat and bulging paunch and wielding his double-bore greener stopped just over the threshold, turned to his boss, and scowled. "Joe, what in holy blazes are you—?"

He stopped when he saw the look on Mannion's face.

"Not you, too," Mannion said in disgust.

Henry and Rio shared an exasperated glance.

"Both of you go on home," Mannion ordered. "Your day is done. I'm staying here tonight in case someone else comes gunnin' for me. Me and Cletus will hold down the fort."

Resisting the urge to correct his boss's English, Henry said instead, "Y-you mean, you're gonna stay *here*...all night?"

"What's Miss Jane gonna say about that?" Rio wanted to know.

"If either of you see her, tell her I rode out after rustlers."

Again, the two deputies shared a glance.

Again, Buster meowed.

Mannion's wolfish gaze settled on his junior deputy. "Henry, that new fella in town, Ferguson, will be bunking over at Ma Branch's Rooming House. Get to know him, will you? Pal around with him a little. I want to know more about him but be sneaky about it. I want to know what he's up to here in Del Norte...what his interest in the Davises might be."

"Hell," Rio chuckled, glancing again at Henry. "I can tell you what his interest in the Davises might be."

"I have a sneaking suspicion," Mannion said, mashing his cigarette out in an ashtray, "that he might be more interested in Norm than Laura. I want to know for sure."

"You got it, boss." Again, the young deputy winced, knowing he was treading in shallow water. "You, uh...you sure—"

"You're both dismissed."

Buster, meowed.

Mannion looked at Rio then canted his head toward the cat. "After you've fed him. Henry, you can go."

"All right," Henry said with a sigh. "See you in the mornin', Marshal."

He glanced once more at the whiskey and the cigarette then reluctantly left the office. As he walked down the porch steps and into the street, setting his Winchester on his shoulder, he hoped like blazes he didn't run into Miss Jane. Talk about being caught between a rock and a hard place!

He tugged his hat down low on his head, as though he thought it might keep her from recognizing him if she saw him—ha!—and hugged the street's left, eastern, side as he made his way south toward his boardinghouse run by the persnickety Ma Branch, a preacher's widow. Though it was after five, traffic was still relatively steady on the main drag, on both sides of the "consarned rail-road tracks," as Bloody Joe was wont to call them. "Wont"—that was another word Grace Hastings had taught him, though he certainly wouldn't hold it up above anyone who didn't know that.

As he walked, he kept a habitual eye out for suspicious strangers from beneath the low brim of his hat. He spied three through the dust roiling in the lee of a passing lumber dray.

They were three men in traditional trail garb lounging a little too leisurely, each shouldering up against an awning support post on the street's opposite side, each giving him the too casual once-over then quickly turning away, turning to each other as though to continue a conversation. They were roughly a half a block ahead of him.

He kept walking south.

As he did, a freight wagon drawn by a six-mule hitch passed on his right.

When it had passed, he glanced through the dust boiling up behind it.

All three men stood directly across the street from him, nearly shoulder to shoulder, facing him with hard looks in their eyes, right hands closed over the hoglegs holstered either on their hips or their thighs. The man in the middle glanced at the men to each side of him, moving his lips, speaking, before turning back to Henry.

All three jerked their pistols from their holsters and crouched to fire.

But not before Henry had pulled his Winchester down from his right shoulder and fired three times quickly from the hip.

CHAPTER 14

HENRY BLINKED THROUGH HIS OWN WAFTING POWDER smoke.

A ranch wagon passed between him and the three gunmen, the driver of the wagon shaking his fist at both Henry and his three attackers, cursing them for almost catching the wagon driver in a crossfire. When the ranch wagon had passed, Henry saw his three opponents lying on the opposite side of the street, one lying across the legs of another.

That man lay quivering as he lay face up on the other man's knees, hatless, giving up the ghost.

Two horseback riders had been about to pass but now, seeing the carnage and Henry still holding his smoking Winchester straight out before him, reined up and switched their wary gazes from one side of the street to the other. Folks walking on both sides of the street stopped to gawk, staring at Henry incredulously.

The deputy felt just as skeptical.

He'd taken down all three men before he'd known what he was doing. His speed with the Winchester had him just as surprised as everyone else in the vicinity seemed to be.

He held up a hand, palm out, to hold the two horseback riders and the traffic behind them, then strode across the street to kick the weapons away from his three attackers, though none seemed capable of further threat.

"Henry!" The female cry came from the boardwalk fronting a ladies' dress shop on the same side of the street Henry was on. He saw Molly Hurdstrom run toward him in her green satin gown and white shirtwaist, shining brown hair dancing on her shoulders. "Henry, are you all right?"

"Molly, don't...don't..."

She stopped at the edge of the boardwalk and gazed down, wide-eyed, the smooth, peach-colored cheeks of her heart-shaped cheeks flushed, at the three dead men. "I just happened to be pinning up a dress in the window. I saw the whole thing. You took them all down—bang! bang! bang!—just like *that*!"

She looked at the rifle Henry now held straight down against his right leg as though it were a venomous snake he was holding. Her surprised gaze trailed up to peer into his eyes as though she were surprised to see whom they belonged to.

"Just like *that*," she said, quietly this time, awfully.

"I know," Henry said, his own baffled gaze returning to the three dead men.

"Do you know them?" Molly asked, a crowd gathering around her, on the boardwalk behind her, a hum of conversation rising.

Still scowling his own incredulity, the young deputy said, "Never seen 'em before in my life." He looked at the men and women gathered on the boardwalk behind Molly. "Any of you know who these three are?"

His question was met with only shrugs and obligatory head shakes.

"What in blue blazes...?" came a familiar voice behind Henry.

He turned to see the marshal and Rio Waite, who'd voiced the exclamation, stride across the street toward Henry and Molly and the three piles of fresh, bloody beef, two lying together with their astonished eyes wide, the third sitting up against an awning support post, chin dipped to his chest as though he'd just sat down to catch a few minutes' shut-eye. Blood matted the front of his checked shirt, between his brown leather suspenders.

"Henry, what the hell happened?" his boss, the marshal, wanted to know as he strode around to each of the dead men, peering down at them.

"I don't know what to tell you, Marshal," Henry said, hearing the bewilderment in his own voice. "They just drew on me's all. I saw them over here, giving me the woolly eyeball. A couple wagons passed and then all three were standing side by side, hands on their six-shooters. Then they crouched and drew and somehow I got the drop. Don't ask me how. Never knew I could fire the Winchester that fast. I don't even remember levering a round in the chamber. But I reckon when you have to, you have to."

Mannion looked at his junior deputy with no little awe and—what? Admiration in his gaze. Henry felt his cheeks flush as though he stood suddenly by a warm fire. He felt a little sheepish for basking in it. But then, who wouldn't bask in the admiring gaze of Bloody Joe Mannion?

"Well, I'll be," said Bloody Joe, who then turned to the crowd gathered behind Molly and said in his deep, commanding baritone, "Do any of you people recognize these three?"

"Not me," said one man, shaking his head.

Another said, "I thought at first they looked like drovers from Bill Wilson's spread, but havin' gotten a closer look, I can see they ain't."

"Nope," said yet another, who held a soapy beer schooner from one of the near saloons in his knobby, brown fist. "Never seen 'em before an' I know most. Strangers in these parts or I miss my guess."

"All right," Mannion said, raising his commanding voice sternly. "Everybody go about your business."

When the crowd began to disperse, except for Molly who stood gazing concernedly at Henry, Mannion turned to his junior deputy and said, "Looks like I'm not the only one with a target on his back." He glanced at Rio standing beside him. "We all three...including Cletus... best grow eyes in the backs of our heads. At least, we all four need to assume we've been targeted...for one reason or another."

He saw Harmon Haufenthistle standing nearby, gawking at the dead men, and told the young odd-jobber to fetch Bellringer.

"Another payday for the cold meat man!" the boy intoned, and trotted away, adding, "I'm in the wrong business!"

Mannion turned to Henry and, frowning, glanced at the rifle the deputy now held on his shoulder. "When did you learn to shoot like that? Been practicing on your days off, have you?"

"No, sir." The deputy shook his head. "I reckon I've been practicing without realizing right here in town—you know during a lead swap now and then. I reckon I just got good without realizing."

"Ice in his veins," Molly said, a proud smile dimpling the pretty's girl's cheeks. "I saw the whole thing, Marshal Mannion. He didn't so much as flinch or bat an eye. He just snapped that long gun down and—*bang! bang! bang!*"

Mannion chuckled and, frowning, glanced from the girl to Henry. "I didn't realize you two were back..."

"Oh, we're not," each intoned at the same time, flushing.

Molly frowned suddenly at Henry. "At least...I don't think...we are..."

Mannion chuckled again. "Well, you two better figure it out." He glanced along the boardwalk up the street to the south and said, "Oh, hell. I gotta run. Jane's comin'." To Henry, he said, "Tell her you haven't seen me all day and have no idea where I am."

Henry and Molly shared a laugh. The only person on God's green earth who could spur the marshal into an all-out, running retreat was none other than his pretty, red-headed wife herself.

And here she came, striding along the boardwalk from the direction of the San Juan Hotel & Saloon, holding the skirts of her metallic blue gown above her high-heel-clad feet. She paused before Henry and Molly and, staring in the direction in which her husband had disappeared, said, "Was that him?"

"What's that?" Henry said, suddenly nervous, feeling very much firmly lodged between that rock and a hard place. "Who...?"

"It was him, all right," said Miss Jane, and headed on across the street, holding up her hands to waylay traffic, very much the queen in command of her domain.

Henry nudged his hat brim up on his forehead with the barrel of his still-warm Winchester. "Boy, I'd sure hate to be the marshal right now."

Molly chuckled.

Henry looked at her.

She flushed, sucked in her cheeks, and looked down at the toes of her black patent shoes.

"Miss Molly?"

She looked up at him. "Yes, Henry?"

He frowned with sudden realization. "You know, you're the only one who always called me by my real name."

"You always deserved to be called by your real name, Henry." Molly glanced at the dead men. "I reckon you proved that here today."

"You think there's too much water under the bridge?"

"For what?"

"For us to take a walk together."

She tucked a lock of hair back behind her ear. "I don't think there's ever too much water under any bridge for taking a walk together."

"You're not seein' anybody?"

Molly shook her head. "You?"

"Nope. Not since..."

"Miss Hastings."

"I reckon I proved myself a fool with her."

"She taught you how to read. To talk right. I mean, *correctly,*" Molly hastily corrected herself with a fetching smile.

When she'd refused to marry the boy her moneyed parents had wanted her to marry, her parents—important people in these parts—had sent her away to a school for wayward girls, who'd taught her a few things between cold baths and palm slaps with rulers. She was estranged from her family now, who'd once owned a freighting business but had since left Del Norte in the wake of the scandal involving Molly, the boy she had been ordered to marry, and Henry.

Now, that was some water under a very big bridge...

Could they both get past it?

Henry found himself wanting to know.

He found himself feeling a stirring of his old feelings for this sweet, shy girl. He sensed she felt the same for him.

"What do you say, then?"

"About what?" she asked.

"We take a walk together. This Saturday. Along Funeral Rock Creek."

"Funeral Rock Creek," Molly said with another dimple-cheeked smile. "That sounds so romantic!"

They laughed.

They'd both walked along the creek before. In fact, they'd had quite a time *in* the creek before, frolicking like forest sprites.

"Sure, sure," she said, when their laughter dwindled. "Let's take a walk, Henry." She reached out and touched his hand. "I'd like to get to know you...again."

"That's good," Henry said, brushing his thumb across her knuckles. "I'd like to get to know you again, too."

"At least I know I'll feel safe...with a rifleman such as yourself." Molly narrowed her eyes ironically and said, *Bang! Bang! Bang!"*

"Oh, stop, now, dang it," Henry said, genuinely embarrassed. "I got no idea where that came from."

"Don't worry," Molly said. "It takes more than a man good with a rifle to impress this girl." She gave an ironic smile. "It's a start, though."

"Mrs. Bjornson won't give you grief?"

"Oh, she'll give me grief, all right. But I'm almost

twenty years old. I love Mrs. Bjornson dearly but I won't let her make me a spinster."

Henry felt his ears warm.

"Oh, I didn't mean...I didn't mean...I thought you were going to...!"

Again, they both laughed.

"You never know," Henry said, when their laughter dwindled once more. "I just might." Propose, he meant.

That made the girl turn red.

"Well," Henry said, "before we both stand here trying to pull our feet out of our mouths till after dark, I'd best head over to Ma Branch's place. She'll be dishing up the chicken and dumplings soon, and letting her food get cold is a sin worse than inviting girls into our rooms."

Again, both flushing at the implication, they laughed...

Henry leaned forward and planted a soft, tender kiss on Molly's cheek. "It was nice jawin' with you, Miss Molly. I'll swing by Mrs. Bjornson's place Saturday morning with a buggy. We'll take us a walk."

"All right, Henry."

They turned away from each other.

"Henry?"

He stopped, turned back to her.

"For real," she said, serious lines cutting across her otherwise smooth forehead. "No, uh...expectations. We have to admit there's water under that bridge. Neither of us knows what might happen. We've both learned that."

"No expectations."

Molly smiled. "All right, then."

She returned to the dress shop.

Henry started walking south along San Juan Avenue, his mind and heart suddenly a tangle.

CHAPTER 15

MANNION HURRIED INTO HIS OFFICE.

Buster looked up at him from where the cat sat, lapping fresh cream from the saucer on the floor near the hole where Rio kept it cool. Green eyes glinted in the shadows at the rear of the room.

Buster meowed.

"Oh, hush!"

Mannion closed the door. He knew he was in for an onslaught. He wasn't sure how to handle it. He dearly did not want to lose his beloved wife once more, but he'd be damned if he'd let either Jane or Vangie or both in tandem cut his oysters off. He was his own man.

He was Bloody Joe Mannion!

So, why did he feel like a weak-kneed schoolboy who'd been caught throwing a snake into the girl's privy?

He looked at his desk. The bottle and shot glass were still there near the pad of tax summons. Two cigarette stubs lay in the carved wooden ashtray.

He'd just started to cross to the desk when feet thumped on the porch, the latch was tripped, the door opened, and Jane, red hair a burning halo against the setting sun behind her, stepped into the office.

"Joe!"

Mannion froze, turned slowly. "Oh, hi, honey."

Jane closed the door and stepped forward, placed a hand on his arm, and looked up at him with concern. Surprisingly—no, shockingly—her tone was even, gentle, quiet. "How are you doing, Joe? I've been putting in orders all day and just heard from Vangie about...your heart."

Lines of worry cut more deeply across her freckled forehead.

"Oh, that," Mannion chuckled. "You know, honey, I really think the doc was being overcautious."

Her fingers dug more deeply into his arm. "Joe, he said you had a heart stroke. He's quite concerned."

"Ah, no need for him to be. No need for you to be, either. I feel fine."

"Are you sure?"

"Sure, I'm sure."

"Well, if you think so..."

Mannion stared down at her, his lower jaw hanging in surprise. "Boy, I thought for sure you'd come over here to give me the what-for!"

Jane shook her head and continued to stare up at him, her brown eyes soft, astonishingly equanimical. "Oh, no, Joe. Not at all. I know you're your own man and have a job to do. And you're probably right. Doc Ellison is probably just being a little overcautious. You know—all that schooling?"

"Well, I will be damned. Do you know that's just what I was telling Henry not fifteen minutes ago?"

"Really?"

"Hell, yeah. You know, overeducated doctors are trained to find more than what's really there."

"No doubt you're right."

Mannion turned to face his darling wife, placed his hands on her shoulders. "Honey, I'm so glad you see it my way. I thought you were going to demand bed rest, like the doctor did. And all that nonsense. A man—especially a lawman—can't do his job from a bed!" Joe chuckled.

"Of course, he can't."

Mannion whistled. "Boy, I sure am relieved. I hope you can convince Vangie of the same thing. She was a might heated. Do you know what she said she was gonna do if I died?"

Jane turned her mouth corners down and nodded. "Yes, she told me. She, as you said, was just a little overwrought. She doesn't understand. She sees you as only her father. She doesn't realize that you're Bloody Joe Mannion. Town tamer of great renown. Why, you came to Del Norte and filed the horns on this town nearly single-handedly."

"Hell, when I first came, I *did* it single-handedly!"

"I know, Joe. I was here, remember?"

"Yes, honey. I remember." He kissed her cheek. "You know who I am."

"Of course, I do. You can't let one doctor's—albeit a Harvard-educated doctor's—"

"An *overeducated* Harvard doctor's...!"

"Yes, an *overeducated* Harvard doctor's diagnosis keep you from your work." Jane glanced at the desk. "You can't let an *overeducated* doctor keep you from drinking whiskey and smoking cigarettes...even if he said you should definitely not drink and smoke with the pills he gave you."

"My point exactly! Hell, you need something to wash them down with, and you know I hate water!"

"I know, Joe. I know." Jane took his arm in her hand. "Come." She pulled him toward his desk, pushed him down in his chair. "You sit down and let's have a drink."

Sitting back in the spindle-back chair, Mannion frowned at her curiously. "Really?"

"Sure." Jane rummaged around in a drawer until she found an extra shot glass. She looked into it, winced, blew the dust and a dead spider out of it. "That's disgusting."

"Yeah, well..."

"Never mind." Jane sat in his lap, picked up the bottle, topped off his glass then filled her own. She handed him his glass, clinked hers against his, smiled, and said, "Cheers!"

"Cheers," Mannion said with another chuckle.

"Oh, god!" Jane said when she swallowed half the whiskey, swallowing again and again to keep the rotgut down. In a strangled voice, she said, "If that hasn't killed you by now, nothing will!"

Mannion laughed and threw back half of his own shot.

Jane set her glass on the desk and reached for Joe's makins sack. "Let's have a smoke."

"Really?"

"Why not? I see you've had two before I came."

"Why not? I feel fine."

"One more might even make you feel better. Leastways, it can't do any real harm—now, can it?"

"My point exactly!"

"If you're going to smoke while on nitroglycerine tablets, well, then, I will smoke with you. No point in you smoking alone."

"Now, I like the sound of that!"

Jane took her time rolling each smoke in turn. She slipped the first one through Mannion's lips then rolled her own, again taking her time, sitting on Joe's lap. When she'd finished rolling the second one, she fired a lucifer match on the top of Joe's desk...when she could find a clear spot...touched the flame to first Joe's quirley and then to her own. She drew deeply, wincing a little at the acrid smoke peppering her lungs. She smoked occasionally herself, but her cigarillos were made from a finer, mellower tobacco than her husband's cheap grade of Durham.

She leaned back against his shoulder with a sigh.

Mannion filled his own lungs with the smoke, exhaled, then threw back the rest of his shot. He held the empty glass to her. "Shall we have one more, honey?"

"Why not?"

Jane refilled their glasses.

Mannion said, frowning at her, "I sure am glad you see this my way."

"What's the point of fighting? I'd lose," she said, lolling back against his shoulder. "Like I aways have. Married to you, Joe. I've become a fatalist."

"A fatalist?"

"Yeah—you know. What you're going to do, you're going to do." She glanced up at him. "I love you, anyway. I'll always love you, Joe."

"I'll always love you, honey."

"Even when you're gone."

Mannion frowned. "Huh?"

"You're going to die, Joe. The way you live. Not listening to anyone but yourself. But that's all right. I'm with you. No matter what happens, I'll always love you. It's the burden I carry. But I'm not going to fight you anymore. You're Bloody Joe Mannion, after all. The man I love. Despite all your faults. Just as you love me... despite my faults."

"You don't have any faults, dear Jane."

"Oh, I have a few." She chuckled. "Loving you is one of them. But what's a lady to do? I'm just along for the ride, I reckon." She reached up and placed her hand on his cheek, kissed the cleft in his chin. "When you're gone, I'll grieve. Along with Vangie. But we'll both go on, knowing we loved a good but stubborn man. But it's been a hell of a ride, Joe Mannion. I wouldn't exchange it for anything."

"Ah, hell." Mannion kissed her temple. "I'm not gonna die. I'm too stubborn to die."

"That's what you tell yourself. It goes along with your legend. But you'll die, Joe. I wish you'd resign, turn the badge over to Rio or Henry or someone else. I wish you'd move with me to Denver. We could start a new life together. But I know that's not the man you are. I know that. And I love you, anyway. And, yes, I'll grieve you when you're gone. But I'll have the memories. With those, I will go on."

Jane finished her whiskey, set the glass on the desk, took one more drag off the quirley, and mashed it out in the tray. She wriggled off Joe's knee and said, "Well, I'd best get back to work."

"Be careful out there, honey."

"Oh, I will."

"Here." Mannion set his glass on the desk, his cigarette in the tray, and rose. "Let me help you to the door. Someone's gunnin' for all of us, it seems." He placed himself between Jane and the window as he escorted her to the door.

At the door, she stopped, turned to him, wrapped her

arms around his neck, and kissed him deeply and with great affection. She looked up at him longingly, but she said nothing more. She opened the door and left.

Mannion stepped out onto the porch and watched her go.

He'd just held his beloved in his arms, but he'd never felt so lonely in his life.

When Jane was gone from view, he went back inside, sat in his chair, and was about to pour himself another glass of whiskey. But then he frowned at the bottle and set it back down on the desk. He picked up his makins sack, studied it closely, then opened a drawer and dropped it inside. He dropped the bottle inside, as well, and kicked the drawer closed.

He sat back in his chair, ran a hand down his craggy face, and said with great weariness, "Bloody Joe Mannion, your wife is way smarter than you are. All the women in your life are smarter than you are. Always have been, always will be."

———

"HENRY MCCALLISTER, YOU ARE LATE FOR SUPPER *again*!" exclaimed Ma Branch, stomping a heavy, black, square-heeled ankle boot down hard on her kitchen floor. She was standing at the range, stirring a big, steaming pot of chicken and dumplings.

Henry had just shot three would-be assailants—*bang! bang! bang!* as Molly would say—dead in the street, but he inwardly cowered at the browbeating of this matronly woman with her pinched up gray-blue eyes and heavy jowls and who always seemed to smell like liver tonic, wood smoke, and perspiration.

"I...I..."

"And skulking in the back door, no less!"

True, he often snuck in the back door which gave access to the rambling, old house's rear stairs. This time of the afternoon, Ma was usually serving the other boarders in the dining room so he could at least delay a haranguing by taking the rear stairs to his third-floor room where he'd wash quickly before descending to the dining room to join the other boarders for supper. Ma's harangues were usually less severe in front of the others. That Henry was a deputy of Bloody Joe Mannion meant no difference to the bosomy, gray-headed widow. He might as well have been a rock breaker or a street sweeper. Ma served supper at five thirty every day and if Moses himself were late, he'd get a good, old-fashioned scolding until his chin would sag in shame to his chest.

Ma set aside her long, wooden spoon and walked toward Henry, pointing an arthritic, accusing finger at her young boarder and narrowing both eyes in castigation, saying, "And you can tell that new boy—what's his name?—that he'd best get his keester down here, too, or I'll take his supper and throw it to the hogs!"

Ma and her hired man, an elderly half-Mexican named Augustin, raised hogs in a pen behind the boardinghouse. The pigs stunk up this entire end of town to high heaven, as the saying went.

"Oh, he's up there, I take it?" Henry said, hopefully glancing at the wainscoted ceiling and remembering the marshal's instructions for Henry to pal up with the newcomer.

"Oh, yes, he's late, too. You fetch him as well as yourself. I'll give you an extra minute to wash good, including behind your ears, or both your suppers will go to the hogs!" She spit a little as she spoke in a harsh Swedish brogue. "His room is right across from yours, but I better not hear any high jinks up there from either of you carrying on after nine o'clock—do you understand me, Henry McCallister?"

"You got it, Mrs. Branch! We'll be right down!"

"See that you are!"

Henry wheeled, pushed through a faded red curtain and, smashing his head against the low-slanted ceiling, which he did every time, he climbed the narrow, winding stairs to the third floor. He strode down the hall toward his own room, noticing that the door on the other side of the hall from his was open about one foot.

He slowed his pace and canted his head to glance through the opening then stopped when he saw a blond man a few years older than Henry and clad in trail gear sitting on the edge of a bed, crouched over the .45 Colt revolver in his hands. His head was bowed over the gun, and he seemed so preoccupied with the revolver he didn't hear Henry's approach on the squawky wooden floor.

He was twirling the gun on his finger and obsessively opening and closing the loading gate on each rotation, hardening his jaws as he did. Suddenly, he lifted his head and stared across the room with a far-away look in his dark-blue eyes, as though he were seeing right through the wall.

He was handsome, but his features were cast severely, a flush in his high-tapering cheeks. He must have spied Henry in the periphery of his vision. He suddenly turned toward the partly open door, bringing the gun up and around, as well, and clicking the hammer back, aiming down the barrel at the unexpected newcomer.

"Woah, now!" Henry said, throwing his free hand and rifle out to his sides. "Easy, there. I mean no harm, though I do apologize for intruding. I'm a fellow boarder."

The man stared down his Colt's barrel at Henry for another couple of stretched seconds then, his flush deepening with chagrin, lowered the piece suddenly and depressed the hammer. "Sorry." He gave a coyote-grin, eyes flashing in the light of a lantern flickering on a dresser, and said, "You're the local lawdog who cut down those three hardtails with that Winchester there." The smile broadened. "I didn't see it, just the aftermath. I was heading for the harness shop. Need a bridle repaired."

Henry stepped forward, nudged the door a little wider, and stood in the opening, leaning a shoulder against the frame. "Henry McCallister."

The newcomer rose from the bed, holstered the Colt, snapped the keeper thong home across the hammer, and moved to the door, extending his right hand. "Quentin Ferguson."

Henry shook the young man's hand. "Don't go thinkin' I'm some kind of toughnut myself. I'm not. I'm Marshal Mannion's junior deputy."

"Maybe it's time Mannion made you his senior deputy."

"Oh, no. That role is filled by Rio Waite."

Quentin Ferguson glanced at the Winchester Henry held low along his right leg. "How'd you get so fast with the long gun?"

"Honestly, I have no idea."

"Maybe you practice without knowin' it."

"That's my theory. Del Norte's a rough town. You might keep that in mind."

"I'll make note."

"Anyway, welcome to town. I hear you're workin' for Norman Davis."

Ferguson threw up his hands. "I wasn't even lookin' for work. Just went into the man's shop in search of licorice and an apple." He grinned again. He was especially handsome and innocent-looking when he grinned; Henry had a feeling he was very much aware of just that. "Left with a job off-loading freight, which, I take it, Davis gets several deliveries of over the course of a week."

"He has a healthy business, does Mr. Davis...and his daughter, Laura."

Ferguson smiled at the girl's name. "That's what I understand. No puzzle why the girl does, though her pastries smelled right fine, as well."

"You met Laura?" They were already chatting in the conspiratorial tones of two robust young men, which was what Henry had been aiming for in the fulfillment of his boss's orders. Not that it was all that hard for him, a young man with a young man's thoughts and desires of his own.

"Oh, yeah. Sweet gal."

"I don't think she's seein' anybody—if you're interested, I mean."

Ferguson frowned. "What about the big, yellow-haired fella who was in her café—Lars?"

Henry winced. "Don't mind him. He's a thug. Everybody knows it. Him and his pal, Dave Coffee, wrangle horses on Lars's father's ranch just outside of town. Olaf Gunderson. No-accounts, all. Laura knows that. Pretty girls like Laura attract all kinds."

Ferguson stood before Henry, grinning knowingly, arms crossed on his chest. "I see, I see."

"If you feel like askin' her out, I'm takin' a walk along Funeral Rock Creek this Saturday with a young lady I'm sorta sweet on. You two could join us. Might help you break the ice. I mean, if you have any intentions that way..."

"Who wouldn't have any intentions that way?" Ferguson pursed his lips, nodded. "She might be more inclined...her pa, too...knowin' we'll be chaperoned, as it were, by Mannion's junior deputy." He glanced at Henry's rifle. "And his trusty Winchester."

"Sounds good, then, Quentin."

"Thanks for the invite, Henry."

They shook hands again. "Not a problem, Quentin. Say, I'm headin' downstairs for supper. Mrs. Branch is likely waitin' on us, tappin' her foot. She don't cotton to dawdlers."

Ferguson shook his head. "Nah. I like to eat alone." He grinned again, slyly. "Don't cotton to crowds, myself. I have some bread an' cheese. That'll do me."

"Are you sure?"

"Certain-sure. Me, I'm used to lonely campfires. Not dining room tables with a cabinet clock a-tickin' and old ladies hoverin' over my shoulder."

"I see, I see. I'll let her know." Henry slapped his new friend's shoulder. "We'll see you Saturday mornin' if not before."

"Sure, sure. Good night, Henry."

"Good night."

Henry turned away as the door closed.

Moving across the hall to his room, he remembered the flinty, determined expression on young Ferguson's face just before he'd spied Henry in the doorway. That look told Henry his boss's suspicions were right. Quentin Ferguson wasn't as interested in the beautiful Laura Davis as he was—who?

Her father?

Why?

He hurried into his room and washed, knowing he was going to get one hell of a tongue-lashing downstairs.

CHAPTER 16

MAKING NIGHT ROUNDS SEPARATELY WITH CLETUS Booker, his night deputy, Mannion crossed a side street, stepped up onto a boardwalk, stopped, and leaned against an awning support post. He winced and reached up to loosen his neckerchief.

He was feeling that damn tightness in his chest again, making it hard to draw a complete breath. He reached instinctively for his makins sack then, remembering he'd left it at the office, vowing off both tobacco and whiskey until that crab in his chest released his old ticker for good, if it ever would, let his hand drop to his side.

Why in the hell had this had to happen to him, anyway?

He'd expected to go out in a hail of hot lead. Not in bed, his life dwindling one painful breath at a time. Maybe that's why, instead of taking a long night's nap in his chair at the office, he'd decided to join Booker making night rounds, rattle door handles and making sure no one was trying to break into anything, breaking up the occasional fights in Del Norte saloons, most of which stayed open either all night or until their business had tapered off enough that it wasn't worth staying open any longer.

He didn't want to die in that damn chair.

Not only that, but he wanted to find out who was out to send the Del Norte police force toe down, and why. So far, no one in town had reported recognizing any of the four would-be assassins propped up in their coffins outside of Bellringer's place, each one sporting a wooden sign around his neck.

Coincidentally, just as Mannion glanced over his left shoulder at the bank one door down from Jane's San Juan Hotel & Saloon, he saw a shadow move in the darkness on the bank's far side. It was the bank he suspected had been targeted by a pack of robbers who might have wanted to obliterate the Del Norte lawmen before they struck. A fairly common practice so not an unexpected one.

"Hmm," Joe said, drawing a deep breath as he turned and squared his shoulders toward the Del Norte Stockmen's, one of only two banks in the town and the most popular, thus wealthier, one. Bank owner and president Edwin McCloud didn't mess with small deposits, so most of the squareheads and honyockers who didn't stuff their meager earnings in their mattresses patronized the Rocky Mountain Bank & Trust.

His heart picked up its beat a little. The crab in his chest didn't entirely release its hold but it did loosen up a little. To give it some help, Mannion reached into his shirt pocket for the small, flat tin Ellison had given him, plucked out one of the several small, gelatin tablets, laid it on his tongue, and swallowed. It would have gone down better with whiskey but the common sense Jane had inoculated him with, however minimally despite her subtle, measured force, had made him realize that the whiskey combined with the nitro might blow him up from the inside out, had made him swear off the brew.

He hoped it stuck. The Who-Hit-John could get a nasty hold on a man.

He'd fought it before. He'd likely fight it again.

Tonight, however, he needed a clear head and ticker. Especially if he had possible bank robbers on the lurk.

He'd just started to walk back in the direction from which he'd come when a man's scream erupted from behind him now as he faced south.

"Booker, no—I changed my mind! I'll come peace—"

A loud, bearlike roar issued from the north. Joe grinned. Another scream and then he saw a man come flying through the batwings of the Three-Legged Dog Saloon, the watering hole's windows lit with flickering umber lamplight. The man formed a shadowy human missile arcing out over the boardwalk to strike the street six feet beyond it with a resolute thud and a groan.

"Booker, now, hangit," bellowed another man. "Put that damn bung starter away. I got a pigsticker, an' I know how to—"

The man's warning was clipped off abruptly and became yet another scream. There was a loud *clank!* as the knife hit the floor. That man, too, came flying through the swing doors, ripping off one of the doors as he, too, arced over the boardwalk to land in the street beside the first man. Both men lay groaning and whimpering, trying feebly to gain their feet.

Heavy footsteps sounded behind them. A big, shadowy bear of a man who could only be Cletus Booker himself in his long, canvas coat and floppy-brimmed hat stepped through the sole remaining louver door to stand on the boardwalk, tapping the hide-wrapped bung starter he held in his right hand against his left palm, pondering the two human vermin—miners, most likely—panting and sighing in the street before him. The big deputy moved forward, tossed away his infamous club, and reached down to haul both men to their feet by the backs of their shirt collars.

Both men groaned louder, clawing at Booker's big, paw-like hands, pleading for mercy.

The giant deputy laughed deep in his throat. It was a grizzly-like laugh—if a grizzly could laugh. Booker swung to his left and half carried, half dragged both men off in the direction of Hotel de Mannion, where they would no doubt be spending the night on the town council's dime—at least until they paid the fines Mannion would set for them in the morning. That was all right. Buster was the basement cellblock's sole occupant at the moment, chasing and terrorizing rats and mice. Being a social albeit savage beast, Buster would welcome the company.

Chuckling to himself, Joe continued south along the east side of San Juan Avenue, the rails of the Colorado Springs & San Juan Line glistening in the light of oil pots placed here and there along the avenue and in the lights of several saloons on both sides of the street. A block beyond where he'd started, he crossed the street at a slant, stepping over the consarned rails and unsheathing the big, silver-chased Russian holstered for the cross-draw on his left hip.

Ahead and on his left was Jane's place from which the low hum of midweek conversation issued as well as the melodic tinkling of a piano in the main drinking hall. Nothing too raucous going on in there. If there had been earlier, it had likely dwindled quickly as Cletus had passed through, saying, "Hmmm...hmmm..." while tapping the bung starter in his open left palm.

Cletus had a way of quieting down the town himself just fine.

A known head breaker was Booker. That's why Joe had hired him. Joe was only out here to check doors and clean up whatever stirred in the big man's wake. Which appeared to be what Joe might be doing now.

He strode past the broad, wooden steps of the San Juan, seeing shadows moving behind the lit windows of the large, rambling building's first story, hearing that conversational hum, the melodic pattering of the piano likely being played by Jane's old piano player and former stage actor, veteran of mining camp opera houses in Virginia City, Deadwood, and Leadville—Vernon Hersch, whom in his mind's eye Joe could see playing the piano in his eyeshade and sleeve garters, ashes dripping from his cigarette as he leaned over the keys, swooning, canting his head this way and that, blinking slowly and smiling, the music as alive in his head as that rising from his long, tobacco-stained fingers expertly manipulating the ivories.

Mannion walked past the hotel and the dark candy shop just beyond it.

At the far corner of the candy shop, he stopped, pressed his right shoulder against the clapboarded front wall, and edged a look down the side of the building, through a dark, brush-stippled break in which the sign for an old, long-vanished opera house—one of Del Norte's original businesses constructed of logs and adobe bricks and long since razed to make way for the San Juan —lay up against the candy shop's stone foundation.

Mannion squeezed the Russian in his hand, which he held just above his shoulder, barrel aimed at the murky, star-sprinkled sky. He switched it to his left hand and pulled the other one, rocking both hammers back. He drew a breath, remembering how he'd started the day with the Mexican, then stepped around the corner of the candy shop, vaguely smelling the caramel apples and fudge inside the place, and began striding slowly through the break, boots crunching weeds and old newspapers blown here by the wind.

He held both Russians straight out before him, sliding them slightly from left to right and back again, watching for movement. So far, the only movement was the breeze bending the brush including bromegrass and sage, a single cedar angling up out of the earth like a crooked witch's finger.

He gained the rear of the candy shop, stopped, looking around carefully.

Not much back here but a leaning privy, more trash, and an abandoned stable that had once serviced the old opera house, its shake-shingled roof now half-collapsed, scrub pines all but concealing its bowed, mud brick walls. A path of bent weeds shone before him, angling around behind the candy shop. Freshly bent. Someone had been here, all right. Mannion followed the weeds to the two-track trail that bisected the rear alley, dropped to a knee, stared down at the slight indentation in the dirt of one of the trail tracks made by a bootheel.

The walker had been heading in the direction of the bank.

Mannion straightened, moved slowly along the trail.

He investigated the barred, stout wooden door at the rear of the bank. Its heavy lock was unmolested.

He looked around again.

Nothing. No movement.

Whomever had been here was gone.

But they'd been investigating the bank, all right. Someone was sizing the place up, likely wondering how they might break in. They'd have to blow the rear door with dynamite; all the windows were stoutly barred, just like the door. Inside, they'd have to blow the safe, as well. During office hours, of course, they might be able to force one of the employees to open it. Mannion knew that McCloud kept the safe's door closed and locked even during banking hours.

All that would take time.

That's why they were endeavoring to rid Del Norte of its lawmen. To give them more time. Those citizens of Del Norte who had their life savings in the bank wouldn't take lightly to it being stolen, but without Mannion and his deputies, it would take them awhile to gather their courage, fetch weapons, and get organized.

Mannion wondered how many robbers were in the gang intending to rob the bank. Probably not that many. Otherwise, they'd just storm it, part of the gang holding off him and the other lawmen and gun-wielding citizens while the others robbed the place, shooting, shouting, cursing, causing chaos that would make the customers and employees and the citizens in the street freeze in their boots.

Joe had seen such escapades before. They were wild, savage, and bloody.

He stretched his lips back from his teeth, deciding that that was likely what he was facing here.

When?

He walked around to the front of the bank, making a mental note to caution his deputies to tread extra cautiously. There would likely be more attacks on their lives.

When he checked to make sure the bank's front door hadn't been fiddled with, he looked around again, pricking his ears, listening, then, holding the Russians straight down against his sides, hammers depressed, made his way north toward Hotel de Mannion.

He met Booker as the big man was just emerging from the front door, having locked up his prisoners in the basement cellblock.

"Havin' a good night so far, Cletus?" Joe asked.

Booker yawned, stretched. "Oh, yeah," the deputy said, as taciturn as usual. "Two downstairs."

Mannion opened his mouth to respond but stopped when a man's voice called from along the street to the south, "Marshal Mannion—got two live ones down here. Threatenin' to carve their hearts out with Arkansas toothpicks!"

Mannion recognized the voice of the manager of the Railroader's Saloon, which sat next door to the Black Cat and was one of the newer watering holes in town and was favored by bullwhackers and mule skinners—big, violent men even when they weren't three sheets to the wind.

Mannion sighed. "You got it, Cletus?" He hated to admit it, but he was played out. He wanted to sit down with a cup of coffee.

"Don't worry, boss."

Joe wasn't.

Booker thumped down the porch steps and stomped off in the direction of the Railroader's and the flickering oil pot burning out front of that saloon and the Black Cat beside it and the figure of the Railroader's manager, Robbie Robertson, silhouetted against it.

Feeling like an old man, hating that perpetual bite in his chest, Mannion walked into the jailhouse and poured himself a cup of coffee.

———

CLETUS BOOKER TRAMPED OVER AND SCOOPED HIS hide-wrapped bung starter out of the street fronting the Three-Legged Dog.

He turned to ponder the Railroader's Saloon sitting beside the Black Cat. He idly tapped the stout end of the club in the palm of his left hand. He could hear men yelling, boots thumping, a crowd of drunks yelling encouragement, no doubt placing bets on which of the mule skinners or bullwhackers would cut the other one's heart out first. One big freight wagon sat out front of the place, the mules in the traces twitching their ears at the commotion. There were six or seven saddled horses tied to the two hitchracks fronting the place, as well.

Shadows moved beyond the big, plate glass window to the right of the batwings.

"Git him," one man bellowed shrilly. "What the hell you waitin' for? You two fightin' or dancin'?"

"Oh, god! Oh, god! Oh, god!" screamed a girl. "Stop this—I hate seein' blood all over the consarned floor!"

"Then git upstairs!" shouted another man. "We got us a good one goin'...if these two would get down to business, that is. I can't figure out if they're fightin' or do-si-doin'!"

Cletus snickered.

He'd make short work of the two knife-wielding drunks who, it sounded like, were losing their nerve. Yep. Short work. He'd have them over to Hotel de Mannion in less than five minutes. Hardly a challenge, really, when they got that drunk. Cletus liked a challenge. The nights could get long and boring if he didn't have enough to do, enough heads to break, enough men to throw into the street.

"All right, all right, all right," the big man said to himself.

He tapped the club in his hand once more then lowered it to his side and strode in his heavy-footed way at a slant across the railroad tracks and over to the Railroader's, the crowd's roar louder now as he stepped around the big Pittsburg freighter and mounted the splintered boardwalk fronting the batwings. He peered over the doors to see two men ducking and feinting and sidestepping in a slow circle as they poked knives at each other—one wielding a Green River knife while the other was poking and prodding and slashing the air with a homemade Bowie with a hand-carved wooden handle.

Neither was all that big. One had long, sandy hair and a matching mustache. The other was taller with dark-brown hair and a patch over one eye. Both were dressed more like range riders minus the chaps than mule skinners or bullwhackers. Obvious mule skinners and bullwhackers surrounded the pair in a ragged circle—big, sun-seared, bearded men in filthy, smoke-stained denims, buckskin, leather, and wool, soiled bandannas knotted around their necks, the lower halves of their faces lighter than the upper halves because of the bandannas they wore up over their mouths and noses against the infernal trail dust kicked up by their mules or oxen.

Right away, Cletus could see that neither fighter meant business.

They lunged at each other, but their knives never got very close to their opponent's chest, belly, or throat. They were likely just drunk and had their necks in a hump over some whore—likely the pretty, little, busty brunette in a gauzy wrap and red hair ribbons cowering back against the player piano, yelling for the pair to stop this nonsense right now.

"This is a civilized establishment!" she yelled.

The rest of the room erupted in laughter.

Scoffing at the two "girls" playing with knives before him, Cletus pushed through the batwings and, tapping the end of the bung starter in his open palm once more, threateningly, bellowed, "All right, you Nancy-boys either cut each other's throats an' make a show of it, or drop 'em an' come with me. If I have to come one step closer, you're gonna wake in the mornin' feelin' like your noggins is broke *rocks*!"

"Ah, let 'em go to it, Cletus!" bellowed one of the mule skinners, a regular named Anderson. "Hell, they ain't even given us a show yet!"

"Drop 'em!" Cletus bellowed again, hating it when he wasn't obeyed right away.

Most knew he meant business, and they knew what kind of business he meant, too. Nasty, hurtful, a whole-world-of-ache kind of business! Most knew not to trifle with Cletus Booker, Bloody Joe Mannion's chief head breaker...

Looked like he was going to have to break a couple of heads here tonight, though.

Booker moved forward.

Suddenly, the "fighters" stopped moving. As one, they turned toward Cletus.

Booker stopped suddenly. He didn't like the smirks he saw in the fighters' eyes.

The room fell suddenly silent. To a man...and girl... everyone slid their own puzzled gazes between the fighters and Booker.

At first, Cletus had thought the pair was turning their horns in.

Now he realized his mistake.

Both men smiled at him, coyote-like. They dropped their knives, closed their hands around the grips of their holstered hoglegs.

"Oh-oh," Cletus heard a warning voice murmur inside his head.

A murmur rose inside the saloon, as well—among the dozen or so men forming a ragged circle around the two supposed knife fighters...who were not knife fighters at all.

They'd only been pretending.

Another man separated himself from where he stood with two others at the rear of the room, unsheathing the hogleg thonged low on his right thigh. The two men nearer Cletus unpouched their own irons. As they did, Cletus, exasperation making his heart pound, dropped the bung starter and reached for his own Remington holstered high on his right hip, bellowing a sudden burst of rage at having been lured into a trap...and that he'd walked right into it.

He did not get the Remington clear of its holster before all three shooters began shooting, the guns bucking and stabbing flames, the bullets cutting into the big deputy's broad chest, sending him wailing and yelling and stumbling straight back through the batwings, knocking both doors off their hinges just before he was blown across the boardwalk and into the street, dead before he hit the ground between two frightened, whinnying horses pulling at their reins.

CHAPTER 17

MANNION HAD JUST LIFTED HIS STEAMING CUP TO HIS lips when gunfire hammered to the south along San Juan Avenue.

He jerked with a start, burning his lips, spilling coffee. Rising, he quickly set the cup on his desk.

His logy ticker quickened as the shooting continued —one loud, angry blast after another. A deep voice wailed in anger and agony.

Booker!

Joe hurried out from behind his desk, setting his hat on his head and grabbing his rifle from where he'd leaned it against the wall by the door. Pumping a round into the action, he fumbled open the door and ran out onto the jailhouse's front stoop in time to see a large, shadowy figure stumble back out through the batwings of the Railroader's Saloon. Booker's arms flapped as though they were wings working desperately to keep the man upright.

To no avail.

As both batwings were ripped off their hinges, Cletus stumbled back across the boardwalk. Bullets continued to chew into him until he flopped back into the street with one last, angry wail, horses to each side of him stomping and pulling at their reins.

Mannion leaped down the steps and into the street then started running in the direction of the Railroader's lit by the burning oil pot and the saloon's large, plate glass window to the right of the batwings. As he did, three men ran out through the open doorway. They leaped Booker's inert figure and ran into the street, turning to face Mannion.

Light from the window and the oil pot glinted off the steel in their hands.

Mannion adjusted his course, angling hard to his left and diving toward a stock trough just as the three killers' guns began flashing and barking. The bullets tore up street dirt and finely ground horse manure just behind Mannion's boots a quarter second before he piled up behind the trough. As he pulled his legs in with the rest of him, the bullets chewed into the face of the trough, sending wood slivers flying in all directions.

The guns barked loudly. The bullets thumped into the trough.

Joe kept his head down, gritting his teeth, rage making his aching ticker buck in his chest.

When the barking stopped, he tried to lift his head and Yellowboy over the top of the trough to return fire, but he found that his chest was aching as though his ticker had been caught in a bear trap, and his right hand and arm had gone stiff.

Beyond him, men shouted. Horses whinnied. Hooves thumped. Tack squawked.

The hoof thuds grew louder.

Finally, hand pressed against his chest, trying to quell that crab torturing his ticker, Joe managed to lift his head to peer over the top of the bullet-pocked trough.

The three shooters were mounted and reining their horses out into the street. They turned them sharply, spurred them, whipped them with their rein ends, and galloped off down the street to the south, quickly consumed by the murky darkness at the edge of town and beyond, the hoof thuds dwindling quickly.

Cursing, suppressing the pain in his chest, the stiff-ness in his arm, Mannion heaved himself to his feet. He ran, heavy-footed, over to the horses tied before the Black Cat and the Railroader's Saloon, ripped the reins of the first mount he came to off the hitchrail, and swung up into the saddle. Men were spilling out of both saloons onto the boardwalk, shuttling their wary gazes between Mannion and Cletus Booker lying in the street out front of the Railroader's. That he was dead, there could be no doubt. He wasn't moving, and no man lived after being shot as many times as Cletus had.

He'd been lured into a trap, and Joe, in his growing feebleness, had let him walk into it solo.

Cursing himself, Joe reined his borrowed mount into the street and booted it into an instant, hard gallop to the south. In seconds, Del Norte had slipped behind him including the ragged outskirts of cabins, warehouses, and stock pens. He rode hard for nearly a quarter mile before the waylaying hand of reason reached up inside him, and he slowed the mount before stopping him, curveting the sorrel and gazing in frustration through the murky dark-ness cloaking the trail ahead.

If he kept riding, he'd likely be playing right into the killers' hands.

Getting shot out of the saddle wasn't going to do him or Cletus any good, and that's likely what the killers' planned to do—hole up in the rocks and bluffs ahead and fill him, as they had Cletus, full of lead.

Rage was a galloping stallion inside of the lawman. He could feel it clawing at his heart, burning in his veins, ringing in his ears. The last thing he wanted to do was give up the chase, but he had no choice. By daylight, the three killers' trail will have gone cold, but Mannion had a pretty good idea he'd see them again.

They wanted the Del Norte lawmen out of the way, so they could rob something big—likely the Stockmen's Bank.

In town, a larger crowd had gathered in front of the Railroader's Saloon.

As Joe approached on his borrowed sorrel, he saw Henry and Rio out there, as well. Holding his Winchester on his shoulder, Henry stepped out away from the horses. The freight wagon had been driven off; Mannion had met it on the way back to town, the driver deciding, after witnessing the horror in the Railroader's, to continue on to Alamosa, even in the darkness.

"Heard the shootin', Marshal," Mannion's junior deputy said, grimly. He shook his head somberly. "Poor ol' Cletus."

Rio stepped up beside Henry and said, "I got descriptions of the three shooters, Joe. Nobody knew 'em. They weren't local. Judging from their descriptions, I don't know 'em, either."

Mannion swung heavily down from the saddle. "You two keep a sharp eye out, careful not to get lured into any traps like the one they set for Cletus. I can't afford to lose any more deputies."

He stepped between the two men and approached Booker lying with his arms and legs spread wide, blood glistening on his neck, chest, and belly. Annoyed at the gawking crowd, Mannion told them to scatter. When they were slow to obey, he lost his temper and repeated the order, barking it out at the tops of his lungs, mindless of that claw squeezing his heart.

When the crowd had dispersed, some returning to the saloons, some heading off to bed, and it was just Joe, Henry, and Rio left, Mannion dropped to a knee beside the big man sprawled before him. With a slightly shaky hand, he closed Booker's eyes, let his hand linger on the man's big face already turning cold now in death.

"Ah, hell, Cletus." Emotion formed a knot in the lawman's throat. He tried to swallow it down, but it wasn't going anywhere.

He just now realized he knew nothing about the man he'd sent into death's jaws. He'd never known any man more tight-lipped. Cletus had never shared with Mannion two words about his personal life. Joe had no idea if he had any family, much less where he might find them. He doubted either Henry or Rio knew anything about him, either. Joe doubted he or his other two deputies had ever shared more than a half dozen complete sentences with the taciturn head breaker. It wasn't because Booker was stupid. Mannion had seen a wry intelligence in his eyes. He was just private, preferring to live inside the myth he'd cultivated as a hard, emotionless giant—no man to mess with.

Until tonight, it had been a successful strategy.

Mannion wished he'd thought to inquire about him.

But now he was dead, and no one knew anything about him except that he'd been a big, formidable, quiet man. Nothing about family, nothing about where he might have come from.

"It's not your fault, Joe," Rio said, both him and Henry standing over Mannion and the dead man now. "Sounds to me like they faked a fight, baited him in."

"Of course, it's my fault. I was on night duty, too. I

should have backed him." Mannion picked up a small stone, slammed it angrily down in the street. "I should have backed him!"

"You'd likely just be dead, too, then, Marshal," Henry said.

"Then so be it."

Rio started to say something more, but Mannion cut him off with: "Send for Bellringer. I want Cletus taken care of tonight, buried in the morning. I want him to have a good marker, too. The town council will pay for it. If they squawk, I'll shoot 'em."

"Uh…" Henry hesitated. "Bellringer don't like to be woke up anymore, boss. I'll send for his hired men. They live in the back of the—"

"No. I want Bellringer out here pronto. I want him to take care of this man personally." Mannion looked up at his junior deputy. "Send for him. Wake him up in that fool mausoleum of his. If he squawks, tell him I'll shoot him, too!"

"You got it. I'll fetch him myself. He'll likely shoot anybody else who rides up there this time of the night."

Henry's coyote dun, Banjo, stood tied at the hitchrack. He mounted the gelding and galloped off in the direction of the bluff atop which Bellringer's impressive house stood.

When he was gone, Mannion glanced up at Rio. "Go back to bed, Rio. You're gonna need to be wide awake tomorrow. Trouble's afoot. We have to be ready to meet it head on."

"I'll wait here with you, Joe."

"Go to bed. I'll wait here with Cletus."

Rio sighed. "If you say so."

"I say so."

———

THE NEXT DAY, MIDMORNING, MANNION SQUATTED near the grave still being dug by one of Bellringer's men on the cemetery sprawling along the side of a low butte on the northeast side of Del Norte.

His bay stallion, Red, stood nearby, idly cropping the short, spring grass, bridle reins dangling. The only sounds were the *snick-snick-snicks* of the gravedigger's shovel, the breeze ruffling the leaves of the large cottonwood behind Mannion, and the crunching sounds of Red munching the tender green shoots from wet patches where snow had recently melted, occasionally giving his tail a switch at pesky flies.

The mule hitched to the gravedigger's wagon hung its head in the traces, also switching its tail at flies drawn by Cletus Booker moldering in the simple, pine coffin beside the grave. Mannion had made sure Bellringer had thoroughly cleaned the man's body and wrapped him in his saddle blanket. Joe had considered buying him a suitcoat, the largest one available at Wilfred Drake's Mercantile, but had nixed the idea. He doubted Booker had ever worn a suitcoat in his life. Knowing he'd be buried in a jacket more appropriate for church would have embarrassed him. No, the man's own saddle blanket was more fitting.

At least Joe had made sure he'd been cleaned up, though Booker wouldn't have known the difference between being cleaned up and buried in his own blood, no more than he'd have known whether he was buried in a suitcoat or in his saddle blanket. It was all just the useless working of a busy mind. Of a guilty mind. Of a sorrow-racked mind.

Cletus Booker was dead and Mannion was going to

miss him, though he'd known so little about him. Though he'd rarely even thought about him when he'd been alive. Had never even thought to inquire about his personal life, his past.

Death put such a damn hard end to things, made you consider things you never would have considered before it showed its ugly countenance in the form of a man walking into a trap in a murky saloon in Del Norte, Colorado Territory, and was blown out the batwings in a hail of lead.

When the gravedigger finished the grave, Joe helped him lower the coffin into it with ropes levered over their shoulders.

When the coffin was settled at the bottom of the grave, Mannion glanced at the gravedigger, a big, bald man named Stanley, who held his black, felt hat down in front of him with cursory deference to the dead he was around so much. Mannion said, "Come back and fill it in later, will you? I'd like a few minutes alone."

Stanley frowned at him, vaguely puzzled.

"I figure he deserves someone to be here with him... for just a few minutes before he's forgotten about for the rest of time."

Stanley stared at Mannion as though he were wondering if the lawman had gone mad.

Joe smiled as he stared at the grave. Maybe he had. His logy heart felt large, swollen, as tender as an exposed nerve. The lump that had lodged in his throat hadn't softened any over the past several hours that he'd sat in his office, in vigil of sorts, waiting for the sun to rise and for the big, inscrutable man to be planted.

Stanley climbed up into his wagon, released the brake, shook the reins over the mule's back, and followed the two-track trail down the bluff through the tilted wood and stone markers. Stanley had to pull the buckboard off the side of the trail to make way for a leather-seated buggy climbing the bluff. The buggy was driven by Jane herself. Vangie sat beside Jane, both women dressed in somber-colored gowns, black hats with black net veils pinned to their piled-up hair.

Mannion regarded the pair as they approached, Jane's handsome black gelding in the traces friskily shaking its head and twitching its ears.

"Whoa," Jane said, drawing back on the reins.

The chaise stopped near Mannion, both women gazing down at him sympathetically, maybe a little incredulously.

Mannion rose, holding his hat down low by his side.

"How are you, Poppa?" Vangie scowled through her veil.

Mannion shrugged.

Jane glanced around. "No funeral?"

Again, Mannion shrugged. "He didn't know anybody. Hell, he didn't even know me, Rio, or Henry."

Jane smiled sympathetically, nodded. "Well, he wasn't really all that approachable."

"No, he wasn't."

Vangie said, "It wasn't your fault, Poppa. I heard all about it."

"He was my man. It was my fault."

"Joe, don't do this to yourself," Jane said. "Don't torture yourself for no reason."

"It's my right."

"Is this about you, Poppa?" Vangie asked. "Or Cletus?"

"Hell, I don't know."

"How are you feeling?" Jane asked.

"I'm alive."

"That's not enough, Joe," she said.

"No, it's not. But at the moment, it's the best I can do."

Jane stared at him, deeply troubled. So did Vangie.

"We were going to sit here with you," Jane said. "Pay our respects."

"Thanks for the thought." Joe gave a wan smile. "I'll be down shortly. Just want to be here with him. He sure as hell wouldn't expect it." He chuckled. "He probably wouldn't even want it. But I want to do it. Just a few more minutes."

"Joe?" Jane said.

"Yes?"

"It's not you in that box. Cletus had a run of bad luck. It's him in that box. You're still alive. Hold on to every minute." Jane dipped her chin, narrowed a commanding eye. "Take care of yourself. Get some rest. You look pale, gaunt."

Mannion nodded. "Like I said. Just a few more minutes."

Jane nodded. She and Vangie shared a glance.

Jane shook the ribbons over the black's back, swung him around, and they rattled off down the hill.

Mannion turned back to the grave. He stared down at the simple, pine coffin, its lid nailed down tight. His mind recoiled at the dead man locked inside, in all that darkness.

In all that endless, unyielding darkness.

He remembered his dream, shuddered.

Had those bullets been meant for him? Likely for both him and the big man.

He pondered the dead man, the darkness, his dream for a long time, holding his hat in front of him, worrying the brim with his fingers.

Jane was right. There was no point in torturing himself.

He didn't know the man. That wasn't about to change now that he was dead.

He wasn't sure why his death affected him so.

But a large part of him was glad it did. At least he could give Cletus...and himself...that.

He picked up a chunk of dirt, ground it between his fingers, dropped it into the grave.

He mounted Red and headed back toward town and the job he had waiting for him, keeping himself and his other two deputies alive.

CHAPTER 18

THREE DAYS LATER, QUENTIN CAMPBELL, ALIAS Quentin Ferguson, unloaded a fifty-pound sack of cracked corn from the supply wagon he'd driven over from the train depot and set it carefully atop the neat stack he'd already piled in the supply shed flanking the Davis' South-Central Colorado Fresh Meats & Dry Goods.

It was a hot day. Quentin had taken off his shirt, and beads of sweat glinted like honey in the sunlight as they dribbled down his chest and back.

He'd just swung back to the wagon in which a half dozen such sacks remained when he heard his name called. He stopped and cast his gaze toward the rear of the main store. Mr. Davis himself, Norman, stood just outside the open rear door, pulling his customary white apron up over his head.

"Yessir?" Quentin replied, finding it a little difficult to call the man "sir" in light of whom he thought he was— the leader of the bluecoats who'd butchered his family.

Wadding up his apron in his right hand, Davis scowled in disgust toward his new hired man and said,

"Denver shorted me a half dozen sacks of buckwheat and two crates of sorghum. I'm gonna head over to Western Union to fire off a telegraph." He glanced at the half-open door behind him. "Since you're still back here, I'm going to leave this open. When you're finished, will you lock it for me?"

"You got it, sir."

"Then help Laura stock the canned goods, will you? It's a big job and she's been busy in the café, too. News of the chili she made for lunch has made its way around town, and it seems half the businessmen in Del Norte have decided to take midafternoon breaks to try a bowl." He smiled, chuckled.

An affable man. Certainly not the man Quentin had cowed in his family's barn that grisly day.

Or was he?

The thing was the man's easy demeanor never seemed to quite make it into his eyes, which Quentin was roughly eighty percent sure were the eyes of the man who'd been standing in the barn's open doors that day, obscured partly by smoke from the burning cabin.

"Oh, sure, sure," Quentin said. "Not a problem, Mr. Davis. I'll make sure nobody gets in and then I'll lock up as soon as I'm done here."

"All right, then. Thanks, son."

Davis gave a wave with the hand holding the apron then disappeared inside the storeroom flanking the main part of the store.

Quentin stood staring at the door.

Davis's office opened off the storeroom just beyond that door. Sometimes the office door was locked, sometimes it wasn't, because usually the shop's rear door was closed and barred from the inside. Was it locked now?

If not, this was likely as good an opportunity the

young man was going to get for investigating the office, looking for anything that might tie Davis to the group of former Union soldiers who'd attacked the farm of his family over ten years ago now. He didn't know what he'd look for. Some memento, say. An old cavalry saber, maybe? A photograph, official papers of some sort betraying his true identity...

He wouldn't know until he started looking.

He figured he had a good half hour to do so. That's how long it would take Davis to make his way to and from the Western Union office on the other end of town. It sounded as though Laura was busy at the front of the shop, between serving customers in her café and stocking the canned goods in the main part of the store. She shouldn't be a problem. He didn't want her to catch him rummaging around in her father's office.

He finished unloading the wagon, closed the tailgate, and looked at the door, which Davis had pulled closed but hadn't latched. His heart quickened. Sweat broke out on his palms. He wiped them on his denims, looked up and down the alley, as though someone might be out here and suspect his intentions.

Of course, that was ridiculous. He was just nervous. He'd waited so long for this moment...of finally tracking down the man who'd led the gang who'd murdered his family. He'd taken satisfaction in finding and killing four after letting them know why they were being killed. But he'd especially savored the prospect of finding and killing the captain—especially the leader with his distinctive eyes and pinky ring.

Those were Davis's eyes. He was sure of it. He just needed confirmation.

Then what?

Kill him. He'd have to. That had been his intention

for the past fifteen years, every day of which he'd been haunted by, driven by the prospect. He couldn't be swayed by the fact the man was Laura's father.

Again, rubbing the sweat from his palms on his trousers, Quentin looked both ways along the alley. He crossed the alley to the small stoop fronting the shop's rear door. He drew the door open, stepped into the storage room aromatic with the smell of flour, cornmeal, sausages, and hams. A side of fresh beef hung near the front of the room, aging, already paid for by a man for his daughter's upcoming wedding party. There was more fresh meat in the keeper shed behind the warehouse. Davis was the most popular purveyor of fresh meat in Del Norte.

He was a valued, respected man.

And Quentin might have to kill him.

Now as he approached the door to the man's office, which was ahead and left, in a boxlike room partitioned off from the rest of the storage area, he found himself hoping he would discover that Norman Davis was not the man he'd been hunting for over half his lifetime. He'd been so intent on the hunt...on the search...that he hadn't considered all the implications of actually finding that man, who of course hadn't, unlike Quentin, lived in a vacuum over the fifteen years.

He'd been living a life that included others. Hopes, dreams, friends, family relationships, love for that family...possibly a business. At least, a job. He'd been moving among others, affecting others who, in turn, had affected him.

Please, let the door be locked, he found himself wishing. He glanced toward the door leading to the main part of the store, glad it was closed. He extended his hand toward the knob of the door to Davis's office, stretched his lips back from his teeth as he twisted the knob. He was able to turn it one full half turn.

The bolt clicked, free.

Shit.

Hinges squawked as he pushed the door halfway open, glanced once more, heart thudding, toward the door leading to the main part of the shop. He stepped forward into Davis's office, then slowly closed the door behind him until the bolt clicked quietly home.

One window in the far wall, its curtains drawn back, offered plenty of light.

A rolltop desk lay to the left of it. There was a table and two chairs. A small safe squatted to the left of the desk. On the other side of the desk were two tall wooden filing cabinets, each drawer outfitted with a lock. On the table, to Quentin's right, to the left of the door, were stacked newspapers and two coffee mugs, an ashtray with a half-smoked cigar in it.

Those were the room's only furnishings.

Quentin crossed the room to the desk, began opening and closing drawers, riffling through papers which were mostly bills of ladling, order forms, catalogs, account books, and other business-related paraphernalia. In one he found a dead mouse and droppings.

He turned to the filing cabinets. He wiped his sweaty palms on his pants and moved to the one nearest the desk, pleasantly surprised to find only one drawer, the bottom one, locked. That was likely the one which held anything of interest, but he quickly went through the others, finding nothing more than neatly labeled files with customers' names on them.

He came to the bottom drawer. His heart quickening anxiously, he produced his small pocketknife from his pants pocket, and picked the lock, hoping Davis wouldn't notice. He returned the knife to his pocket, quickly flipped through files of inscrutable financial documents and what he assumed were bank bonds. At the very bottom of the drawer, he came upon a timeworn, water-stained manila envelope stamped with a large, black U.S.

Quentin's already fast beating heart beat faster.

His right hand shook as he closed his thumb and index finger around one corner of the envelope and started to pull it out from the neat stack of files and outdated account books it was buried under.

He stopped, heart bucking painfully. He'd heard the door to the main part of the store open.

Laura's voice, soft but echoing around the cave-like storeroom just outside the office: "Quentin?"

Quentin jerked his hand out of the drawer.

Silently, he cursed. He straightened, stiffening.

He didn't say anything. Maybe she'd think he was still working out back and would return to the counter.

That didn't happen.

Footsteps sounded, growing louder.

Laura's voice again: "Quentin?"

His mind raced.

She was approaching the office.

"In here!" he said, quietly closing the drawer, wincing dreadfully at the lock he'd picked. He had no key; he couldn't relock it.

He moved to the door, drew it open. Laura turned to him, frowning. Then she blushed.

He followed her gaze to his bare chest. In his urgency to investigate Davis's office, he'd forgotten to put his shirt back on when he'd finished unloading the freight wagon.

"I think I heard a rat," Quentin said. "I don't think your father would want rats in the storeroom."

"No." The girl's gaze ran quickly, furtively down to his flat, corded belly then back up to the hard, twin slabs of his chest still damp with sweat. Her flush touched her ears as she returned her eyes to Quentin's. "But unfortunately, they're in here, all right. I've heard them myself."

"I'll set out some traps."

"Please do. We've had cats but at night they go out and become meals for the coyotes."

Quentin smiled. It was a smile of relief. She'd bought his story. It helped that she seemed rather distracted by the fact of his bare chest and belly.

She said, "I was wondering if you would come up and watch the counter for me. I have several ladies from the Del Norte Abstinence League holding a meeting in the café, and, well—"

"Laura?"

The man's voice was familiar.

Quentin turned to see a tall, broad-shouldered figure standing in the door opening onto the main part of the shop. It was the tall, rangy, yellow-haired Lars, his battered, funnel-brimmed Stetson shoved up on his forehead.

Lars scowled at Quentin, rolled a matchstick between his thin lips. His hard eyes sized up Quentin and then they slid to Laura as he crossed his arms on his chest, canted his head to one side, and said, "Was wonderin' if you wanted to go to the barn dance tomorrow. Homer MacGregor an' his boys'll be playin'."

The obvious toughnut smiled but given Quentin's unwanted presence, it was a brittle expression. "Figured you should let your hair down a little." The smile faded as he rolled the match from one corner of his mouth to the other and his eyes returned to Quentin. "You work too hard, girl. I figure you could use a night out. Harley Gibbs is roastin' a hog."

He straightened his head, lifted his chin, his eyes boring into Quentin's. "You, Mister, should have a shirt on. Show the girl some respe—"

"Oh, thank you, Lars," Laura said, smiling deferentially at the hard-eyed blond man as she took a step toward Quentin and brushed her fingers across his wrist. "Quentin has already asked me out for Saturday."

True, he'd asked her out just that morning and, to his surprise given they hadn't known each other long, she'd accepted. Just like he'd wished the door to her father's office had been locked, he halfway wished she hadn't. It was as though he found himself playing a game he now realized he wasn't prepared for.

"Oh, he has, has he?"

"Yes. Thank you, though, Lars. Maybe some other time."

"That's what you always say."

Lars looked at Quentin again. He looked at Laura once more as well, his eyes hard and sullen, angry. Then he turned and strode away.

Laura turned to Quentin and shuddered. "I swear, that man makes my skin crawl. He's asked me out several times. I've never accepted. There's no attraction for me. Still, he keeps coming over here. Him and his friend Dave. He keeps asking then goes away angry."

As if of their own accord, her eyes flicked down to Quentin's belly again before returning to his own.

"You should have your father ban him from the shop."

Laura shook her head. "I'm afraid to make him angrier than he already is. I'm afraid of what he might do. I wouldn't put it past him to set fire to the place some night."

"Talk to Marshal Mannion. He'd know what to do."

Again, Laura shook her head, dismissively. "Will you help me up front?"

"Of course."

She glanced at his chest again. Again, a slight flush rose in her cheeks, and she chuckled. "Best put your shirt on. Don't want the ladies from the sobriety league having unclean thoughts. They might order a belt of whiskey."

Laughing, she returned to the door Lars had left standing open.

Quentin stood gazing after her, admiring the way her body moved inside the dress. He'd be damned if he didn't like the girl, didn't lust for her. He didn't want to, but he did.

His mind returned to the manila envelope in the cabinet drawer.

Somehow, he had to see what it contained. He had a feeling that whatever it was would give him a clue as to Laura's father's true identity.

CHAPTER 19

A WARM PLATE COVERED WITH A RED-AND-WHITE checked napkin in his hands, Henry McCallister climbed the stairs in Ma Branch's boardinghouse to the third floor, strode down the morning-quiet hall, and lightly tapped on the door across the hall from his own.

"Rise an' shine," he said, turning his head to listen through the panel. "Breakfast is served!"

From inside the room came a startled grunt, a cough. Bed springs squawked. Bare feet tapped the floorboards. A key turned in the lock, the door opened. Quentin Ferguson blinked sleepily as he gazed through the opening, his longish blond hair mussed from sleep. He snorted, frowned at the plate in Henry's hand, brushed a fist across his nose.

"What...?" He was clad in only his longhandles.

"Room service. I figured after a week here in Del Norte, it was time you had a proper breakfast. Especially since we're goin' a-courtin' in just a few hours." Henry smiled.

Quentin stared at the plate as though he feared a live snake might be coiled under the napkin.

"It's not poisoned, if that's what you're thinkin'. Ma Branch can be right colicky, especially when her boarders don't go downstairs for their meals, but I don't think even she'd poison anyone for such a sin. I told her you were shy but that being as it may, it was time you had a proper breakfast. Fortunately, she agreed and filled a plate for you." Henry paused, frowned at the man frowning skeptically back at him. "Can I come in?"

"Oh, sure, sure." Quentin stepped back and drew the door wide. "Sorry. I was, uh...I was..."

Henry walked into the room and set the plate on the small, square table on the room's opposite side, fronting the room's single, curtained window. "Sleepin' in?"

It was nearing eight thirty. Mrs. Branch served breakfast promptly at seven. Henry had lingered over his own, palavering with some of the old-timers who boarded here and always seemed to want to talk over morning coffee, telling stories about the old days which was their way of reliving those "shining old times," as well. Henry enjoyed such tales as well as giving an ear to the old salts who seemed to need it. He hoped some young man would give him the same courtesy when he was their age.

"Yeah, I reckon." Quentin placed his fists on his hips and stretched his back, making a face. "Mr. Davis gave me an extra hour this mornin'. My poor ol' back needed it, I reckon. I slept hard."

"He's keepin' you busy, is he?"

"I'll say he is. A lot of goods go through his store. Game hunters keep bringing in game that needs hanging and butchering. I do that, too. Do you know a ranch lady —Mrs. Shatterly—came in yesterday and bought over a hundred dollars' worth of fresh elk, oysters, venison and nearly as many pounds of coffee, sugar, and flour? All in one fell swoop!"

Henry chuckled. "The Shatterlys' old foreman is retir-ing. I heard most of the other ranchers in the county were attending the all-day, all-night hoedown out at the Shatterly Ranch. The Shatterlys can throw one heck of a good, old-fashioned stomp. Story has it that when the fiddles an' guitars start up after dark, even the hosses in the corrals dance!"

He and Quentin laughed.

Quentin groaned again and said, "I feel every pound of that bill in my back! I filled her carriage for her."

He sat down at the table and removed the napkin from over the steaming plate packed to overflowing with eggs fried sunny side up, fried potatoes nicely browned in butter, biscuits and sausage gravy, and three thick slices of bacon that had, of course, come from the Davis' store as had everything else on the plate.

Quentin scowled up at Henry, deeply incredulous. "You didn't have to do this."

"I wanted to. As hard as you work, you should eat more than just jerky and apples in your room." Henry felt a little guilty. He had an ulterior motive for bringing the man's breakfast. He wanted to get to know Quentin better, wanted to learn his reason for visiting Del Norte, for going to work for the Davises. He and Marshal Mannion both had a feeling it was more than just that the young man needed a grubstake.

Quentin shrugged as he took up his fork and knife. "I reckon I've been so tired of late I don't realize how hungry I am." He started shoveling the food into his mouth and glanced at Henry, saying around a mouthful, "Sit down, sit down!"

Henry used a boot to slide the second chair out from the table and slacked into it, habitually reaching down to adjust the old Remington on his hip, forgetting that he hadn't strapped it around his waist yet. Ma Branch's first and foremost rule was no wearing of guns on the premises. Not even Bloody Joe Mannion's junior deputy.

Henry watched the young man eat for a time and then said, feigning a casual conversational tone, "You like working for Davis, do you?" He smiled. "Or might there be some other reason you've lasted longer than most of the other men who signed on with the man?"

Quentin glanced across the table at him, one brow arched. "Others haven't lasted?"

Henry chuckled. "Davis can be quite the slave driver, I've heard. A might surly, as well. And protective of his daughter."

Quentin frowned as he forked more biscuits and gravy into his mouth. "I haven't seen that. He's been good to me, the man has." His frown cut deeper lines across his forehead. "And if he balked at my askin' Miss Laura out for that walk along the creek we're takin' today, Laura didn't mention it to me."

"Hmm," Henry said, tapping his fingers on the table. "He must cotton to you, all right. He rarely lets Laura step out with anybody. Word has it he and Mrs. Davis are savin' her for the son of a fellow businessman. Possibly the son of one of the men who owns the railroad."

Inwardly, Henry grumbled. He knew a thing or two about arranged marriages, since Molly Hurdstrom had herself gotten caught in that whipsaw and had ended up killing the young man her parents had promised her to. Doing that, she'd saved Henry's life.

He didn't want to think about that now. In fact, he'd just as soon not think about it ever again. That was a complication from the past he worried might come between them again despite him knowing they both still had real feelings for each other.

Suddenly, swabbing the last of the gravy from his plate with a ragged chunk of biscuit, Quentin looked pointedly across the table at him, his dark-blue eyes deeply pensive. He hesitated as though not sure he should say what he wanted to say then, forking the gravy-soaked piece of biscuit into his mouth, went ahead with: "What do you know about Mr. Davis, Henry?"

Ah, here we go...

"What do I know about him?"

Quentin shrugged as he wiped his mouth with the napkin and slid his plate, as clean as though a dog had licked it, away from him. "Yeah...you know. Where are they from, the Davises?"

Henry thought it over, offered a shrug of his own. "Well, you know," he said, "I really don't know. I don't know the man other than to talk to him or Miss Laura when I've gone over for cartridges or jerky. The Davises make the best jerky in town. Always fill my saddlebags when I have to ride out after rustlers or some such. He's never mentioned anything personal about himself, and I've never asked. You know how it is out here."

Come to think of it, he'd never heard any such information relayed by the marshal, either. And Mannion was pretty good friends with the man. Leastways, Henry knew they played poker together occasionally. Occasionally, Henry had seen them having a beer together at Miss Jane's San Juan or at one of the lesser watering holes surrounding it.

"Hmm," Quentin said, shifting sideways in his chair and casually hooking an arm over the back of it. "Must've fought in the war...on the Union side, judging by that ring he always wears." He looked off as though he were just indulging in idly speculative chitchat.

Henry knew it wasn't idle.

His new friend was curious about his boss. That wasn't so unusual. But most folks in Quentin's situation would have just gone ahead and asked the man about himself. Or his daughter. He knew them both well enough by now. If he was just idly curious, that was. Henry had a feeling Quentin hadn't inquired with the man or his daughter because he hadn't wanted to risk tipping off either one that he was more than just idly curious.

"Most likely," Henry said. "I'm sure they're from somewhere in the north." He frowned at Quentin, it being his turn to feign idle curiosity. "Why are you wondering?"

Quentin glanced at him. "Huh? Oh—just wonderin'." He gave a sly smile. "Can't help bein' curious about the girl I'm sparkin'."

"Are you sparkin' her?"

Quentin's smile grew. "Who wouldn't? I got me a feelin' half the young men in town would like to spark her."

"That's true," Henry said. "Her parents watch over her pretty well, though."

"But they're letting me take her out," Quentin said, a puzzled frown stitching his brows over his cobalt eyes. "Imagine that." Idly, he dug a fingernail into the edge of the table. He seemed genuinely curious about that. Maybe there was more than curiosity in his eyes. Maybe —what?

Suspicion as to Norman Davis's own motives?

Henry knew from the marshal that Davis himself was curious about the young man's interest in him, which

Quentin, caught off guard, had betrayed the day he'd first ridden into town and had been standing at the bar with Marshal Mannion when Davis had entered the saloon.

Henry decided to stop beating around the bush. Why not come right out with what was on his and the marshal's minds?

"Quentin," he said, placing his hand palm down on the table before him, beside an unlit hurricane lamp, "why are you so interested in Norman Davis? I have to be honest here, since we've become friends an' all. The marshal noticed you acted a little odd when you first saw Davis walk into the saloon the other day. Davis noticed it, too."

He splayed the fingers of the hand resting on the table, a little apprehensive about what his new friend's reaction to the question might be.

"He did, did he?"

Henry did not respond. He held Quentin's gaze with his own, waiting.

Quentin drew a deep breath, filling up his lungs, and let it out slowly.

"Can you keep a secret, Henry? I mean, hold it real close to your vest? Not even tell your boss, Mannion?"

Henry pondered that. He was a man of his word so if he promised he'd keep the secret, he'd have to do it. He couldn't even tell the marshal. That would be hard, because he was eternally loyal to his boss, but if he didn't make the promise to Quentin, he wouldn't learn what he'd been assigned to learn.

"I can keep it for a while," he said. "But just awhile. He is my boss, and he does want to know."

Quentin pursed his lips, gazed over the table at Henry, nodding, thinking it through.

"All right," he said, finally. "Give me a few days before

you tell Mannion. Eventually, he's going to have to know, because he'll be wondering, sure enough."

"Wondering what?"

Quentin's eyes hardened. A slight flush rose into his cheeks. "Why I might have to kill Norman Davis."

CHAPTER 20

HENRY LEFT THE BOARDINGHOUSE FEELING DEEPLY conflicted.

As well as troubled.

Who wouldn't be troubled by the story he'd just heard from Quentin Campbell, a.k.a. Ferguson?

Rifle resting on his shoulder, he headed out to start making his morning rounds, keeping an especially sharp eye on the Stockmen's Bank, which Marshal Mannion believed had been targeted by the gang of robbers who, it seemed, wanted to clean out the local lawmen before they struck. Midmorning, he almost literally ran into Rio Waite as the older deputy made his own way along the congested boardwalks of Del Norte, making his own rounds and sticking particularly close to the bank.

Since it was ten thirty, the pair decided to sit down together over a cup of coffee and a piece of pie at the appropriately if unimaginatively named Ida's Good Food. They palavered about suspicious-looking characters they'd both spied on their rounds, indulged in their usual friendly banter and then, suddenly, Rio stitched his shaggy, gray-brown brows together at the younger man.

"Say, what's eating you, Hank? You don't look your normally carefree self this mornin'?"

Rio always called Henry "Hank." He was the only one who did. Rio was like that. Those he felt especially close to, he gave special nicknames, though around Del Norte that mainly included his favorite whores. It made them... as well as Henry himself...feel special. Which was exactly what it was meant to do.

Henry had just taken a last bite of his dried peach pie. Now he swallowed, sending Rio's frown back across the table at him. "I do?"

"You do."

Of course, he did. Henry had always had trouble hiding his moods, and he had to admit, if only to himself, that he did, indeed, feel a little colicky in the wake of the gruesome story he'd heard from Quentin. He wanted to share that story with Rio in the worst way, but he'd given his word he'd keep the secret, so he had to do just that.

Henry shrugged, sagged back in his chair. "It's probably just Mrs. Branch's breakfast gravy. Sometimes it's a little rich for my blood." He smiled. "Especially if I eat too much of it."

Rio wasn't buying it. He arched a suspicious brow and opened his mouth to speak but closed it when the marshal himself walked up to their table, a mock look of admonition on his big, handsome face with those long, wolfish gray eyes. "Well, lookee here," Mannion said, stopping at the table and crossing his arms on his chest. "It's none other than my two deputies slacking off on the job."

"No, no—we ain't slackin' off, Joe," Rio said, playing along. "We're both fortifying ourselves for the long day ahead and, besides, we got us a table right here by the window so's we can keep a close eye on the bank." He jerked his chin toward the Stockmen's Bank sitting catty-corner to Ida's place.

"I see, I see," the marshal said, cracking a smile. "I had the same idea myself. Pretty quiet out there today... so far."

"That'll likely change tomorrow," Rio said. "The train's due to pull in about this time tomorrow morning."

Mannion scowled. "Consarned contraption!"

"You gonna replace Cletus, Joe?" Rio asked, his tone suddenly dour.

"There's no replacing that big mountain of head-breaking granite," Mannion said. "I'm afraid it's gonna be just the three of us. Leastways, until the next town council meeting and I can make a plea to hire someone else. The way things have been going lately, though, I don't reckon donning a deputy marshal job here in Del Norte is gonna be all that appealing. Especially when I can't pay more than what I know the skinflints on the council are gonna let me offer."

"Speaking of that, Marshal," Henry said. "I'm gonna stay here in town today. You need both me an' Rio, an'—"

"Nonsense." Mannion leaned forward, placing his big fists on the table and giving his junior deputy a hard, level look. "You haven't had a day off in weeks. I want you and Ferguson to go ahead with your picnic with those two pretty girls you're both sparking. You're young...with young men's blood...and taking an afternoon off will make you fresher for the week ahead. And, like I said, it seems pretty quiet out there today. It has for the past several days. Rio and I'll keep a lid on the town. I know a few toughnuts I can deputize temporarily if I need to."

Henry frowned, puzzled. That wasn't like the marshal. He was usually no-nonsense about such a situation as the one they were facing now—men out to kill them and get them out of the way so the robbers could rob the bank relatively unfettered.

"Besides," Mannion explained. "Like I said before, I want you to find out what young Ferguson's interest in Davis is. If Norm's who he's interested in."

Rio said, "You think he might be here with that gang we think is out to rob the bank, Joe?"

"I don't know," Mannion said, straightening. "My gut tells me no. But he did ride into town around the same time that Mexican took that shot at me."

"True enough," Rio said.

Mannion looked at Henry. "What've you learned about him so far?"

There it was. The question Henry had been dreading but had known was coming.

He hated like hell to lie to his boss—a man he eminently respected. Hell, Bloody Joe was his hero, though he knew that if he lived a thousand years, he'd never be able to fill the man's boots. But he'd given his word to Quentin. He had to keep it. For a time.

"Nothing so far, boss," Henry said, hearing the wooden tone of his voice. "I'll likely learn more this afternoon."

"All right, then," Mannion said, kicking out a chair and sitting down, doffing his hat and setting it on the table, running a big hand through his long, thick hair. "All the more reason for you to go ahead. Like I said, Rio and I'll hold down the fort. Go on. Get outta here. Get yourself cleaned up and rent a buggy from Nordstrom. It'll be noon before you know it."

Henry hesitated, feeling awkward and unwieldly with all he had on his mind.

Quentin Ferguson. Molly Hurdstrom.

The information he was keeping from Bloody Joe.

"Go on, boy," Rio said. "Go on back to Ma Branch's place." He grinned. "Don't forget to change your underwear and scrub behind your ears."

He gave the younger man a playful kick under the table.

The marshal gave him another direct look with those wolfish gray eyes. "And watch your back."

———

QUENTIN "FERGUSON" GRINNED AS HENRY McCallister pulled his red-wheeled, two-seated rented carriage up in front of South-Central Colorado Fresh Meats & Dry Goods, on the front stoop of which Quentin stood with the arm of Miss Laura Davis's arm hooked through his own.

On the front seat with Henry sat a pretty, brown-haired, gray-eyed young lady holding a brown parasol above her head in a brown-gloved hand. The young lady smiled fetchingly at both Quentin and his date for the day, the cheeks of her heart-shaped face dimpling beautifully.

"Good day, Laura. Good day...Mr. Ferguson, I assume...?"

On the other side of Miss Hurdstrom, Henry set the brake and leaned forward to see past his date the two standing on the stoop before him. "Mr. Quentin Ferguson, Miss Laura Davis, allow me introduce you to Miss Molly Hurdstrom."

"Pleased to meet you, Miss Hurdstrom," Quentin said, stepping forward to gently shake the pretty brunette's hand.

"Molly, nice to see you again," said Laura, also stepping forward to give Miss Hurdstrom's hand a ladylike squeeze.

"Laura and I know each other well," Molly told Henry. "We went to school together for a few years—did we not, Laura?"

"And you helped me get through fourth-grade arithmetic," Laura said. "Without your help, Molly, I'd still be back in that classroom, being browbeaten by the poor, long-suffering Mrs. Nordekker."

Molly laughed. "She was a little uncompromising, wasn't she?"

"Climb aboard, folks," Henry said. He lifted the wicker basket covered with oilcloth wedged on the seat between himself and his date. "Miss Molly went to the trouble of frying us a passel of chicken and whipping up an even bigger passel of potato salad. Mrs. Bjornson even contributed dill pickles and pickled eggs. Just thinking about it makes my belly growl as though it's certain-sure my throat's been cut!"

Mrs. Bjornson ran the young ladies' boardinghouse in which Molly had rented a room since her estrangement from her family.

"Oh, Henry!" Molly playfully admonished the deputy who, Quentin saw, was not wearing his five-pointed, silver-chased badge. It was the first time since Quentin had ridden into Del Norte he'd seen the young deputy without it.

Quentin did notice, however, that Henry was wearing his six-gun thonged on his right thigh and that his Winchester rifle resided in a leather sheath beneath the carriage's front seat. That made Quentin feel better about wearing his own six-gun thonged on his own right thigh.

He'd worn the gun so long, every day for the past fifteen years, in fact, that he would have felt naked without it. Neither Laura nor her father, who was likely peeking out a front window of the shop at the four young people, had questioned him about it. That had made him a little curious, but it had also made him feel relieved. He was so accustomed to having the weapon on him that he didn't think he could have taken two steps outdoors without it.

Maybe Mr. Davis was glad that his date was prepared to defend his daughter, if need be. Or maybe Davis...who Quentin suspected was actually the Union-sympathizing gang leader named Dalton...knew why he was carrying it —in case he, Quentin, realized whom he was working for. Maybe he didn't want to tip off Quentin that he knew.

Anyway...this was a day to forget about those things. This was his afternoon off to enjoy free time in the country with three other young people like himself. Over the course of his young life, in the wake of his family's brutal murders, he'd had no time for socializing let alone stepping out with a pretty girl. Of course, totally letting go of the past would be impossible today as it would any day. He'd be in the company of Davis's...or Dalton's... daughter, after all. But he'd do the best he could. Laura, who worked so hard in the café part of her parents' business, deserved to have a good time...even if she didn't know that one of the two men she was having that good time with was here to possibly kill her father.

Of course, that wasn't fair to her. But then, having his family butchered before his very eyes hadn't been fair to Quentin.

He helped Laura into the buggy's rear seat, taking her hand, which he then realized was the first time he'd touched her—he liked the sensation—and then he climbed in after her.

"All aboard," he told Henry.

"All aboard!" yelled Henry, obviously feeling buoyant despite the grisly tale Quentin had shared with him earlier, detailing that horrible, carnage-ridden afternoon years ago, leaving nothing out. Henry reached over and squeezed Molly's hand then shook the ribbons over the steeldust in the traces.

They were off, Henry steering the gelding around the block and then negotiating the midday Saturday traffic before the bustling town slipped behind them and they were heading north along the main trail that hugged the railroad tracks for a mile before the relatively recently laid rails swerved off to the east where they eventually dropped down out of the mountains, cutting through the canyon of the Arkansas River and onto the plains just north of Colorado Springs. There, they intersected the tracks of the Atchison, Topeka & Santa Fe Line and thus most of the rest of the country.

Henry swung the buggy onto a secondary trail and then the large, gray formation of Funeral Rock loomed before them. Quentin had heard from one of the old salts in the boardinghouse, who'd stopped him one day in the hall to chat, that the Utes had at one time buried their dead atop the formidable crag. It had been, and in some cases still was, the Indian way to bury their dead high above ground, away from predators. Now, as the buggy rattled and meandered along the curving trail, the mountain shifted before him and his fellow sojourners—large, formidable, and appearing closer than it really was in the lens-clear, high-country sunlight.

It seemed to Quentin that the mountain was very much like his quest over the past ten years—stalwart, formidable, prepossessing...always before him no matter where he went. And here it still was now even on a day when he didn't want to think about it.

What Quentin assumed was Funeral Rock Creek glistened straight ahead, cutting west to east through its shallow wash sheathed in pines and aspens whose leaves flashed like newly minted nickels as the breeze drifting down from the Sawatch Range brushed the white-stemmed trees and made the pine boughs bounce and sway.

An idyllic day for a picnic.

But then, he did not see the two horseback riders sitting among pines on the shoulder of a near ridge, the tall, yellow-haired rider sitting a black-and-white pinto, studying Quentin's party through a spyglass...

CHAPTER 21

FOR THEIR PICNIC, HENRY PICKED OUT A HORSESHOE bend in the creek, a small clearing in the trees yet one still shaded enough to spare them from the intense summer sun.

He stopped the buggy and unhitched the horse, hobbling the gelding so it could freely graze and draw water from the creek. Blankets were spread in the grass only a few feet from the glistening brown water of the stream. The picnic basket was hauled out, the food laid out upon oilcloth, and the sojourners lounged on the blankets, in the shade, the stream making rippling sounds beneath the quiet rustling of the breeze.

Here they got to know one another quietly, gently, speaking in at once jovial and intimate tones, their hair and the corners of the blankets ruffled by the wind. Quentin learned about how Henry and Molly had first come together but neither elaborated on what had driven them apart, though Quentin sensed it had been painful as well as dramatic for them both. Laura's story was almost bucolic. Hers had been a happy childhood in a much smaller Del Norte than the town it was now. While she had a hankering to see the rest of the world one day, for the time being she was happy running the café, working side by side with her father. Her shy and retiring mother remained mostly in her office, keeping the books, not a small chore for a business that had grown to the size of the Davis'.

Quentin had met the woman only once, and, while reserved and a bit formal, Mrs. Davis had seemed warm and friendly enough. Quentin realized then where Laura had gotten her looks, for her mother, also lilac-eyed and flaxen-haired with only a few streaks of gray, was handsome in her early middle age. Her figure, though mature, showed all the signs of an earlier perfection, like her daughter's.

All four picnickers were made hungry by the fresh, mountain air and by the adventure of their outing and the normal anxiousness of their getting to know each other. The food was quickly consumed among much chuckling and laughter. When there wasn't even a morsel of anything left in the basket, the girls cleaned up, stowed the basket away in the buggy, then strode off hand in hand, laughing, into the brush away from the river to tend nature.

Quentin found himself staring after them, as, dappled by the sunlight angling through the trees, they gradually drifted from view.

"Nice girl," Henry said.

Quentin smiled. "I like her."

"Complicates matters, doesn't it?"

Quentin drew his mouth corners down. "It does."

Henry narrowed a gently admonishing eye at his new friend. "No matter what you find out, you can't kill him, you know?"

Quentin looked at him, the earlier merriment gone from his gaze.

"You have to let the law handle it," Henry said.

"It would be his word against mine. You know that, Henry."

"Still, if you kill him, it's murder. You'll hang."

"Small price to pay."

"You say that now. I doubt you'll say that when you watch them building the gallows on San Juan Avenue, within view of the cellblock window. Usually takes them about two days. Imagine two days of hearing the carpenters jawing and laughing and the constant pounding of hammers."

"You weren't there that day."

"What about her?" Henry said, jerking his chin to indicate where the girls had gone.

"I admit it's complicated."

"Whoever Davis was at one time, and I just can't believe he had a hand in your familys' murder, he is no longer that man. He's a good, God-fearing, family man. Hell, look at the young lady he sired."

"You haven't carried what I've carried for the past fifteen years. What I'll carry for the rest of my life. Those eyes I saw in the barn doorway. That ring on the man's finger. He still wears that ring!"

"Anyone who fought for the Union—hell, even the frontier army—could wear that ring!"

Growing heated, Quentin raised two fingers to his face. "His eyes, Henry! His eyes!"

"Whose eyes?"

Both men jerked with starts as Laura and Molly stepped around a pine and into the clearing, frowning curiously.

Quentin felt a flush rise in his cheeks. He hesitated.

Henry said, "We were just talkin' about some ranny who rode into town yesterday. Quentin thinks he has an outlaw's eyes. While I don't disagree, we can't go around lockin' someone up because of a look in his eyes."

He cast a quick, meaningful glance at Quentin, whose face grew warmer.

"Uh...no, no. I reckon not." Quentin cast the young deputy his own meaningful glance. "I'd keep an eye on him, though, Henry. I've been around enough to know who looks like trouble, and I say he's trouble."

"Hey," Molly said, scolding in her eyes as she sank to her knees on the blanket. "No talking about serious stuff today. Either of you." She leaned back on the heels of her hands and shook her hair back from her face with aplomb. "Today is a day of rest and relaxation. No grim talk."

"I agree," Laura said, as she stepped onto the blankets but was casting her frowning, curious gaze toward something on the far side of the creek. She was shading her eyes with her hand. "Except...who do you suppose they are?"

"Who?" Quentin said, turning to follow the girl's gaze with his own.

"Those two."

Then Quentin saw them—two riders sitting two horses maybe two hundred yards away, beside a large, columnar rock jutting up out of the shoulder of a low ridge. As Quentin watched them, unable to see anything distinct about either rider from this distance, one raised a hand to his mouth, leaned his head back, and yammered like a coyote.

"Oh!" Molly said, turning her suddenly frightened gaze to Henry. "Who do you suppose they are?"

The yammering continued for several more seconds.

Then the yammering rider lowered his hand and turned to the other one. They reined their horses around, rode up to the top of the ridge and disappeared down the other side.

Laura gave a shudder.

Quentin rose and put his arm around her. "It's all right. Just a couple of drunk range riders, no doubt."

Again, Molly turned to Henry. "Did you recognize them, Henry?"

Henry shook his head, frowning. "Couldn't see either one clearly."

Molly's voice quavered a little. "You don't suppose they're...part of the same bunch who tried to kill the marshal and shot Mr. Booker the other night, do you?"

Henry wasn't sure how to respond to the girl's query. But that was exactly what he himself was wondering.

"If so," Molly continued, hesitating, her quiet voice brittle with apprehension, "they might be out to try to do the same to you..."

"I don't know." Henry heaved himself to his feet. He went over to the buggy, pulled his rifle out from under the seat, shucked it from its sheath, and tossed the sheath back into the buggy.

Gazing off toward the ridge over which the two strangers had disappeared, he said, "Quentin, you stay here with the ladies. I'm gonna ride the steeldust over there, check it out."

He knew the gelding was broke both for pulling and riding.

"You sure you wanna do that alone?" Quentin asked.

"Don't have a choice," Henry said, levering a live round into the Winchester's action then lowering the hammer to half-cock. "One of us needs to stay here with the girls. I'm gonna check those two out. I don't want any surprises on the way back to town."

Not with the girls in the buggy.

"Oh, Henry," Molly said. "Do be careful!"

"Yes, be careful, Henry," Laura chimed in.

"I will."

He leaned the Winchester against a tree then went over and unhobbled the steeldust. It wore a hackamore with a rope attached. That was all he needed for a short ride. He swung up onto the gelding's bare back, and Quentin handed him his rifle.

"Don't take any chances," Quentin said, quietly adding so the women couldn't hear, "Those two might be leading you into others. If they want you dead, that is."

Henry nodded.

He reined the steeldust around, batted his heels against its ribs, and put it into the stream, which was only a foot or so deep. Horse and rider climbed the opposite bank then Henry booted the horse into a trot. He wanted to gallop, but he hadn't ridden bareback enough lately for a hard run. He'd likely fall off and make a damn fool of himself in front of the girls. As a kid, he rode bareback all the time, and there'd been no art to it then. Now, especially with his bum hip incurred when a bronc he'd been trying to break had thrown him, it was a bit of a trick...

He rode up the ridge and past the columnar rock.

Several yards from the ridge crest, he slowed the steel to a slow walk and slowly, carefully edged a look up over the top of the ridge and down the other side, wary of an ambush. Seeing no sign of danger, he put the gelding up and over the ridge and down the other side, scouring the ground with his gaze, looking for sign.

The trouble was the ground here was covered in

short, brown grass growing up out of a thin crust of hard soil. It didn't easily accept a print. In fact, he found none. He rode the steeldust across a broad, deep bowl toward a wide crease between two shelving mesas straight ahead of him, figuring the riders had probably ridden that way, since that was about the only route available.

Unless they climbed one of the several mesas or bluffs rising on both sides of him, that was. That didn't seem likely; he saw no sign of the riders on any of those formations. He kept riding until he entered the mouth of the gap then slowed the steeldust, tightening his right hand around the neck of the Winchester, thumb on the hammer, ready for the first sign someone might be drawing a bead on him, intending to blow him out of the saddle.

He rode ahead slowly, casting his gaze from left to right and back again.

A thumping, crunching sound rose suddenly.

He reined the steeldust up sharply and jerked his head to the slope on his right, taking the Winchester in both hands and thumbing back the hammer. Aiming down the barrel, he eased the tension in his trigger finger, lowered the rifle.

He released his held breath as a big, mule deer buck ran out from a berry thicket, bounding straight up the ridge, flicking its small, back tail.

"Damn," he muttered.

The two riders must not have ridden this way. If they had, that buck would have spooked earlier.

He hipped around in his saddle, frowning edgily.

If they hadn't headed this way, east, they must have circled around the bluff they'd been on and headed—

The troubling thought had not finished raking over his brain plate when a girl's shrill scream rose in the west.

CHAPTER 22

QUENTIN STOOD AT THE EDGE OF THE STREAM, GAZING in the direction Henry had ridden a good twenty minutes ago. He was wondering if the deputy had picked up the trail of the two strangers when a shrill scream behind him and to his left made his heart buck.

He swung around, right hand dropping to the grips of the revolver holstered on his right thigh.

"No, no, no—don't do that, mister, or you're gonna get yourself shot out of your boots!"

It was the tall, rangy, yellow-haired toughnut Laura had called Lars. He was just then riding up through the aspens with his sidekick—the big, beefy, bearded man with long, sandy hair and whom Laura had called Dave. Both men walked their horses with menacing casualness, swaying easily in their saddles, Winchester carbines resting across their saddlebows. Lars just now aimed his rifle straight out from his right hip at Quentin, narrowing one malicious eye, an evil smile quirking at the corners of his mustached, thin-lipped mouth.

"Lars!" Laura intoned. "What in blazes are you doing out here?"

Lars and Dave reined up ten feet from Laura and Molly, both of whom had gained their feet and were staring at the two newcomers fearfully, eyes darting to the carbines Lars and Dave wielded.

"Dave an' me—we seen you ride out of town with that boneheaded deputy and this stranger, who, as soon as he rode into town, came trespassing on my territory."

Dave cut his eyes at Lars and smiled inside his thick tangle of beard.

"*Your* territory?" Laura said in exasperation. "I am no man's territory. Least of all *yours*, Lars."

"Now, that ain't very nice. Especially since you been carryin' on like you liked me. Maybe even set your hat for me. Or..." Lars's gaze turned hard again. "Maybe you was just leadin' me on. Or maybe you was tryin' to make me jealous so I'd ride out and save you from this stranger an' that hoople-headed deputy." He smiled again, lewdly, his eyes sliding across the nicely filled corset of Laura's shirt-waist. "Well...I'm here now, sweetheart."

"Don't you call me that. You have no business being here."

Before Lars could respond, Quentin said, "The girl's right. You have no business out here. Obviously, Laura doesn't like you as much as you thought. So, it's time to ride on."

Lars cut his enraged gaze to Quentin. "Shut up, you! It's a free country."

"We'll ride where we want," Dave added. His voice was deep and thick, eyes glassy from drink. "Like Lars said, it's a free country."

To Quentin, Lars said, "Unbuckle that pistol belt, toss it away."

"No."

"You want one in the guts?"

"Lars!" Laura said. "Just because I was polite to you at the café does not mean I 'set my hat for you.' Ride away or I'll tell my father and he'll have Marshal Mannion take care of you!"

Ignoring her, Lars looked again at Quentin. "You haven't dropped your pistol belt. Drop it...now..." He cocked his carbine one-handed and aimed down its barrel again at Quentin's belly.

Laura glanced at Quentin. "You'd best do it."

Quentin stared into the toughnut's flat brown eyes that contrasted sharply the deep tan of his long, bony face. He could tell the man meant business. He didn't see that he had a choice. He drew a deep breath, let it out slow then unbuckled his shell belt and tossed it away.

"There, now," Lars said, sheathing his Winchester then swinging down from his saddle while Dave kept his Winchester aimed at Quentin. "That wasn't so gallblasted hard—now, was it? You might have just saved your life."

"Go to the devil, Lars!" Laura barked at the man, leaning forward at the waist and clenching her fists in fury. "You have no business being here!"

Lars tossed his reins up to Dave then strode forward. "I don't like your tone, princess. Not one bit."

"I don't care what you like and don't like, you pig. Go to hell!"

Lars kept walking toward her. His eyes smoldered.

"Leave her alone, Lars," Quentin warned.

Dave said, "You done had your horns filed, pilgrim."

"I'm warning you, Lars," Quentin said.

The man ignored him. Lars stopped three feet in front of Laura. He turned to Quentin, gave a coyote smile then turned his gaze back to Laura once more. She took one step back in fear. Quentin could see her throat move as she swallowed.

Lars took one more step forward then, so suddenly that Quentin could see only the blur of quick movement, reached up, took the neck of Laura's frock in his hands, and ripped it clear down to her waist. He ripped the camisole, as well, so that suddenly the girl stood before him with her pale, upturned breasts laid bare.

Both Laura and Molly screamed.

Laura stumbled backward two steps and crossed her arms on her tender orbs.

Dave threw his head back and laughed.

As Lars took another step toward the girl, rage exploded inside Quentin. He lunged forward, wheeled to his right, and launched himself into a dive off the heels of his boots. Dave's Winchester barked but the bullet sailed wide as Quentin landed belly down, unsnapped the keeper thong from over the barrel of his .45, and pulled the revolver from its holster.

As Dave cursed and recocked his carbine, Quentin aimed at an upward angle at the big man. The .45 thundered. The bullet punched through Dave's lumpy chest and sent him flying over the tail of his lineback dun. At the same time, Lars wheeled toward Quentin, ripping his own pistol from its holster.

Again, Quentin's .45 spoke.

Lars stumbled backward with a scream, dropping his Colt and looking down in horror at the blood spraying from his chest. He looked at Quentin, eyes wide and white-ringed, mouth forming a large, dark *O*. Quentin's Colt spoke again. The bullet punched a puckered blue hole in the man's forehead. He flew straight back and piled up in a quivering heap at the base of a large cottonwood.

Quentin stared at the man through his own wafting powder smoke.

He looked at Dave who lay unmoving, the big man's horse galloping away and shaking its head, reins trailing along the ground to each side of it.

Quentin turned to Laura.

Still holding her arms over her breasts, she stared back at him in shock.

So did Molly.

Neither girl said anything.

Behind Quentin, a horse blew. He wheeled, extending his .45 once more and clicking the hammer back. He eased the tension in his trigger finger when he saw Henry McCallister sitting his coyote dun in the middle of the stream, water glistening on the horse's legs. Sunshine glinted off the barrel of the deputy's own Winchester, the barrel of which he slowly lowered now. The deputy stared at Quentin with much the same look of incredulity as the girls.

———

No one said anything on the way back to Del Norte.

Henry and Quentin sat in the front seat, Henry driving. The girls sat in the seat behind them, Laura with a blanket wrapped around her shoulders. Molly held her arm around the girl as they bounced along the trail. The horses of the two dead men followed close behind, reins tied to the carriage. They were wrapped in their bedrolls though parts of their heads and feet could be seen at either side, bouncing with the movement of the horses.

Henry dropped Laura off at her family's store, then he and Quentin waited while Molly escorted the girl, pale and silent with shock, inside to her parents.

Henry took Molly over to her boardinghouse and led her up to her room.

At her door, Molly turned to face him and said, "Don't worry—I'm all right. I've been through trouble before. You know that. It's Laura I'm worried about."

"Yeah, me, too."

"I think she'll be all right." Molly frowned up at Henry, shaking her head. "Who is he, anyway?" Henry knew she meant Quentin.

"I don't know. I'll find out."

"That was some shooting."

"I saw. Never figured him for a cold-steel artist."

"I'm at once grateful and..."

"I know. Curious about who Laura might be tumbling for."

"I'm sure her parents are, too."

"Like I said—we'll get to the bottom of it. We'll take Lars and Dave over to the marshal's office. I'm sure the marshal will have some questions. He'll get answers."

Molly nodded.

Henry leaned forward and pressed his lips to her cheek. "Sorry the day had to end this way."

Molly laid a hand against his cheek. "I hope there will be another time." She smiled weakly. "A better time."

Henry smiled, then, too. "There will be. I'll see to that."

Again, she nodded and then Henry set his hat on his head and walked off down the hall and out to where Quentin waited in the carriage.

As silently as they'd ridden into town, they wheeled over to Hotel de Mannion.

The marshal must have seen them through the window because Henry was just setting the brake when Bloody Joe stepped out onto the porch, scowling at the two horses tied to the carriage, packing their grisly cargoes.

"Who do you have there?" the marshal asked. He held a steaming granite mug of coffee in his hands. "I thought you were going on a picnic."

"Change of plans, Marshal," Quentin said, stepping down from the carriage. "I shot those two men."

"Lars Gunderson and Dave Coffee," Henry told Mannion. "They attacked the girls."

Mannion drew a deep breath. "Well, I wouldn't put it past 'em. I've seen Gunderson over at her family's store, sort of hovering around like a fly that couldn't find its way out."

"Yep, that's him," Henry said.

"You shot 'em?" Mannion asked Quentin.

Henry answered for him. "Displayed some fancy shooting, too. Dave had him dead to rights." He shook his head and turned to Quentin. "Didn't do him much good."

"Were the girls hurt?"

"Gunderson ripped Laura's dress. Would've ravaged her."

Mannion glanced at Gunderson's horse. "Well, I guess that'll be the last girl he attacks. He's done it before, but the girls were too afraid to give statements, so I couldn't hold him."

"I had no choice, Marshal."

"Come in."

Mannion turned and walked into his office. Henry and Quentin shared a glance then followed him in.

"Fresh pot of coffee on the range," the marshal said, easing into the chair behind his desk. "Rio made it and if it doesn't sear a hole through your plumbing, it'll likely turn your hair black." His traditional, high-crowned, brown Stetson was pegged by the door. He ran a hand through his dark-brown hair liberally flecked with gray and said ironically, "Hasn't done as much for me, though, damn the luck. Not even Rio's mud can turn back the clock."

"I'm fine," Quentin said.

"I'll take a cup." Henry hauled a mug down from a shelf and filled it.

When he and Quentin had both taken a seat at the table Mannion's deputies used for a desk, the marshal said, "How'd you get so good with that hogleg?"

He sipped his coffee while holding Quentin's gaze over the rim of his mug.

The younger man leaned forward, elbows on his knees, hesitating.

"Tell him," Henry prompted him then took a sip of his brew.

Quentin frowned at him. "Tell him what?"

"Everything starting with how you got so good with that Colt. What you intend to do with it."

Quentin scowled, suddenly angry. "Now, look, Henry —I told you what I told you in complete confidence!"

"That was before I knew how easily you could kill. How mad you could get. Lars didn't need that extra bullet. He was already dead." Henry jerked his chin toward Mannion. "This is the marshal's town. He needs to know who's in it and why."

"Why are you here, son?" Mannion said. "Why are you after Norm Davis?"

Quentin flushed, again angry. "How did you know...?" He glanced accusingly at Henry.

Mannion said, "He didn't tell me a thing. It was obvious as hell from the reaction you had when Norm walked into the Three-Legged Dog. Norm saw it, too. He hired you to keep his possible enemies close, to find out just what your interest in him is."

Quentin stared at the marshal, incredulous.

"You're fairly transparent," Mannion told him, and took another sip of his brew. "And we older fellas aren't as stupid as you might have pegged us for."

Still, Quentin stared at him, seemingly tongue-tied.

Henry said, "Tell the marshal what you told me. He might be able to help."

Quentin leaned back in his chair with a sigh.

He told Mannion everything he'd told Henry—starting with that afternoon he was picking berries near his family's ranch then detailing the eyes of the man he'd seen in the barn doorway, the ring on the man's little finger, and seeing the man, Dalton, who was now calling himself Norman Davis walk into the Three-Legged Dog.

He topped off his story with, "I'm sure it's him. I'm sure it's that former Union man who murdered my family, burned our cabin. Cut my sister's throat with a Bowie knife."

"And you intend to kill him," Mannion said. It wasn't a question.

Again, anger blazed in the young man's eyes. "Wouldn't you?"

"Of course," Mannion said.

CHAPTER 23

"BUT YOU'RE NOT GONNA DO IT," MANNION ADDED. "Not in my town."

Mannion saw fury blaze in the younger man's blue eyes as he rose from his chair and stood before the marshal's desk, one fist clenched at his side, the other hand raised, index finger pointing at the window above Mannion's desk. "If you think I'm gonna allow that killer to get away with murdering my family, Marshal, you got another thing comin'!"

"I know how you feel," Mannion said, mildly. "But you're not judge, jury, and executioner. If Norm Davis really is this Union captain you think is Dalton, the law will have to handle it."

"But it'll be only his word against mine! And who am I? I'm a stranger here in Del Norte. Davis is a prominent businessman!"

"I'm sorry, but that's how the law works."

"It's easy for you to talk from your position...*Bloody Joe*!"

"Hey, easy, Quentin," Henry intervened from his chair

across the cluttered table from that of the enraged newcomer's.

Mannion held out a waylaying hand to his deputy. "It's all right, Henry. He has a point. I've often taken justice into my own hands." He looked up at Quentin standing over him. "It's not fair. But what kind of lawman would I be if I let you play Judge Colt and kill Davis on my turf?"

"Must be nice—hidin' behind your badge, Marshal."

"It has been. But sometimes there was no other way to keep the lid on the towns I was brought into tame. Besides, before I killed a man, I made certain-sure he deserved it. You don't know that about Norm Davis."

Mannion spied movement out on the street. "Speak of the devil," he said, scratching his chin and rising in his chair a little to see the proprietor of South-Central Colorado Fresh Meats & Dry Goods angling across the busy main street, heading toward the jailhouse. Davis paused to let a big lumber dray pass, pinching the brim of his bowler hat at the driver before crossing the Colorado Springs & San Juan rails and continuing toward the jailhouse.

"What is it?" Quentin said, crouching a little to see out the window.

"Davis. Or Dalton. Maybe it's time we found out which one he really is...before you shoot him and hang for it."

Quick footsteps on the porch.

Lying curled in his open cage on a shelf above the deputies' table, Buster meowed. The cat was often like a barometer, gauging the level of the pressure in Mannion's office. The cat seemed to be saying it was about to go up. Mannion had no doubt it was.

Two quick knocks on the door. Quentin turned to it. So did Mannion.

The door opened and Norm Davis poked his head inside, eyes widening in surprise to see the young man who'd likely saved his daughter's honor, possibly her life, standing before him.

"Oh, good," Davis said, stepping into the office and closing the door behind him. "You're here."

"I'm here, all right," Quentin said.

"Sit down, son," Mannion said.

Quentin glanced at him, his eyes hard but also vaguely uncertain. He opened and closed his hands at his sides then retook the chair across the table from Henry.

Taking another couple steps into the office, Davis cut his glance from Mannion to Quentin. His own long, craggy face with its dark eyes—a killer's eyes? Mannion wondered—was flushed from the walk over here and likely from his concern about his daughter.

"I heard what happened from Laura and Miss Hurdstrom," he told Quentin, softly, his voice quavering a little. A concerned father's voice. "I wanted to hear it from you. They both said you were mighty fast with that pistol of yours. Gunslinger fast."

When Quentin just stared up at him, Mannion said, "He's been practicing for the day he finally meets the man who led the men—former Union bluecoats and an Indian, likely a scout—against his family."

Davis stared curiously at Mannion then turned to Quentin again. "I see..."

"Do you?" Quentin asked the man, his voice bitter.

"All right," Davis said, his voice hardening and quickening with strained patience. "What's this about?"

Quentin rose to stand facing the man. "Are you the captain who led those men, Mr. Davis. Is your real name Dalton? Your eyes and that ring on your little finger tell me you are."

Davis just stared at him, his eyes deeply befuddled behind the glinting lenses of his glasses.

Mannion said, "Where did you live before you came to Del Norte, Norm? I've never heard. Not sure anyone has. As long as you've been here, most folks would likely know by now."

The befuddlement and indignation grew on Davis's craggy face. "No big secret. Albuquerque. We came from Albuquerque. I owned the San Francisco Mercantile there."

Quentin turned to Mannion. "My family's farm was southeast of there, in the foothills of the San Francisco Mountains."

"Figured it probably was," Mannion said. "I heard about former Union soldiers going on the rampage nearly twenty years ago." He scratched his neck as he studied the businessman suspiciously. "Got fed up with all the former Southerners moving into the area, homesteading on land the former Union soldiers—mostly Yankee ranchers and businessmen—claimed was their own."

"The man I've been lookin' for," Quentin said, "wore a U.S. ring just like that garnet ring of yours, Mr. Davis."

Davis raised his hand, looked at the ring. "Do you know how many former soldiers wear a ring like this?"

"So, you did fight on the side of the Union during the war," Mannion said.

"Yes. Like so many others. Then I spent two years in the frontier army, fighting Apaches out of Fort Bowie in Arizona. The army gave me this when I mustered out." Davis turned to Quentin. "Look, son. I heard about the marauding that went on in your neck of the woods, as well. I thought each one should have been hunted down and shot by firing squad. Let me assure you that I am not one of them. President Lincoln wanted us to unite, not keep fighting ten years after Appomattox."

Quentin stared at him skeptically, but Mannion thought his resolve was beginning to weaken.

"I take no offense that you thought I might be one of them," the businessman went on. "If I were in your shoes, I'd probably think so, too. But do you think the man who cut your sister's throat could have raised a girl like Laura? You know her. You saved her today, in fact. Probably both her and Miss Hurdstrom. For that, I will be eternally grateful. Now, if you still want to work for me, the job is yours. We'll forget our discussion here ever happened."

Quentin glanced at Mannion. The marshal arched a brow at him.

Quentin turned back to Davis, sighed. "All right. I reckon I made a mistake. No, I don't think any man who raised Laura could have murdered my sister. I guess I should've thought it through. That bein' so, I reckon I'm still on those killers' trail." He hardened his voice as he shuttled a dark look to Mannion. "There's three left."

"It's a cold trail," Mannion told him. "You know that as well as I do. That happened more than fifteen years ago. Those men are likely either dead or scattered to the four winds. Don't waste your life, son. Don't risk being hung for murder. You're young. Keep the job. Who knows—you might even decide to settle down here in Del Norte."

He glanced at Davis.

Davis said, "Who knows?"

"How's Laura?" Quentin asked.

"Very shaken up." The businessman drew his shoulders back and filled his chest with air. "But I know she, as well as I, are grateful for what you did. I'm not saying you two have a future—we have the son of a business associate picked out for her, but...well, you never know. I do think she could do worse. You're a man of passion, Mr. Ferguson. I admire that." Davis smiled at Quentin, nodded at Henry and Mannion then turned and left the office.

Mannion turned to Quentin. "What do you think?"

"It's him." The young man pursed his lips and nodded. "He's cunning, shrewd. He's a liar." Again, he nodded. "It's him, all right."

―――――

THAT EVENING AROUND TEN O'CLOCK, JANE MANNION was counting the day's earnings in her office at the rear of the San Juan Hotel & Saloon when a soft knock sounded on her door.

Jane set the wad of greenbacks she'd been counting on her desk, opened the drawer in which she kept a short-barreled Colt Lightning .44, and turned to the door, frowning curiously, apprehension touching her, as she closed her hand around the Lightning's ivory grips.

"Who is it?"

"It's Vangie," came the familiar voice on the other side of the door.

Jane released a relieved breath, closed the drawer, and rose from the velvet upholstered chair fronting her rolltop desk.

"Coming, honey."

She unlocked the door and opened it.

"Sorry...I know it's late," Vangie said. She wore her usual attire when working with her horses—plaid wool shirt, wide brown belt, boots, and denims. She wore a denim jacket over the shirt; even in the summer, the nights were cool in Del Norte.

Jane drew the door open wider and stepped back. "No, no, come in. I was just finishing up for the night. Would you like some tea?" She glanced at the china tea server sitting on her desk, beside her painted china cup. "I can run and grab another cup from the bar."

"No, thanks," Vangie said, entering the carpeted office and glancing self-consciously at her boots. "Not sure my boots are clean. I was riding late."

Jane studied the girl, concern touching her. Vangie seemed down, her tone unusually demure, with none of the jovial playfulness she usually exhibited. She also looked pale. Her brown hair was pulled back into a queue, making her look even more pale and severe. "Don't worry about it. Have a seat."

Vangie walked over to one of the brocade armchairs encircling a small coffee table fronting a brick fireplace in which a small blaze burned, warming the room. She sat down, rested an elbow on an arm of the chair, and crossed her legs, swinging a booted foot edgily. Jane retrieved her teacup from her desk and sat down in a chair across the table from her stepdaughter.

"You don't look well, my dear. Are you getting enough sleep?"

"Sleep—ha," Vangie said with a dry chuckle. "I've been doing nothing but tossing and turning at night. I think I've been keeping Ben from sleep, too."

Jane sipped her tea and looked at the pretty girl over the rim of the cup. "Well, we have that in common. Lack of sleep, I mean."

Vangie looked at her. "Pa?"

"Yes."

"I take it he's not sleeping here?"

"Not for well over a week. I'm not sure he's even sleeping in his office."

Vangie winced, shook her head. "That man."

"I'm not sure what to do about him. He thinks he's protecting us by staying away. He doesn't understand it's having the opposite effect. We're racked with worry. I'm having food sent over, but I'm told he hasn't been eating much of it. I've stopped in a few times to check on him, but I've stopped cajoling him. There's no point. He's going to do what he's going to do, the rest of us be damned."

"He's going to have another heart attack. Ben says the next one might kill him."

Jane heaved a weary sigh.

Tears came to Vangie's soft, brown eyes. One slid down her pale cheek, glinting like honey in the dancing firelight. "What are we going to do without him?"

That brought a sheen to Jane's own eyes and a lump in her throat. She'd been trying not to think about that. She honestly didn't know what she would do without the big, handsome, stubborn Bloody Joe Mannion in her life. She didn't know what Vangie would do, either. But there was only one thing either of them *could* do.

"Carry on," Jane said, trying to swallow the knot in her throat to no avail. "That's all we can do. Fortunately, we're both strong."

"All my life, it's just been him and me. I mean, until he married you."

"Now we both have him. In spite of who he is, he's been a blessing, Vange. We both know there's no other man like him."

"It's almost like he has a death wish."

Jane shook her head. "No. It's not that. He's *afraid* of death. On the outside, he's a big man...*all* man...but inside he's like a little boy afraid of the dark. He thinks if he keeps moving...pinning that badge on his shirt every day and making his rounds, meeting the train to scrutinize newcomers...he won't die. Keeping moving keeps him from thinking about dying."

"He doesn't think he *can* die."

"Yes, he does. He knows it very well. He's terrified by it, so he shoves it to the back of his mind."

"That little boy afraid of the dark."

"What's worse is he's afraid of *us* dying. Taking a bullet meant for him."

Vangie leaned forward in her chair, taking her face in her hands. She sobbed.

Jane set her cup down, rose, walked over to the girl, dropped to a knee, and took her in her arms. Vangie cried against her shoulder. Jane chewed her lip to keep from crying herself. She had to be strong for Vangie.

They needed to be strong. Vangie was. Jane knew she was. She would be all right.

They both would.

She wasn't sure she believed that, but she had to tell herself that because that was the only bastion she had to stand against the darkness of a world without Joe Mannion in it.

Vangie pulled away from Jane. She swabbed tears from her cheeks with the backs of her hands.

"I'm going to go see him," she said thinly, rising from her chair. "I keep thinking when I see him it might be the last time, and I want go see him again...in case."

"He might be making his rounds."

"I'll run him down," Vangie said, her tone touched with wry humor again. "I'd like to run him down and hogtie him, but at least I can give him a kiss on the cheek."

"Give him one for me, too."

Vangie smiled, nodded, pressed her lips to Jane's own cheek, and started for the door. Jane had locked it again. She always kept it locked because of the money she usually had inside the office. "Good night, honey," she said, turning the key in the lock. "It's late. Lots of drunks out there on the street."

Vangie wiped another tear from her cheek, sniffed, and smiled. "They won't mess with me. They know I'm the daughter of Bloody Joe Mannion!"

Both women laughed.

Jane opened the door and gasped when a tall man dressed in black stood before her, aiming a big revolver on her. He spread his mustached lips, narrowing his dark eyes, and said tightly, "Bloody Joe's wife *and* daughter." He glanced at the heavyset man standing beside him, also holding a gun on Jane and Vangie. "We get two for the price of one, Parker."

The jowly Parker spread his lips inside his salt-and-pepper beard and clicked the hammer of his silver-chased revolver back.

CHAPTER 24

"WHERE IN THE HELL ARE YOU TAKING US?" VANGIE barked at the two men sitting on the driver's seat of the buckboard wagon that rattled violently along a two-track wagon trail barely lit by wan starlight.

As they'd done ever since they'd left Del Norte, Jane and Vangie sitting with their backs to the front of the wagon, ankles tied before them, wrists tied behind them, neither man said a thing. They just sat staring straight ahead over the backs of the two horses hitched to the buckboard, the man called Parker sitting to the right of the bigger one Parker had called Thorn, who was driving.

Sitting beside Vangie, staring at the desert southwest of Del Norte bristling darkly around them, Jane could feel the fury radiating off the girl. It was a crazy, wild anger. Her father's anger. Though she rarely displayed her father's heated emotions, she was Bloody Joe Mannion's daughter, after all. Jane knew how she felt. As they'd sped out of Del Norte under cover of darkness, Jane had wanted to scream out for help in the worst way. But the two men had told them to stay quiet or one of them "would be gutshot and thrown from the wagon to die hard along the trail."

They needed only one of the two women.

Apparently, they'd slipped into the back room of the San Juan, intending to kidnap only Jane. Vangie had just had the lousy luck of being in the wrong place at the wrong time.

Jane had no idea why they'd wanted to take her. She assumed they had some bone to pick with Joe. They probably knew he'd come for her...and now for Vangie, as well...and ride into the trap they'd likely set for him.

Fear engulfed Jane as she knew it did Vangie sitting to her left, occasionally casting her stepmother dark, terrified, frustrated glances.

She leaned toward Vangie and said into her ear, "Calm down, Vange. Don't draw attention to us. I've been working at the ropes tying my wrists together, and I'm making some progress."

Vangie flashed her a surprised look. "You *are*?"

Jane nodded, stretching her lips back from her teeth as she continued working desperately at the rope wrapped twice around her wrists and knotted tightly. Using her fingers, nearly ripping off the nails of both index fingers, she was gradually loosening it. Once she got free...*if* she got free...she had no idea what she'd do. She'd cross that bridge when she came to it.

Maybe get hands on one of the pistols holstered on each man's hip.

Blast them both in the backs of their ugly heads!

She lifted her chin, drew a deep breath, calming herself. She was letting herself get as enraged as Vangie. She had to keep her head so she could think rationally, move methodically. If she was not successful, she might very well get both her and Vangie killed.

A front wheel of the wagon banged against a rock, making the wagon sway violently and causing Jane and Vangie to jerk hard to their right, their backsides aching even worse from the torturous ride than before. The hard wooden floor of the wagon was not padded. A rear wheel of the wagon struck the same rock that the front one had, and both women groaned as their rumps rose from the wagon bed and slammed back down on it.

Both men on the driver's seat laughed.

Vangie cursed them both, using words that Jane had never heard her use before. Her father had used them. Joe could have written a dictionary chock full of foul language. But Jane had never heard Vangie use them before, and despite the direness of their situation, she found herself feeling a little shocked but also impressed.

Her shock at her stepdaughter's language and her indignation at the wagon's abuse of her backside was short-lived.

It had been that second violent blow that had caused her fingers to jerk the knot free. Heart quickening, she unwrapped the rope from her wrists and, keeping her hands behind her back, turned to Vangie, who she could tell was still fuming, jaws hard, nostrils flared. Vangie turned to her. When she saw the smile on Jane's lips, the younger woman frowned, curious.

Jane brought her free hands around to her lap, opening them, showing them to Vangie, whose eyes widened, her lower jaw sagging in shock.

Jane glanced at the two men behind them as she and Vangie faced the buckboard's tailgate then, seeing that they were staring straight ahead over the horses, gestured for Vangie to give her back to her.

Vangie twisted around, and Jane went to work on the knot binding her wrists together. Vangie's knot was especially tight. Jane could see that her hands were swollen. Quickly, desperately, Jane worked, not knowing how far ahead lay her and Vangie's kidnappers' intended destination.

Finally, the knot was free. Jane tossed away the rope.

Both women glanced at the men on the driver's seat. The kidnappers, sure their female charges were tightly bound and defenseless, stared straight ahead, shoulders sliding left and right with the wagon's sway. The bearded man drew on a cigarette, the exhaled smoke tearing away on the wind. Jane and Vangie exchanged hopeful glances then leaned forward to work at the ropes binding their ankles together. Those ropes weren't as tight as those that had been binding their wrists. Vangie had her ankles free first, tossed the rope away, and looked at Jane just as the older woman pulled her own rope away from her ankles, as well, and tossed it to the rear of the wagon box.

Jane gave Vangie a determined look, chin dripped, savage resolve in her gaze.

Hardening her jaws, the burn of rage rising in her chest, Jane hipped around and rose onto her knees, facing forward. The gun of the black-clad man driving the buckboard bristled on his right hip, in a hard black holster, the steel band at the end of the grips glinting in the starlight. Jane slid her right hand forward, closed it around the grips of the gun and, freeing the keeper thong with her right hand, jerked the piece from the holster.

She pressed the barrel against the back of the black-clad man's head, just beneath his hat.

"Stop the wagon!"

Both men jerked with starts, turned their head toward Jane. The bearded man closed his hand around the grips of his own, silver-chased, holstered revolver but froze when Jane clicked back the hammer of the gun in her hand and pressed the barrel harder against the head of the driver, shoving his head forward.

"You want a runaway wagon?" she said, sliding her hard gaze to the bearded man.

His eyes went soft. He removed his right hand from the gun on that side and raised it before him, palm out.

Jane pressed the barrel of the gun in her hand harder against the head of the black-clad man. "Stop the wagon or I *will* blow your head off, you sonofabitch!"

"All right, all right, all right, you crazy bitch!"

Jane pulled her pistol away from the back of his head.

As she did, he straightened in the seat and drew back on the reins, yelling, "Whoahh! Whoahh...now...!"

Kneeling to Jane's right, Vangie pulled the silver-chased Colt from the holster on the heavyset man's right hip. She slammed the barrel across the man's head, knocking his hat off, and, as the wagon drew to a halt, said, "Where in the hell were you taking us?"

Holding the reins taut in his black-gloved hand, the man called Thorn turned a smirk to Vangie and said, "Now, that's real simple. Real simple." He turned his head forward. "See those lights just ahead? That's a cabin. Either of you decided to pull those triggers, you're gonna have a whole passel of men just like us swarmin' up your skirts like hornets from a holler log!"

Jane followed the man's gaze.

Sure enough, three separate, dull, umber lights shone ahead in the darkness. They were vaguely square in shape.

Jane could make out the outline of a cabin framing the lights, which, she saw, were three lamplit windows in the cabin that lay down a slight slope maybe a hundred yards ahead, beyond cottonwoods standing along both sides of the trail.

She looked at Vangie. Vangie looked at her.

She thought she could hear the younger woman's heart hammering beneath the hammering of her own.

Vangie's face was drawn and pale. Her lips moved, forming the silent question: "What are we going to do?"

Jane's mind raced.

It came up with the only answer.

She turned to the two men hipped around in the driver's seat, staring at her, faint smirks on their mouths.

Jane gestured with the pistol in her hand. "Out," she said, tightly. "Out...now!"

"What?" said the driver, Thorn, scowling at her incredulously, defiantly.

Jane aimed the pistol at his head. "Out. Or take one between the eyes!"

"Lady, you're crazy," said the bearded man. "All we gotta do is call out, an'..."

"I know," Jane said, reaching across the distance into her husband's mind. What would Bloody Joe do? What would his only option be?

She turned to the black-clad man staring at her, that smirk returned to his muddy black eyes above his long, hooked nose. "That's why I can either let you climb down off the wagon, let you call to the others, or I can shoot you right here...right now...culling the herd, so to speak, and take my chances with the others."

The black-clad Thorn and the bearded man, Parker, looked at each other, eyes growing wide in sudden realization that the end was near.

They turned back to Jane and then the bearded man reached for the rifle lying on the seat between them. Jane swung Thorn's pistol at him and shot him. He wailed, throwing both hands up as the bullet lifted him up off the seat and threw him off the wagon's right side. He struck the trail with a grunt.

Coolly, Jane turned to Thorn, recocking the Colt in her hands.

"Wait! Wait!" Thorn pleaded. "No!"

Bang!

Thorn screamed and flew over the wagon's dash-board, bounced off the hitch with a wooden, crunching thud, and struck the trail between the front wheels.

"Oh, my god," Vangie said, staring at her stepmother in shock.

"Vangie, hurry!"

Jane stepped over the wagon box's front panel and onto the seat.

She saw Vangie still gazing at her in shock and said, louder, "Vangie, climb up here!"

That jerked Vangie out of her stupor. She stepped fleetly over the wagon box's front panel, dropped her knees onto the seat, then swung both feet to the floor of the driver's box. Both horses were whinnying and pulling against the two breaking blocks pressed snug to the front wheels, jerking the wagon forward.

"Hold that," Jane said, shoving her smoking Colt at Vangie, who took it stiffly, gazing at Jane incredulously.

She turned to the two men lying dead in front of and beside the wagon and said, tonelessly, "That was good thinking, Jane...I reckon..."

"You can thank your father for that," Jane said, releasing the break handle with a grunt then shaking the reins over the backs of the two horses in the hitch, yelling, "Hy-ahh! Hy-ahhh, there, fellas—*goooo!*"

As Jane reined the team around sharply, standing in the driver's box now, expertly manipulating the reins, Vangie said beside her, "But Pa's not even here..."

"Oh, yes, he is," Jane said, laughing manically as the horses jerked the wagon around and Jane whipped the reins violently against their backs once more. "Oh, yes, he is!"

She laughed again as the buckboard shot up the trail, heading back north, the direction from which they'd come. As the horses started around a bend in the trail, between large rocks and cedars along the trail's both sides, Jane heard men shouting behind her, in the direction of the cabin.

Jane sat in the driver's seat, glancing back over her shoulder. "I do believe we've prodded that hornet's nest."

Vangie turned to her. "I had nothing to do with it." Her lips shaped a faint smile in the darkness.

Jane gave her a smirk, manipulating the reins in her hands.

"Are we going to make it?" Vangie said above the thunder of the horses' hooves and the wagon's ironshod wheels. She'd shoved both pistols under her thighs and was holding onto the seat for all she was worth, afraid of being pitched out which, at the speed Jane had the horses galloping, was possible...even likely...at any second.

"We can't keep ahead of horseback riders for long." Again, Jane turned to Vangie and smiled. "But we can say we did the best we can!" She shook the reins over the team's backs again, and yelled, "Hahh! Hahh, there! First one back to town gets the biggest bucket of oats, you cayuses!"

"Jane!" Vangie cried when they'd struck a particularly large rock in the trail and nearly overturned, "It's not going to mean much if *you* kill us!"

Jane frowned as she stared over the horses, pensive.

She pursed her lips and drew back on the reins.

"Right you are," she said, slowing the team. "Right you are, dear girl."

Vangie sighed in relief when the team was only walking, blowing and shaking their heads, sweat lather showing silver in the starlight.

She gasped when men's shouts and horses hoof thuds rose behind them.

"They're coming," she said to Jane, voice pitched with fear.

"Of course, they are."

Jane swung the buckboard off the trail, bulling through cedars and small cottonwoods and into the desert beyond.

She needed to find somewhere to make a stand, however feeble it might be.

Two women with two revolvers against who knew how many armed men...

CHAPTER 25

WHEN THE WAGON'S WHEELS THUNDERED LOUDLY OVER several large rocks, making the wagon pitch violently, Jane knew they weren't going to get far from the trail in the wheeled contraption.

Only maybe fifty yards from the trace, that fact became even more apparent when two large, pale boulders formed a narrow corridor before them. Much too narrow for the wagon, and choked with more large rocks and stunt cedars, besides. Jane thought they might have already broken an axle because in addition to the loud barking of the wheels, a weird, low whine rose from the undercarriage and the horses in the traces had to lean farther forward against their hames, grunting and blowing as they muscled the contraption along through the desert.

"Whoa, Whoa." Jane didn't have to pull back very hard on the reins to stop the exhausted beasts. In fact, just the command stopped them. The poor animals stood wearily, breathing hard, shaking their lathered heads, tails drooping. She glanced at Vangie. "This is the end of the line," she said.

"We're better off on foot." Clutching one of the kidnappers' pistols, Vangie nodded. "We're better off on foot." Fleetly, she swung down her side of the wagon and gazed warily back toward the trail.

Jane climbed down her side of the wagon, stuffed her own pistol behind the wide, black leather belt she wore over the waistband of her long, wool skirt, and stood gazing back in the same direction as Vangie. "Hear anything?"

Vangie shook her head. "Not yet."

The last word had no sooner escaped her lips than the rataplan of galloping horses sounded back in the direction of the trail, muffled with distance at first but growing quickly louder.

"Yep!" Vangie said.

Glad she was wearing short-heeled boots instead of the high heels she usually wore when she was working in the saloon/hotel, Jane clambered up a stone outcropping rising off her side of the wagon. She hadn't climbed far before she felt a hitch in her chest, and her breath grew labored—a reminder of the bullet courtesy of Ulysses Xavier Lodge residing too close to her heart for Dr. Ben Ellison to have removed it safely. Ironic, she vaguely reflected, that she and Joe might both shed their earthly shackles due to logy tickers.

Ignoring the strain in her chest, she pulled herself up onto the crest of the scarp, rose, and gazed back in the direction of the trail. Just as she did, she saw jostling shadows moving quickly from her right to her left—the indistinct shapes of at least a half dozen riders, riding fast. The group past quickly, the thuds dwindling until they were lost in the darkness back in the direction of town.

Jane adjusted the pistol wedged behind her belt and

clambered back down the scarp to stand beside Vangie, who stood where she'd been standing before, gazing back in the direction of the trail.

"How many?" Vangie said, keeping her voice low as though she feared their stalkers might hear her.

"Six. Seven, maybe. I think we're in the clear for now as long as…"

Jane let her voice trail off as the thunder of galloping horses rose again as they had before—quietly at first but growing quickly louder.

Jane cursed.

Vangie said darkly, "If they see where we left the trail…"

"Yeah," Jane said, her heart quickening. "Then we've come to the end of ours in more ways than one."

"I think we best hotfoot it, as Pa would say. Find a place to hide."

"Yep," Jane said. "As far away from the trail as we can get, the better."

She and Vangie strode quickly up around the horses and started clambering through the rocks between the boulders. They hadn't gone far before Vangie, moving over the rocks to Jane's right, said, "Jane, are you all right?"

That was when Jane realized she was breathing hard, wheezing like a woman twice her age. Jane drew a deep breath, shook her head, and continued moving, tripping as they both scrambled over the rocks. "I'm fine, I'm fine."

"You don't sound fine."

"Vangie, I'm fine. Keep moving."

At the end of the corridor between the boulders, they came to a dry wash. They both stopped and stood staring down at it, Jane with her fists on her hips, trying to catch her breath and trying to suppress the gnawing pain in her chest. "Should we take the wash?" she asked her stepdaughter.

"Soft sand down there. They'll be able to track us. We best stick to rocky ground." Vangie moved up close to Jane, wrapped her left arm around Jane's waist. "Let's head straight across and find a place to hole up. You need to rest, dear Jane."

Jane wrapped her arm around Vangie's shoulders, gave her a quick hug. "Good thinking. Don't worry about me. I'll be fine."

"It's your heart." Vangie said it in such a thin, fearful tone, that it chilled Jane to the bone.

Dear God—please, please, please, don't let me die out here. Not on Vangie. I know what she's thinking. She's liable to lose her beloved father as well as her stepmother.

Jane could fairly feel the fear atremble in the young woman's slender body.

"I'm fine, Vange." Jane took her hand and together they strode down the shallow bank into the wash. "Let's go!"

When they'd crossed the wash and had climbed the opposite bank into the thin fringe of willows sheathing it, Vangie squeezed Jane's hand then released it. "Wait."

Vangie looked around then broke off a couple of leafy willow branches. Wielding each, she scrambled back into the wash to the other side, backing toward Jane as she used the branches to wipe out their tracks in the arroyo's sandy bottom. She was halfway across when a man's voice rose clearly in the near-silent night, back in the direction from which they'd come.

"Here! The wagon's here!"

Jane's heart leaped. Vangie stopped, gave Jane a dark,

fearful look then quickly finished her job and tossed the branches into the brush.

She took Jane's hand. "Let's go!"

Hand in hand, they made their way through rocks, creosote, and spindly cedars. As they did, they heard a horse whinny and then men's voices pitched in anger. Ten minutes later, as they continued moving, another man's voice rose amid the distance-muffled thudding of horse hooves.

"This way! She came this way!" They were assuming the wagon had been carrying only Jane.

"Damn," Jane said, breathless. "They're good."

"Too good."

When they came to the top of a low ridge, Vangie stopped, took Jane's hand again, and said, "Can you keep moving?"

Jane nodded and started down the slope, Vangie moving along beside her. Jane could see Vangie casting her frequent, worried glances. Jane hated that she had to be the source of worry to the girl, on top of the fear of the cutthroats stalking them. She cursed the bad luck of Vangie happening to have visited her when the kidnappers had come for her.

When they'd crossed another low ridge and were making their way around two more, at the base of a rocky dike that rose like a half-buried dinosaur spine, Vangie stopped suddenly.

"There," she said, grabbing Jane's arm, stopping her. "Maybe we can hide in there."

Jane followed the young woman's pointing finger to a hollow in a boulder snag, just ahead on their left. Jane couldn't deny she needed rest.

She nodded. "Worth a try."

They strode quickly over to the hollow. It was actually a corridor through the rocks, though Jane couldn't see how far it went because about twenty feet away, it turned sharply left. Inside, it smelled gamey. Jane hoped no wildcat had made it home. If so, she and Vangie had leaped from the frying pan into the fire. Still, she moved into it, crouching because the ceiling was only a little over five feet high, and she stood five feet four. Vangie had to crouch, too. A few yards inside, Jane stopped, sighed, slid slowly down against the stone wall, sinking to her butt onto the corridor's stone floor and extending her legs straight out in front of her.

Vangie sank down beside her, kissed her cheek, and hugged her.

"Who are those hardtails, anyway?"

"I don't know for sure, but I think they probably wanted to take me for ransom. It's the only thing I can think of."

Vangie sighed. "Makes sense. You are, after all, the most successful business *person* in Del Norte."

Jane squeezed her hand. "I'm just sorry you had to be there when they came for me, honey."

"I'm not. I wouldn't want you to go through this alone."

"Do you have any idea how fortunate I feel to have you as a stepdaughter? I love you more than anything in this world, Vange."

"Even more than Pa?" Vangie said with some surprise.

"That old bastard?"

They both had a good, quiet, snickering laugh at that.

Then Jane, sobering, said, "Listen..."

They both turned to look toward the mouth of the gap in the rocks. Men's voices grew. So did hoof thuds, then came the squawk of tack and rattle of bridle chains. A horse blew, and then the hoof thuds stopped. Jane knew their stalkers were close. They stopped their horses nearby.

"How we gonna find them in the dark?" one man said from maybe fifty yards away, close enough that Jane felt a shiver ripple through her bone marrow.

"We'll find 'em," said another. "Let's split up. Mick, you check those rocks over there. Charlie, you and Bone investigate the base of that ridge. McCluskey, check south. They might be huddled in the wash over there. Rip an' me'll continue west. If you find 'em, don't shoot 'em. They're worth nothing to us dead."

"Who do you think the second one is?" asked another toughnut.

"I don't know. Judging by the size of the prints, another female. Maybe one of Jane's working girls. Maybe Mannion's daughter. Those were bootprints. Having Mannion's daughter out here would be better yet. All right, let's split up. If you find 'em, fire two shots."

Hooves clattered. Tack squawked. Saddlebags slapped against the sides of the horses as the riders continued their savage quest. Soon there was the sound of only a single rider, slowly approaching the jumble of boulders Jane and Vangie were in. The smell of tobacco smoke touched Jane's nostrils. Mick was smoking a cigarette, riding slowly, casually. To him, his female prey was defenseless. Maybe he and the others hadn't noticed the guns of the wagon men were gone. Or maybe they didn't think their female quarry would use them. As Jane and Vangie gazed dreadfully toward the mouth of the corridor, the smell of a hard-ridden horse and saddle leather accompanied the smell of the smoke on the still night air.

As the clacking of the hooves on rock grew louder, Jane pulled the Colt pistol from behind her belt, and cocked it. Vangie looked at her then did the same with her own gun, resting it across her thigh.

Mick was occasionally stopping the horse, likely looking around.

Then he continued forward.

Jane drew a sharp breath when she saw the front legs of the horse he was riding, one with one white sock. Then she saw the stirrup with Mick's brown-booted foot snugged inside it. Tobacco smoke wafted into the corridor, and then she saw the horse's right rear leg, which bore a scar across the hock, then the swishing tail as horse and rider drifted past the corridor.

Jane and Vangie gave a collective sigh of relief.

Just beyond the corridor, the thud of hooves stopped again.

A long silence.

Then Mick said, "Hmm..."

Jane and Vangie shared a wide-eyed, fateful look.

"Hillbilly," Mick said, "let's go take us another look. "I got me a sneakin' suspicion."

"Oh, shit," Jane whispered.

Hooves thudded, growing louder as Mick and Hillbilly approached the mouth of the corridor. The horse stopped just outside the corridor. Jane could see its broad chest with breast collar, and both front legs.

"Come on, Vange," Jane said, rising and tugging on Vangie's arm.

Vangie rose and said tightly, "We could just shoot the son of a bitch."

"And draw the others? Come on!"

She gave the girl's hand a hard tug and, crouching beneath the low ceiling, made their way back deeper in the cavern's deeper shadows. Jane moved quickly, wanting to gain the bend that lay ahead before Mick moved into the cavern. She'd just made it, pulling Vangie along by her hand, when a man's voice echoed off the corridor's walls behind them.

"Knock knock." Pitched with jeering menace. "Anybody home?"

CHAPTER 26

VANGIE GASPED WITH A START JUST AS JANE PULLED her back against the cavern wall beside her, on the other side of the slight bend in the corridor, which was lit by a rising moon peeking in from above the slabs of rock.

Jane looked to see if there was any escape route beyond them, but there was only the darkness of a stone wall. They were trapped.

Her heart thudded heavily. Vangie saw what she'd seen, which was only solid rock and turned her own concerned gaze to Jane, the girl's brown eyes glinting in the moonlight.

"Hello, hello," came Mick's voice from back in the direction of the cavern's mouth. "Anybody here?" His boots clacked on the corridor's stone floor. "Just payin' a friendly visit's all!"

He snickered an evil laugh.

"Don't know how friendly. Maybe that's up to you. Maybe not..." Again, that evil laugh.

The man's footsteps grew louder.

"Seen what you done to Parker an' Thorn," he said, just as his man-shaped, hatted silhouette came into view, moving around the bend, so close now to Jane that she could smell the smoke, horse, and man-sweat on him. "That weren't nice. That weren't nice atall!"

Jane turned to face him; he hadn't seen her yet. She rammed the barrel of her six-gun against his soft belly and said tightly, "You want the same thing, you gutter-crawling son of a bitch?"

He stopped with a start, eyes dropping to the gun in Jane's hand.

He started to raise his own six-shooter but stopped when Jane pressed her own pistol still harder into his guts. "Drop it!" she ordered.

"Hey, now. Hey, now," Mick said, backing up a step, lowering his own six-gun back down against his right leg. "Ain't no reason to get—"

"I said drop it or take one in the guts!"

"Okay, okay. Don't get excited." There was a thud as he opened his hand and the six-shooter fell straight down to the cavern floor. He raised both hands to his shoulders, palms out.

Keeping her pistol rammed taut against his belly, Jane said, "Why did you men take me?"

"Uh, well..."

"Tell me."

"I don't reckon...I don't reckon..."

"You don't reckon you want to die? If not, tell me, you gutter snipe."

"It wasn't so much about you as Mannion?"

"Joe? Why?"

"Now, that I can't tell ya."

"Get down on your knees."

"What?"

"Get down on your gallblasted knees!"

"Why?"

Jane enjoyed hearing fear in Mick's voice now, the tables having been turned.

"Now, that I can't tell ya," she said, mocking the man, who was about her height and with several days' worth of stubble on his homely face. "But if you don't drop to your knees now, I will shoot you in the guts. You saw what we did to Parker and Thorn."

"All right, all right."

He'd no sooner dropped to his knees than Jane flipped the gun in her hand, taking it by the barrel and swinging it back behind her shoulder. With a grunt, she swung it forward, ramming the butt solidly against Mick's left temple, knocking off his battered Stetson.

"Ow!" he cried, listing to his right.

With another grunt, Jane rammed the six-gun's butt against his temple once more, harder this time.

Mick gave another grunt and tumbled onto his shoulder and lay still.

"Well," Vangie said, standing to Jane's left. "That's one way to skin a cat." She looked at Jane. "Should've maybe told us why they wanted Pa."

"He wouldn't have told us. The rest of his bunch would have killed him slow. Besides, we know enough. They wanted to lure Joe up here, likely to assassinate him."

"In that case, I hope Pa doesn't come."

"Oh, he'll come," Jane said with certainty. "As soon as he learns we're gone. Unless we can make it back to town and stop him. And that, young lady, has to be our first priority."

Jane kicked Mick onto his back, unbuckled his shell belt, and yanked the belt and holster out from under him. It was outfitted with a knife sheath, too. What appeared a homemade skinning knife jutted up from it. There must have been at least twenty extra .44 shells in the loops on the belt.

"Now we have an extra gun and plenty of ammo," Jane said, shoving Mick's pistol into the holster and looping the belt over her right arm.

"Let me take that," Vangie said.

"What? Why?"

"Do you hear how hard you're breathing?"

Then Jane realized that very thing. Her heart was hammering, and she was breathing as though she'd run a long way uphill. She was also sweating.

"Good point," Jane said, handing the shell belt and filled holster over to her stepdaughter, who looped it over her own right shoulder.

Please, please, please. Don't let me die. For Vangie's sake if for no one else's.

Jane drew a deep breath, swabbed sweat from her forehead with the sleeve of her blouse.

"Now," she said. "Let's get the hell out of here."

"And then what?"

"We start making our way back to town."

"You do remember there are five more men out there —right, Jane?"

And your heart is pounding like a tom-tom. Vangie didn't have to say it. Jane could read her mind.

Chin up, Jane said, smiling like the cat that ate the canary, "We have Mick's horse. And I'll bet there's a carbine on the saddle."

Vangie smiled, nodding.

They hurried around the bend in the stone wall and back in the direction of the cavern's mouth—two women, three guns, a knife, a horse, and probably a rifle.

"Wait—slow, easy!" Jane said, grabbing Vangie's arm.

In the darkness tempered by the light of the rising

moon, she could see the horse standing about ten feet out from the entrance to the cavern. The horse was lowering its head to peer into the corridor, twitching its ears, working its nostrils. Probably wondering where its rider went.

"Easy, boy," Jane said, stepping ahead slowly. "Easy, now..."

"Yeah," Vangie said behind her. "Easy, boy."

"It's all right," Jane cooed, setting each foot down in turn, smiling, holding up her hands palms out as though to show the beast she had nothing in them.

The horse stared at her, head low, eyes dubious.

Jane took another step.

The horse snorted, shook its head.

"Easy, Jane," Vangie said.

Jane stopped. "It's all right, big fella. Everything's all right. Your rider's just taking a little nap."

Vangie snickered.

Jane took another step forward. She was about six feet from the entrance now.

The horse whickered, took one step backward.

"Don't be afraid," Jane said, taking another slow step forward.

The horse watched her, doubtful.

Jane took another step forward. Another.

As she crouched through the entrance and out into the night, the horse whickered again, took another step backward. Jane lunged forward, reaching for the reins. As she did, the horse whinnied, swung around, and lunged off its haunches. Jane hurled herself forward, grabbed the reins with both hands.

To no avail.

The horse jerked them free and bolted off into the night.

"Damn!" Jane said, belly down in the dirt.

Vangie ran out to crouch down beside her. "You all right?"

Jane looked around, spying no movement around them. "I think so. Damn the luck!"

"Damn the luck is right."

Jane frowned at Vangie. Vangie hadn't said it. A man's voice had said it.

They both turned in dread to watch Mick duck out of the cavern, the pistol in his hand glinting in the moonlight. He grinned. He was wearing his short hat, which he'd reshaped after Jane had brained him. "Had a hideout in my boot."

It was a small, silver-chased pistol. But just as deadly as a big one.

"Kindly drop my pistol belt, Missy," he told Vangie. "Both of you toss your own hoglegs down, too."

They both stared at the man in shock.

He held his snub-nosed pistol on Vangie and turned to Jane. "Do it. She's Mannion's daughter, ain't she? I can tell by the way she's dressed. Horse girl. She could use a ribbon in her hair for my taste, but I reckon Joe'd be right lonely without her."

Vangie narrowed her eyes at him.

Jane glanced at her as she slid her own six-shooter out from behind her belt and tossed it away. "Do it, Vange."

"We couldn've killed you, you know," Vangie told Mick.

"Should have," Mick told Vangie. "Drop 'em, horse girl!"

Vangie told him to do something physically impossible to himself and then dropped his shell belt and six-gun at her booted feet. She followed it up with the six-gun she'd appropriated from one of the men who'd taken her and Jane in the first place.

Mick lifted his chin and gave a wild coyote howl. He triggered his snub-nosed pistol in the air twice.

Vangie took advantage of the foolish man's distraction.

She crouched to grab the pistol she'd taken off one of the wagon men.

"No, Vange!" Jane cried.

Too late.

Vangie hurled two chunks of .44-caliber sized lead into Mick's guts.

Mick stumbled back toward the cavern entrance. "Oh," he said, dropping his snub-nosed hogleg and looking down at the two holes in his paunch, one in the flap of his vest, the other just above his belly button. He closed his hands over both holes that turned dark with oozing blood. He took another stumbling step backward. His eyes were wide with shock.

"Oh," he repeated. "That *hurts!*"

He dropped to his knees.

He stared at Vangie, incredulous. "Even no ribbon would fix you. You ain't no lady at all..."

Jane glanced at Vangie as she grabbed her pistol up off the ground, her heart thumping painfully against her breastbone. "Come on, Vange. We gotta get out of here —*fast!*"

Already she heard men shouting in the distance around them.

Vangie stood frozen in shock, staring at the hard-dying Mick, still extending the pistol in her hand. Smoke curled from the barrel.

"Vangie!" Jane cried, gaining her feet.

"Right," Vangie said, lowering the Colt then picking

up Mick's gun and shell belt and slinging the belt over her shoulder.

She glanced at Mick once more, as the man knelt sobbing and trying to hold in his guts with his hands. "No lady atall," Mick cried. "No lady atall..."

"Vangie!" Jane shouted as the men's shouts grew louder around her and she could hear the growing thunder of galloping horses.

Vangie lurched forward.

"Straight ahead!" Jane said.

Her stride faltered when behind them Mick yelled in the collective voice of all human agony, "They killed me boys! *I'm leavin' this world*!"

Running beside Jane, breathing hard, Vangie said, "I think that's a bit dramatic—don't you?"

Ahead, just beyond a shallow wash Jane was heading for, she saw the shadow of a rider galloping straight toward her and Vangie, from the direction of the high, stone ridge that was a black wall in the night, its crest painted with the milky hues of the moon. He held a rifle straight up from his right thigh.

"Ahead, Vange! Beyond the wash!" Jane stopped and dropped to a knee.

She raised the Colt in her hand just as Vangie, kneeling beside her, raised her own.

"Shoot the son of a bitch!"

Both women fired at the same time—once, twice, three times.

The shadowy rider leaned sharply back in his saddle, pulling back on the reins. The horse screamed, curveted, and fell in a heap, whinnying shrilly. Its rider, pinned beneath its thrashing body, bellowed painfully.

Jane and Vangie dropped into the arroyo and ran to their right. The arroyo cut through the jumble of boulders—a twisting course choked with rocks and flood debris in places. In some sections the boulders leaned like giant dominoes over the wash, and they had to nearly crawl under them. But those "dominoes" would keep horseback riders from following. They had to stop to catch their breaths several times, hearing men shouting behind them. The shouts were dwindling.

They were outdistancing their stalkers.

That quelled the painful pounding of Jane's heart.

"You think we're gonna make it, Jane?" Vangie asked as they continued, walking fast.

"I think we already have," Jane replied with buoyant smile, taking Vangie's hand in her own, swinging it with glee.

Two horseback riders thundered out of intersecting arroyos to either side of them, blocking their way, their horses whickering. Jane ran into the one on the right, bounced off the man's right leg and stirrup, and went stumbling backward, falling onto her butt, dropping her pistol. Vangie screamed. Both men extended carbines at her and Jane one-handed, drawing sharply back on their reins.

The man on the right was tall. Astride a beefy cream horse, he wore a gray shirt under a denim jacket, and a high-crowned gray Stetson. He stretched his black-mustached upper lip back from his teeth and said, "Evenin', ladies. And I use that term very loosely."

CHAPTER 27

"HOW YOU WANNA PLAY IT, JOE?" RIO WAITE ASKED Mannion midmorning of the next day.

"Not sure yet," Joe said, gazing through his field glasses at the L-shaped, shake-shingled cabin, an old, log mine office shack in the hollow below.

The shack lay across a narrow, shallow stream that glistened in the lemon morning sunlight, fronting the mountain behind it honeycombed with the dark, round portals of abandoned mines. A sprawling, falling down wooden tipple flanked the shack, on the slope above it, at the base of the broad field of slag plundered from the mines. Steel rails ran down the slope from the tipple, and several ore cars sat rusting on the rusty rails, above three big, derelict ore drays rotting in the hollow below it, wagon tongues that hadn't been hitched to mules in a good fifteen years drooping like the tongues of weary dogs.

This was the old Aunt Ethel Mine, long abandoned by its eastern and British investors since its riches had been plundered from Mount Ethel flanking it and looming over it, like a giant skull that had been ravaged by carrion eaters.

Two men sat on the halved-log stoop that ran across the front of the shack, kicked back in chairs and smoking cigarettes, stone coffee mugs in their fists. Another man sat on the pitched roof of the shack, also smoking and drinking coffee, a rifle resting across his thighs. He had a pair of field glasses hanging from a leather strap around his neck. Every few minutes, he lifted the glasses and took a long look around, smoke from the quirley in his lips wafting around his head. Once when he was peering through the glasses, he let go the rifle and it slid down the pitched roof. He'd lunged for it and nearly fell off the roof himself. He'd scrambled sheepishly back to his perch, looking around to see if anyone had witnessed the clumsy act.

Mannion had. Joe hadn't smiled. He had nothing to smile about. These men had kidnapped his wife and daughter.

Why, he had no idea. For ransom, possibly. To lure Mannion himself into a lead bath, most likely. They wouldn't be the only ones, after Bloody Joe's long career, to have a bone to pick. Scores to settle.

He'd always known this could happen. He'd lived in dread of it. That dread was a rusty pigsticker poking his logy heart. His belly churned with bile.

He couldn't see them from this vantage, but he had to assume more lookouts flanked the shack. He'd accounted for three of the gang but judging by the hoof prints he and Rio had followed here, after finding a wagon abandoned in the rocks beside the trail, roughly eight miles outside Del Norte, there were a total of five kidnappers. Two were dead and had been dragged to the side of the trail, hidden in the brush. Buzzards had given them away to the two lawmen. There were possibly three more men flanking the shack or squatting inside it, keeping a close eye on the likely very frightened Jane and Vangie.

Mannion lowered the glasses with a sigh. "They're expecting us. Probably waiting for us. I don't see any way in without getting my girls killed."

"Devil of a situation," Rio muttered, peering over the barrel of his old Spencer repeater, sliding a sharpened matchstick around between his lips.

"Doesn't get much worse than this."

"Wait for nightfall?"

Mannion shook his head. "They'll still be waiting. Keeping a sharp eye out. There'll be no way to take them without getting my girls killed."

"Jesus, Joe."

"Yeah."

"Tough situations call for tough solutions."

Mannion crawled down off the ridge he and Rio were on, shielded from the hollow by a thick tangle of evergreen shrubs. He rose, donned his hat, and strode down to where their two horses waited, tied to spruce branches. Rio watched his boss, incredulous. "What're you gonna do?"

Mannion dropped his field glasses into a saddlebag pouch and tightened Red's saddle cinch. "I'm gonna ride down there and see what they want for Jane and Vangie."

"You consarned loco?" Rio hissed. "You know what they want!"

"Then they can have me. As long as they free my gals."

"There ain't no guarantee they'll do that."

"We'll see."

Rio clambered down the slope then donned his own hat, rose, and ambled in his bull-legged fashion down to where Mannion was checking the loads in his two pistols. "Joe, I think you'd best rethink this. I say we wait till dark then crawdad up to that shack and take them out one by one. That's how we usually do it!"

"They don't usually have Jane and Vangie."

"Joe, this is just plum foolhardy. Ol' Bellringer'll be fittin' you fer a wooden overcoat by sunup tomorrow! Me, too, because I ain't gonna let you go down there without backin' your play!"

Mannion placed a hand on his friend and senior deputy's lumpy shoulder. "Don't die for me, Rio. I'm not worth it. This is the life I chose long ago. Now the hounds of hell are nipping at my ass. My back's to the wall. But it's a wall of my own building. I'm gonna do what I can to get my gals out and give the devil the hindmost."

"Give the devil the hindmost, my ass!"

"Yeah, that's probably what he'll get."

Joe smiled, untied Red's reins from the spruce branch, and climbed up into the leather.

"Joe!" Rio said as he watched his boss gallop Red out away from the perch they'd been on, heading west. "Joe, dammit, sometimes you just gotta pocket your pride an' listen to ol' Rio!"

Mannion thew up an arm and kept riding away.

Rio cursed and slapped his battered old Stetson—it hardly even looked like a hat anymore—against his thigh.

"Bloody Joe's last dance is what this is," he muttered, watching Mannion and Red disappear into a mixed grove of pine and spruce. "Bloody Joe's last dance, fer certain-sure."

He set his hat back on his head and looked at his horse.

His lineback dun with one white sock was looking at him with a skeptical cast to his brown-eyed gaze.

"What the hell you lookin' at, Louis?" Rio grouched. "Ain't you never seen a broken-down old deputy town marshal before?"

———

MANNION RODE AROUND THE SHOULDER OF THE HILL from the crest of which he'd reconned the cabin.

He came to a shaggy two-track trail meandering off through the canyon in which the mine office cabin sat, at the base of the mine-honeycombed mountain rising on Joe's right. He couldn't see the hovel from here, for it lay on the other side of a low rise. He stopped Red at the mouth of the secondary trail, gazing along its rocky, curving course, and rubbed his jaw.

If he had any brains, he'd take a minute to consider his options.

On the other hand, he'd never been known for his brains. Just for his ability to plow through a tight spot, shooting. Also, he didn't think he had many options. He might get Jane and Vangie killed, but it was his impulse to ride into the whipsaw in that canyon and figure his moves out as he went along.

It was his way.

He booted Red onto the shaggy trail. He rode up over the rise, saw the cabin with the two men sitting on the peak of the roof, the third one kicked back in the chair by the door. As he rode down the other side of the ridge, three heads turned toward him, bodies stiffening. The two men on the roof stood, raising their rifles to port arms.

"Company," one of them called. "Looks like Mannion!"

The man in the chair rose, also raising his rife and turning toward the lawman as Mannion came down off the rise, Red's ears pricked, tail curled, knowing trouble was about to pop. The bay knew that from his keen sense of the situation and the general nature of his rider. Sometimes Red thought if his fortune had been better, he'd belong to a ranch hand or, better yet, a preacher's widow, pulling her two-wheeled buggy into town every morning to sell eggs or to purchase a fat roast for evening supper.

The bay snorted and shook his head dubiously, gave another snort when he heard his rider pump a live cartridge into his Yellowboy's breech.

"Well, well, if ain't Bloody Joe his ownself," said the man on the porch, racking a round into his own rifle's action.

Keeping one eye on the two men on the roof, one on the man on the porch, Mannion rode up to the front of the cabin and turned Red to face it. Mannion studied all three faces through his long, gray wolf's eyes, rage burning in him, barely able to contain it, barely able to keep from snapping up the Yellowboy and blowing the two men off the roof, the third one off the porch.

As he did, the cabin's front door opened so fast it slammed against the chair of the man who'd been sitting in it, knocking it over. Two men stepped out, shoving Vangie and Jane out before them. Both women were badly disheveled, their hands tied behind their backs. Their faces were pale and drawn, fear in their eyes.

"These two look familiar?" The man behind Jane was dark-haired, cobalt-eyed beneath a cream Stetson, with a long, hooked nose and jutting chin. He held a cocked pistol to Jane's head. The other man, short and squat, with a big belly and a round face, held a cocked pistol to Vangie's head. A low-crowned black hat sat on his head, a billowy, dirty bandanna knotted around his neck.

"Oh, Joe!" Jane said. "You shouldn't have come, Joe!"

"I had no choice, honey," Mannion said, grimly, his eyes hard, jaws taut. To the man holding Vangie, Joe said, "All right—you have me. Let the women go."

"No, Pa!" Vangie said, tears glistening in her soft brown eyes, rolling down her cheeks.

To the men on the porch, Mannion said, "Let them go."

"Drop the rifle first," said the man who'd been sitting on the chair. He was tall and startlingly thin, with long, pale blond hair falling to his shoulders. He held his own carbine straight out from his right hip. The hammer was cocked back.

"Let the women go first," Mannion said.

He noticed Vangie's shoulders twitching slightly as she cast her father a grave, determined look.

"We got you dead to rights, Mannion," said the tall man. "If you don't drop the rifle, we'll kill your women and blow you out of your saddle."

Mannion aimed his rifle at the tall man. "You'll die too, Slim."

"Depends on whose trigger finger is faster," said Slim.

Mannion stared down the rifle at him.

The man holding his pistol to Vangie's right ear grinned devilishly. "You want this to be the end of it all, Bloody Joe? Want to watch your daughter die right in front of you?"

"Your purty wife, too?" said the man holding his revolver to Jane's head.

Staring at Joe, Jane shook her head slowly, meaningfully. Tightly, she said, "We're dead, anyway, Joe. Kill 'em!"

Her jaws hard, Vangie said, "Kill 'em, Pa. Kill 'em all!"

Mannion's heart shuddered. His throat was dry. He considered each rifle aimed at him, calculated his odds. They didn't look good. He had the dreaded feeling he and his ladies had come to the end of the trail. He'd always thought he'd die first. Now, it looked like they'd all die together.

Should have thought it through before waltzing in here, Bloody Joe, he berated himself.

Him and his pigheaded ways!

Grinning sidelong, Slim turned slightly to the two men on his left and the two on the cabin's roof. "Kill Bloody Joe, fellas. *Kill his women!*"

The last word hadn't left his mouth before his carbine roared, smoke and flames lapping from the barrel. As it did, Mannion threw himself off Red's back, striking the ground as Slim's bullet caromed through the air where he'd been sitting an eyeblink before.

Red pitched and whinnied, wheeled, and galloped away.

Mannion rolled onto his belly and raised the carbine in time to see Vangie give an enraged scream, reach up and knock aside the gun aimed at her head, turning toward the man wielding it and savagely thrusting her right knee into the man's groin. At the same time, the head of the man holding his own pistol on Jane fairly exploded, like a watermelon struck by an axe handle. The man's right arm dropped and he triggered the gun into the porch floor.

As he fell, he pulled Jane down with him.

The man behind Vangie wailed and stumbled backward, triggering his own Remington into the porch floor. He was just bringing the Remington up again when Vangie threw herself into him, knocking him back against the cabin's wall, trying to wrestle the pistol out of his hand, screaming.

Mannion shot Slim just as he racked another round into his carbine. Slim cursed and, blood oozing from the wound in his chest, dropped his rife and fell over the porch rail to his right, losing his hat.

Rifles roared from the cabin's roof. Bullets plumed the dirt around Mannion. Joe racked another round into his Winchester's action, rolled to his right and fired two rounds, triggering and levering, until both men on the roof flew back off the other side of the roof, screaming, and out of sight, dropping their rifles which slid down the near side of the roof to drop over the edge to the ground.

Mannion rolled back to his left, racking another round into the Yellowboy's breech. "*Vangie, down!*"

Vangie released her attacker's gun hand and threw herself to the porch floor.

The man aimed the gun at Vangie's head.

Mannion's rifle spoke. Another rifle roared, as well, to Mannion's left. Joe's bullet drilled a hole in the man's forehead. Another bullet smashed into his right ear and exited his left temple, leaving a fist-sized hole leaking blood and brain matter. He dropped to his butt, hollowed out head lolling on his shoulders like the head of a broken doll, and slid sideways to his shoulder.

The echoes of the gunfire chased themselves, dwindling to silence.

Mannion gained his feet and, wincing against the aches in his shoulder and hip from his unceremonious meeting with the ground, and from the ever-present pain in his chest, ran up onto the porch just as Vangie rose to her knees. Jane was sitting up, as well, her hands still tied behind her back. Both women looked bewildered. Joe dropped to his knees, pulled his Bowie knife from its sheath, cut Jane's wrists free, and wrapped his arms around both women, pulling them close.

The thuds of a galloping horse rose to his left.

He turned to see Rio galloping toward the cabin, his carbine resting on his saddlebow, the brim of his battered Stetson pasted back against his wrinkled forehead in the wind. He reined up before the cabin, drawing sharply back on his dun's reins.

"Everbody all right?"

As the women clung to him, one each side, hugging him tightly, Mannion turned a wolfish grin to his deputy. "Rio, you old scudder—I had a feelin' you'd come up with somethin'!"

Rio shrugged. "Yeah, well, this broken-down old mossyhorn still has a *few* tricks up his sleeve!"

Vangie pulled away from Mannion, frowned at him curiously. "Who were they, Pa? Who were those men?"

Mannion shook his head. "I got no idea. I don't think I ever saw 'em before in my life."

Jane said, "They must've had some bone to pick with you, Joe. Are you sure you've never seen them before?"

Mannion thought it through. The attempts made on his life and Henry's, the killing of Cletus Booker...

His aching ticker leaped in his chest.

He pulled out his timepiece, glanced at it. "Oh, my god," he said. He turned to Rio. "The train's due in Del Norte in an hour. It's carrying a special cache of gold coins headed for the mines! *These guttersnipes kidnapped Jane and Vangie to lure us out of town!*"

CHAPTER 28

QUENTIN CAMPBELL, A.K.A. QUENTIN FERGUSON, HELD his hat in his hands as he stood in the doorway to Miss Laura's Café and said, "Miss Laura, I'm riding into town to fetch freight for your father. Do you want I should pick anything up for you?"

Laura had just turned from a table to which she'd just delivered two hot buttered cinnamon rolls to an elderly couple named Harkinson, retired ranchers who had dessert in her café almost every afternoon. Now she stopped and regarded Quentin skeptically, as though she were seeing him for the first time all over again.

It was the look she'd been giving him ever since he'd taken down Lars and Dave that fateful day by Funeral Rock Creek, where she and Quentin had been picnicking with Henry McCallister and Molly Hurdstrom. He hated that look because he'd found himself tumbling for the gal, and he knew she'd been tumbling for him. But the quickness with which he'd dispatched Lars and Dave had told her she had no idea who he really was. And of course, she didn't. Though he'd saved the girl's life, or at least kept her from being savaged, she was wary of him, cautious. And she obviously didn't trust him because he'd been holding back from her his true identity.

But what was he supposed to do—tell her he'd become somewhat of a gunslinger in the aftermath of his family's brutal murder, and he'd come here gunning for her father, whom he'd believed to be the leader of that depraved gang of former Union soldiers? He no longer believed Mr. Davis was that man, but he'd found himself dragging his feet here in Del Norte, anyway.

Because of Laura.

He didn't want to leave here with things unfinished between them, but he just hadn't gotten up the courage to tell her who he really was. He believed her father hadn't told her, either. Davis was probably waiting for him to do it. To be man enough to tell the girl the truth...

He was surprised that Davis, knowing why Quentin had come here, had let him keep his job. More than surprised. It made him feel guilty and to somehow want to make things right before he left to hunt the rest of his family's killers. Or maybe the need for vengeance was cooling inside him?

Maybe he wanted to stay right here and settle down with Laura.

"No, Quentin," she said, starting back to the lunch counter in quick dismissal. "I have everything I need. Thanks for asking."

Then she went to take the orders of two cowboys sitting on wooden stools at the lunch counter. Laura didn't give him so much as a second glance.

Quentin sighed and went out, setting his hat on his head. He'd parked the Davis's freight wagon in the street before the store's loading dock. Now he climbed up into the wagon and was about to release the brake when he was surprised to see Laura step out of the store, regarding him with that quizzical, wary expression in place on her pretty face.

"Quentin," she said, "or whoever you are." She stopped at the edge of the loading dock and cast him a none-too-vague look of accusing, "Where did you learn to shoot like that? Were you in the army or something? Or..." She crossed her arms on her chest and kicked one ankle-booted foot forward. "Maybe you're an outlaw on the run..."

No, Miss Laura. Neither of those things. I learned how to shoot after my family was murdered and I came here to kill your father even after he was good enough to give me a job. Everywhere I go, I've pretty much been out for blood, and I've been living a lie since I was twelve years old.

If he told her that, he thought, that would likely be the end of their relationship right here and now. Laura Davis deserved a better man than him. A *civilized* man. Besides, he just didn't know *how* to tell her. Maybe in the future he'd figure it out.

Damn his luck at having tumbled for her, anyway!

Quentin flinched, sighed. "Can we talk about it later, Laura? I'm, uh...in sort of a hurry here. The train should be pulling in any minute."

She snorted a caustic chuckle. "All right, Quentin Ferguson...or whoever you are. But just know there might not be a later."

With that, she wheeled and disappeared back into the store, the bell over the door punctuating her leaving like the tinny laugh of an amused god.

———

Quentin rolled onto San Juan Avenue just as the train was barreling into town from the north, its whistle blowing like the wails of an ailing dinosaur, the heavy chugging of the big iron wheels reverberating like the workings of a mine mill stamper.

He crossed the tracks then, as the locomotive chugged to a stop in front of the long, low, brick depot building—the newest structure on the south end of town —he pulled up beside the combination's two freight cars, signed the bill of lading handed to him by the conductor in charge of freight, and off-loaded Davis's thirty or so crates of flour and oats while the conductor checked the parcels off on his clipboard. When the wagon was nearly full, he climbed back onto the seat, pinched his hat brim to the kindly old conductor whose name was Vincent Latterby, and put the wagon up through the crowd of detraining passengers.

He saw Henry McCallister sitting on a loafer's bench near the depot building's broad, wooden doors propped open to receive both departing and arriving passengers. Mannion's junior-most deputy was watching several Wells Fargo train guards, wielding shotguns and rifles, milling in front of the Wells Fargo Express car's closed doors, obviously guarding a valuable cargo within, grim sets to their mustached faces.

Quentin pulled the wagon up in front of the young deputy.

"Afternoon, Henry," he said, setting the brake.

Henry looked at him, one brow arched in surprise. "You still talkin' to me?"

Quentin leaped down off the wagon. "Why wouldn't I be?"

"Because I ratted you out to my boss. And he ratted you out to Davis."

"Oh, hell." Quentin mounted the platform and slumped onto the varnished wooden bench beside Henry.

"I reckon I should thank you for that. If you both hadn't done what you did, I might have lost control and shot Laura's father in his office. I reckon I rode into town half-cocked and leaped to conclusions."

Henry hiked a shoulder. "I reckon it's understandable...given your situation."

Quentin sighed, removed his hat, and worried the edge of the brim with his fingers. Henry raked his eyes off the express guards and, fingering the rifle resting across his thighs, looked at Quentin curiously. "What's on your mind, Quentin?"

"Ah, hell. I reckon I could do with a piece of advice if you can spare it."

"Givin' advice is my favorite thing to do." Henry grinned. "It's Miss Laura, ain't it?"

"Yes."

"She find out you came to town to kill her father?"

Quentin flinched at the directness of the question. "No. That's the thing. She doesn't know. All she knows is I'm not the man she thought I was...after I cut down Lars and Dave. She thinks I might be an outlaw on the run."

"Ungrateful women, I tell you," Henry said. "She should be brushin' your hat an' shinin' your boots!" He looked at Quentin pointedly, wrinkling the freckled skin above the bridge of his nose. "You gonna tell her?"

"You think I should?"

"If you're gonna stay in town...and you still want to see the gal...you're going to have to tell her sometime."

"I reckon that's the conclusion I came to, too. I'm just afraid she's gonna see me as the killer I am, an' she won't wanna have anything to do with me."

"I suppose that's the risk you have to take."

"I ain't much for talkin' to women. Haven't had much practice."

"Maybe now's the time to star..." Henry let his voice trail off.

He was staring off along the train where six men wielding rifles and clad in trail garb just stepped off the rear vestibule of the second of the two passenger cars. They mounted the station platform and were too-casually studying the Wells Fargo, blue-clad guards as they hauled out makins sacks and started building cigarettes. All five wore long dusters, the sides of the dusters bulging as though from hideout iron inside.

"What is it?" Quentin asked.

"Not sure," Henry said. "I shouldn't tell you this, but just so's you're prepared if hell pops, that express car is carrying a special shipment. Payroll for three mines owned by the same syndicate in the Sangre de Cristos. Wells Fargo wired the marshal about it just the other day."

"Oh-oh," Quentin said. "You think those men're..."

It was his turn to let his voice trail off when the oldest of the Wells Fargo guards—a big, going-to-seed, heavy gutted man with red-gray muttonchops trailing down from his leather-billed cap—walked toward the five obvious toughnuts and, holding a shotgun up high across his chest, barked, "Hey there! You men!"

One of the six, the youngest of the group, said, "What men? You mean *us*?"

"Wait here," Henry told Quentin. He rose from the bench, and, holding his rifle in both hands, walked toward the six toughnuts and the guard approaching them.

The older guard stopped ten feet from the six. "Move along. We're Wells Fargo." He brushed a gloved thumb across the copper shield pinned to the breast of his wool coat. "No loitering out here. Either get back on the train or—"

Casually, the youngest toughnut opened the flap of his coat. He squared his shoulders at the old guard, raised a double-barreled, sawed-off shotgun hanging from a lanyard from his right shoulder. The savage weapon thundered. The guard screamed and throwing his arms out to both sides, was picked up off his feet and thrown back against the train, which he bounced off to land in a bloody heap beside the tracks. The gaping, bloody hole in his belly was pumpkin-sized.

"Hold it!" Henry bounded forward.

He saw the sawed-off's large, black round maws swing toward him and knew he didn't have a prayer.

Instinctively, he threw himself right, diving through one of the depot's plate glass windows, screeching glass raining down around him as he landed on the brick floor inside, just beyond a bench abutting the window. He hadn't finished rolling when what sounded like a war raged outside, heavy shotguns blasting, men screaming and cursing. Henry started to rise but stopped when one of the toughnuts peered through the broken window, aimed a six-shooter through the shards of glass remaining in the frame, grinned, and said, "Nighty-night, mate!"

Henry heard the heavy, rocketing blast of a Colt .45 and then everything went dark.

———

OUTSIDE, TWENTY FEET SOUTH OF WHERE HENRY LAY unconscious inside the depot building, Quentin bounded up off the loafer's bench, drew his Colt, and dropped to a knee, firing into the melee of smoke-belching blue-clad guards and duster-clad robbers. He shot one of the robbers in the arm before the man, stumbling back against the train, sent one of his own rounds into Quentin's lower right side.

Stunned, Quentin lowered his right arm, the hand grasping the revolver suddenly seeming to weigh as much as an anvil. Screams and more shooting sounded from inside the express car. The heavy doors roared open, and two more guards—or men dressed *like* guards—were kicked out onto the ground beside the tracks, uniforms stained with blood. Yet another guard hunkered behind what appeared a brass-canistered Gatling gun.

The Gatling, looking like a giant steel mosquito, started roaring, smoke and flames lapping from the rotating canister. Bullets tore into the bona fide guards and into the townsmen who'd come running and shooting. As one volley slid across the front of the depot building toward Quentin, Quentin, knowing his six-shooter was no match for a machine gun, leaped to his feet and dove through the window flanking the loafer's bench. He banged his head on the brick floor so that from a haze of agony he heard the roar of the train's whistle and the heavy thumping of the wheels as the train rolled south along the tracks, pulling away from the station.

Beneath the cacophony, a man laughed like a lunatic. "We got it, boys!" he shouted, his voice dwindling into the distance. "We got it all!"

"They're stealing the train," another man nearer Quentin shouted beneath the continuing rat-a-tat of the death-dealing Gatling. "They're stealing the *consarned train!*"

CHAPTER 29

CRACKED BELLS RANG IN HENRY MCCALLISTER'S EARS. The ringing was like an axe handle beating his brain plate, sending excruciating pain through his tender skull, down the back of his neck and into his spine.

Beneath that ringing came the sound of men shouting and cursing and women crying, dogs barking. He opened his eyes, squinting against the daylight angling through a near window. Slowly, the memory of where he was and how he'd gotten here came to him, and seeing the broken window before him, on the other side of an oak bench in the brick-floored waiting room of the new railroad depot on San Juan Avenue in Del Norte, confirmed the memory.

He remembered the grinning face and the long-barreled revolver being thrust through the broken window. He winced, remembering the orange flames lapping from the barrel. He reached up now with his right hand toward the source of his misery—a deep, bloody gash on his right temple stretching up from his forehead to his hairline. The blood had thickened to jelly.

Placing his hands on the glass-strewn floor to either

side of him, he heaved himself to a sitting position. The movement caused his heart to increase its beating, that axe to slam even harder against his tender brain, which felt swollen to nearly twice its normal size. The shouting and the crying, the dogs barking, called strongly to him, making his consciousness swim up through the pain that urged him to lie here and close his eyes and wait for the agony to abate.

But he remembered the duster-clad cutthroats and the shooting as they'd cut down the Wells Fargo guards with shotguns and rifles, the screaming and the cursing of men dying, and he thrust himself to his knees with a groan. From his knees he could see movement out the broken window as well as dead men lying between the depot's brick platform and the shiny steel rails over which another blue-clad body lay, the man's face and chest matted with blood over which flies were already swarming.

The train was gone.

"Jesus," Henry groaned. "Oh, Lordy...what in... tar*nation?*"

"Henry!"

A young woman's familiar voice came to him as though from far away and then he spied movement to his left and he turned to see Molly Hurdstrom kneeling beside him, wrapping an arm around his shoulder as she put her face up close to his, her concerned gray eyes inspecting the gash on his temple.

"Oh, Henry, dear god—are you alright? Don't you dare die on me, Henry!"

Still hearing the chaos outside, he turned to her. "Do you...do you think...you can help me up, Molly?"

"You just stay right here, Henry. The doc's outside, tending the wounded. I'll fetch him!"

She started to rise but Henry pulled her back down. "No. I gotta get out there...see what happened. My god—where's the dangblasted train?"

"They stole it. The robbers took it over, forced the engineer to pull out. There were passengers aboard..."

"Help me up!"

"No—Henry!"

"Help me up," Henry insisted, wrapping his left arm around her shoulders.

"Oh, Henry!"

Molly wrapped her arm around his waist and, leaning into her, giving her half his weight, he planted his boots against the glass-strewn floor and heaved himself to his feet, squeezing his eyes closed against the throbbing in his skull. Standing, he released her. He steadied himself. He was a little dizzy, but he thought he could walk.

"Take him into the Black Cat," he heard a familiar voice say. "I have to dig that bullet out of his abdomen. Have the barman boil some water—plenty of water!"

Henry moved to the window. Dr. Ben Ellison, a stethoscope around his neck, coat off and shirtsleeves rolled up his bloody forearms, was just then rising from where a wounded Wells Fargo man lay beside the rails, writhing in pain, grinding his bootheels into the ground. Around him several other men—more blue-clad Wells Fargo men, men clad in business suits as well as a few in range garb, cowboys off ranches—lay unmoving.

"They shot up this whole end of the town," Molly said. "They had a wicked gun. Blew out the windows of the shop I work in, almost hit Mrs. Taylor who was in picking out material for her daughter's wedding dress." Molly covered her face with her hands and sobbed. "Oh, Henry—it was terrible!"

Henry pulled her against him. "You'd best go home,

Molly. No point in you stayin' out here. I got a job to do, an' I'm gonna do it, by god."

He led her out onto the boardwalk and released her. "Go on home. Have a cup of tea. Lay down an' rest awhile."

Molly looked up at him through tear-filled eyes. "Henry, what're you gonna do? They shot you in the head!"

"It's just a graze. Hurts like blazes, but it's just a graze."

"I'll get to you in a few minutes, Henry." This from Dr. Ben Ellison who was following three townsmen carrying the wounded Wells Fargo man up onto the boardwalk fronting the Black Cat Saloon half a block away on Henry's right.

"I'll be all right, Doc. There's more people hurt worse than I am."

"I have to look at that," the doctor admonished then pushed through the batwings of the Black Cat, on the heels of the townsmen carrying the wounded train guard.

"Henry," Molly said, "you can't go after those men alone. Not even if you were well!"

"Don't worry—I'll be backin' his play."

Henry turned to see Quentin Ferguson sitting on the loafer's bench where he and Henry had been sitting before the toughnuts had started cutting into the Wells Fargo men with rifles and shotguns. Before the massacre had started...

Ferguson's shirt was open, and he was sitting sideways on the bench, leaning forward as none other than Miss Laura Davis was wrapping a length of what appeared a white sheet around his waist, gritting her teeth as she pulled it taut.

"Molly's right—neither one of you is going anywhere,"

Laura admonished. "You both have wounds. Let a posse go after that train. My father's trying to round one up now."

"Mine's a flesh wound," Quentin said, glancing down at his lower right side. "Went all the way through. Just pinched me a little's all." He smiled at Henry, but it was a taut, pained smile.

To Molly, Laura said, "Let's get them both over to my café. I have a back room with two cots. Henry needs that head wound cleaned and wrapped, and they both need to rest. The doctor has his hands full."

"Good idea, Laura," Molly said.

The two women loaded both men into the back of the Davis freight wagon and drove them over to Laura's Café, where Quentin rested on one cot in a back room off the café, and the two young women cleaned and wrapped Henry's head on the other cot. When the women had finished their work and had headed off to have some tea to calm their nerves, Henry turned to see a door in the room's rear wall.

He turned to Quentin lying on the cot on the other side of the room, looking at him.

"You thinkin' what I'm thinkin'?" Quentin asked the deputy.

"You don't have a stake in this, Quentin. Those robbers are my job."

Quentin patted his wounded right side. "This right here says I got just as big a stake as you do."

Quentin sat up, wincing against the pain in his side, and grabbed his gun and shell belt. "I'll fetch my hoss. You fetch yours!"

CHAPTER 30

AFTER A PAINFUL, NINETY-MINUTE RIDE LATE IN THE day, Henry and Quentin reined up at the top of a windy pass and, belly down in the rocks and pines atop the pass, gazed into Tomahawk Canyon quickly filling with shadows as the sun dropped behind the San Juan Mountains in the west. The San Juan River meandering through the heart of the deep chasm was a tea-colored snake writhing between high, rocky banks.

On the opposite side of the canyon lay the tracks of the Colorado Springs & San Juan Line after the line's course had made a long curve west of the canyon, crossed the river via a high trestle bridge, climbed a pass beyond, then turned sharply east to start the descent out of the mountains toward Pueblo. That route was far longer than the old Indian hunting trail Henry and Quentin had ridden cross country.

The shadows were inching up toward the rails.

All that lay on that side of the eerily quiet canyon were birds flashing in the sunlight, including one bald eagle circling the ridge over the rails and plunging occasionally, a winged missile, into the dark-brown river to surface a few seconds later with a silver fish writhing in its beak.

"I don't get it," Henry said, lowering his brass spyglass. "We've waited an hour. That train should be trundling along that side of the canyon by now."

"Must've gotten held up," Quentin opined.

"Or maybe they're not headed down out of the mountains."

"You think they might have stopped farther west?"

"Or south," Henry said. "Somewhere around Alamosa. They might figure they're heading either for the Black Mountains in New Mexico or over to Arizona. From there, maybe push through the Chiricahuas into Old Mexico."

"That means they'd have left the passengers that were aboard the train when they'd stolen it stranded somewhere."

Henry gave Quentin a dark look. "Or worse..."

Quentin chewed his lower lip, nodding. "They are brutal sons of bitches."

Henry rose and compressed his spyglass. "Let's ride west to the rails and follow them south up War Hoop Pass."

"All right." Quentin tried to rise but lay back down on an elbow, wincing and grunting.

"You all right?" Henry asked him.

"No worse than you, I reckon." Quentin looked at the bandage encircling the top of Henry's head. "That wound of yours is bleedin' through the bandage."

Henry nodded. "I can feel it. We'd best stop for the night soon, rest, get somethin' to eat, and tend these wounds before we bleed dry."

"Gotcha. We won't catch up to 'em dead."

They clambered down the ridge to where their horses

waited on the flat below, tied to pines, saddle cinches dangling, bits slipped so they could draw water meandering along the base of the slope and running down the mountain toward the river, murmuring musically over rocks. They tied their saddle cinches, mounted up, and followed another horse trail—probably another old Indian hunting trail used mostly by range riders these days—south to where they intersected the rails in a shallow canyon.

By now it was nearly dark but after pausing to water themselves and their horses and tightening each other's bandages, they pushed south toward War Hoop Pass. They climbed the pass until they came to the old ghost town of Devil's Jaw, so named for the formidable ridge of bald rock overlooking the old mining hamlet, the top of which was colored salmon by the last rays of the dying sun. The purple night shadows filling the canyon made bizarre spectacles of the abandoned, boarded up buildings lining both sides of the street as well as the mountain opposite Devil's Jaw Mountain, pocked with the dark specters of abandoned mines.

A cool wind moved along the street, shepherding tumbleweeds and whistling through broken windows and the gaps between buildings.

"This place always gives me the creeps," Henry said. "The marshal and I have camped here a few times when we've been after owlhoots, like you and I are now, heading south. It's the best place to camp in these parts, though. Well sheltered and there's a well providing fresh water for us and the hosses."

"I don't normally get the creeps," Quentin said, as they clomped along the street, looking for the place where Henry and Bloody Joe had camped in the past, out front of an old, long-abandoned hotel improbably named

The Queen of England. It was well sheltered with another abandoned building sitting adjacent to it, and close to the well, which had hitchracks surrounding it so Henry and Quentin wouldn't have to haul water except up from the well.

They tended the horses, tying them by the well, then set up camp out front of the tall, narrow, badly listing Queen of England, whose windows were boarded up, a single chain over the narrow front boardwalk squawking eerily in the wind. There was plenty of wood abutting the side of the hotel, so they had a good fire going against the mountain chill not long after they'd set up camp. Henry boiled beans and brewed coffee, and they ate the beans and drank the coffee, neither of which had ever tasted so good to each weary, ailing rider.

The wind continued to howl and squawk more than just the one single chain, but both men were so tired that after they'd changed their bandages and had a few sips of the bottle Henry kept in his saddlebags for medicinal purposes—he never drank anything stronger than beer and rarely even beer—they both slept the sleep of the dead. The next morning found them back following the rails south up the gradual incline of War Hoop Mountain.

Pines lined the rails, adding their winey aroma to the cool mountain air.

They were nearly to the top of the ridge and traversing a relatively flat bench in a grassy clearing which a creek cut through, when something whined through the air between the two riders, spanging off a rock just over Quentin's left shoulder. Quentin gave a startled curse as his horse pitched, throwing him off. Just after he'd struck the ground with a resolute thud and a groan, the spanging report of the rifle that had fired it cut through the cool, sunny mountain silence.

———

PAIN SEARED LIKE A BRANDING IRON THROUGH Quentin's wounded side.

He lay stunned but the stunning did nothing to quell the agony in his side.

To his right, Henry cursed as he swung down from his coyote dun's back, slapped the horse in the rear, sending it out of the line of fire, and ran over to Quentin.

"You all right?" Henry asked.

"Hell, no!"

Henry grabbed him around the waist, helped him to his feet, and the two men hotfooted it over to a large rock on the opposite side of the trail from where the shot had come. Another bullet slammed into the face of the rock just as they ducked down behind it, the report rocketing over the clearing a second later.

Sitting with his back facing the rock, holding his hand over his bloody side, Quentin said, "You suppose they've left a few men to scout their back trail, wipe out any possible posses?"

"That's what I'm thinkin'?" Henry jacked a round into his carbine's action and edged a glance around the rock to shout, "Who the hell are you and what do you want?"

"Oh, good Lord!" came a voice from an escarpment roughly fifty yards from the trail, rising in a fringe of pines and firs. "Hold your fire—we're coming out!"

Quentin glanced at Henry. "Where've I heard that voice before."

"I've heard it, too. It is blame familiar."

Quentin edged a look around his side of the rock, aiming his .45 out around it toward where two men scuttled down off the escarpment, one to each side. One was dressed in a business suit complete with gold watch chain glinting in the high-country sunshine. He wore a broad frock coat over a red vest and a black foulard tie. Quentin recognized the man's angular, still-fit build before he saw his face.

"Well, I'll be hanged," he said, glancing at Henry. "That's Norman Davis!"

He looked around the rock again. The other man appeared older—tall and lanky, dressed in sack trousers and a long denim coat, a floppy-brimmed, green hat on his gray head. The second man moved stiffly while Davis fairly ran down the slope, leaping blowdowns and sage shrubs. Both men held Winchester rifles.

Quentin kept his pistol cocked and aimed, cautiously, suspicion growing in him.

"Good Lord—I'm so sorry, fellas," Davis said as he approached the trail between him and Quentin and Henry. Breathlessly, he added, "I thought...I thought you were two of the robbers. I thought maybe they'd left two behind to clear any posse from their trail."

"Stop right there," Quentin said, rising, keeping his cocked pistol aimed at his employer as the other one came up from behind him to stand beside him. The second man was a good four inches taller than Davis's six feet. He had a hangdog look—long-faced, heavy-lidded, unshaven. He had the look of a ne'er-do-well.

"Oh, for heaven's sake," Davis said, scowling his dismay now at Quentin. "That was a mistake. Sincerely. Haven't I convinced you I'm not the man you think I am?"

Henry had walked out from behind the rock to stand beside Quentin. "You make it a habit of shooting first and askin' questions later, Mr. Davis?"

Davis threw an arm out, as though he were a victim of his own bad judgment. "What can I say? I guess I'm jumpy. It's only Shep and I. This is Shep Thompson, odd-job man. We had five others riding with us but when we started getting too far into rough country they got cold feet—afraid of an ambush. Especially given the fact those cutthroats have a Gatling gun, of all savage weapons."

"Why are you out here, Mr. Davis? I never took you for a man-tracker."

Davis laughed. "You'd be surprised what I did in my younger years—when I was fighting in the Indian Wars against Red Cloud, no less. I've ridden in posses before. With Bloody Joe and Henry here himself when they needed an extra hand or two. I don't mind strapping on the old six-shooter and loading my trusty Winchester '73." He patted the long gun of topic.

"That's true, Quentin," Henry said. "Mr. Davis has ridden with us after owlhoots more than a few times in the past. You can't always depend on the other towns-men, but you can depend on Mr. Davis."

Davis was smiling. But Quentin thought he could see that flat, dark, soulless look in the man's eyes. He might have been imagining it, but he thought he could see it—the look he'd seen in the eyes that had gazed up at him from between the barn doors back home at the Circle C Bar while the cabin burned and his sister died. Davis wasn't wearing the ring, but of course, having been suspected of being the killer who had, he wouldn't wear it conspicuously any longer.

Or was Quentin just being paranoid?

Maybe he was catching brain fever from blood loss.

"All right," he said, beginning to believe the latter was true.

"You sit down, Quentin," Henry said. "I'll fetch our horses and change that bandage of yours. You look like you could do with another swig of the forty-rod."

"You can say that again," Quentin said, sagging down against the rock.

"We might as well ride together," Davis said. "Since we're all out here. Shep and I will fetch our own mounts."

Quentin didn't say anything. The dapper Davis and the tall and silent Shep started walking back up the slope from where Davis had fired at Quentin and Henry. What an odd pair, Quentin considered, alone now with his thoughts. He wondered if Davis had any other friends. Come to think of it, he'd never seen the man with anyone but his daughter, Laura. And his oddly reclusive wife, of course. He took an afternoon beer in one of the saloons and palavered with Bloody Joe or one of the other businessmen, but those all seemed like superficial relationships. Nothing close. No one ever stopped by the store just to visit over a cup of coffee.

Being a friendless man, however, didn't necessarily make the man a killer.

But what about trying to shoot Quentin out of his saddle?

Had that really been a mistake?

Whatever the answer, Quentin was going to watch his back.

When Henry returned leading two horses, he quickly dug out a hole, lined it with rocks, and built a fire. He warmed beans, brewed coffee, hauled out his bottle, and rewrapped Quentin's wound.

"That sure looks nasty," he said, wincing and shaking his head. "I think maybe you should head back to town, Quentin."

Quentin took a liberal pull of the Who-Hit-John. "It'll hurt as bad in town as out here."

"Lying around in the boardinghouse isn't the same as riding in these mountains."

"I like to finish what I started." Quentin took another pull from the bottle as Henry drew both ends of the fresh bandage behind Quentin and tied it off tightly enough to stem the bleeding. "Besides," Quentin said, pointing with the hand holding the bottle at the two men, Davis and Shep—riding toward them from the west, Davis on a handsome steeldust, Shep on a sway-backed roan—"I got me a feelin' out here I'm gonna find out once and for all if Davis is who he says he is, or if he's a cold-blooded murderer who needs a bullet in his guts."

CHAPTER 31

NINETY MINUTES LATER THE FOUR-MAN POSSE CRESTED a ridge and Henry, riding point, stopped his coyote dun and raised his hand. "Whoa!"

Feeling better from the whiskey and the tight reban-daging, Quentin rode up beside him while Davis rode up to sit his own handsome horse off Quentin's right stirrup. Shep Thompson stopped his nag behind them and sat there sullenly, quietly, as though knowing his place. Quentin still hadn't heard the man say a single word.

Now they all sat in hushed silence, staring down the ridge at the eight-car combination sitting idle on the tracks ahead of them, shaded by the tall pines and spruces on both sides of the tracks. Quentin saw no one stirring but two men lay unmoving on the right side of the tracks, one halfway in the brush, the other just off the side of the rails.

"Good god," Henry said.

Shucking his rifle from his saddle boot, he gigged his horse slowly down off the ridge. Quentin rode along beside him, sliding his own rifle from its scabbard, cocking it, lowering the hammer, and resting the barrel across his saddle horn.

As the four riders descended the ridge—Quentin and Henry riding side by side, Davis and Shep Thompson riding side by side behind them—all of them riding quietly and with a cautious air, Quentin suddenly spied movement in the open door of the caboose at the end of the train. He and Henry were maybe twenty feet from the yellow-and-red caboose's rear vestibule when a shadowy, man-shaped figure rose from the floor. Quentin and Henry stopped abruptly and raised their rifles. A man clad in the blue wool of a conductor staggered toward the vestibule's back rail, yelling, "Butchers! Ah you filthy butchers!"

He weakly, awkwardly cocked the rifle in his hands, hardening his jaws and gritting his teeth. He wasn't wearing a cap, and a wing of gray hair hung down over his right eye. He slumped against the vestibule's rear rail, trying to aim the long gun in his hands.

Quentin held up one hand, palm out. "Hold on, Mr. Latterby. It's Quentin Ferguson!"

The freight conductor scowled over the barrel of his Winchester.

The man lifted his head a little, squinting. Quentin could see dark-red blood staining the belly of his blue wool, brass-buttoned coat.

"Who?"

"Quentin Ferguson. I saw you in town earlier today, just before the robbers struck the train." He hooked a thumb over his shoulder, indicating his employer. "I work for Mr. Davis!"

Davis rode up and around Quentin and Henry, also holding up a gloved hand, palm out in supplication. "Yes,

Latterby. It's me—Norman Davis from South-Central Colorado Fresh Meats & Dry Goods. You bring a lot of freight to me. Remember? We're not here to hurt you. We're here to help."

The man let the Winchester wilt in his hands. "Oh... oh...well, I'll be hanged. I thought it was them butchers... come back to finish me off." The freight conductor dropped to his butt and sat back against the caboose's rear wall. "Just the same, there's damn little help fer me!"

────────

HENRY SHARED A LOOK WITH QUENTIN THEN SWUNG down from Banjo's back. Quentin followed suit and the two walked over to where the conductor slumped back against the caboose's rear wall. Henry placed one foot on the vestibule bottom step and leaned forward, wincing against the thick blood and viscera issuing from the poor old-timer's belly.

"It's Henry McCallister, Mr. Latterby. What happened?"

The old man rolled his watery, pain-glazed eyes to him. "They killed everybody, is what happened. I reckon they didn't want to leave no witness or...or maybe they just enjoyed it. Killin'! The one the others called Wilkins —big fella, long, curly hair, dressed in buckskins—he stuck a Green River knife in my guts. Smiled while he was doin' it—real mean-like. I told him to finish me. I couldn't stand the pain. He shook his head no, told me to die slow, old man."

Latterby coughed. Blood bubbled out of his mouth, dribbled down his chin. He wiped at it weakly with the back of one hand and continued with: "They shot everybody. Every passenger in both cars includin' one dog and two chickens. Fun is all. They was just havin' fun. Bastards! Then they loaded the two strongboxes on two mules they had waiting with two other men in the woods. Then they all lit a shuck, leavin' me to die *slow*!"

"How many were there?" Quentin asked.

Latterby shrugged a shoulder. "Nine, ten, maybe. A few more dressed like railroad men in the express car. The two express agents was bona fide. The robbers gunned 'em down then turned the Gatling gun on the Wells Fargo men. They waited to get to Norte 'cause they wanted the guards to get distracted by all the other passengers gettin' off, climbin' on...the porters haulin' luggage an' such. There were a whole passel of Wells Fargo men both in the express car and both passenger cars. Wilkins figured he could take 'em all down easier in town then steal the train amid the confusion."

Henry asked, "Which way did they head?"

"Straight west. I heard one of 'em mention a cabin somewhere around Silverton."

Quentin reached out and placed a hand on one of Latterby's bloody ones which he was using, along with the other one, to hold his guts in. "Rest easy, old-timer. I'll stay with you." He glanced at Henry.

Latterby shook his head. "Don't stay with me. Go with the others. You're gonna need every man an' more. Kill me." He hardened his jaws, showing his teeth. "Then kill every one o' them bastards an' mention my name!"

Quentin looked at Henry, a vague beseeching in his eyes.

Henry said to the old man, "Look, Mr. Latterby, I know you're in but..."

"You do it," Latterby insisted. "You're wearin' the

badge. You're the head of this posse. You do it!" He glanced at the old Colt hanging on the deputy's thigh. "Then go find 'em an' kill as many as you can...before they kill you!"

Henry sighed. He turned to Quentin and Davis, looking on in silent shock. "Head west," Henry said. "I'll be along shortly."

Later that night, when they were all camped along the killers' trail and, judging by the tracks the killers had left, several hours behind them, Henry sat staring dully into the fire, a cup of cold coffee in his hands.

Sitting beside him, Quentin asked softly, "You want to talk about it?"

"No." Henry tossed his coffee into the fire, drew up his blankets and rolled onto his side, resting his head against his saddle. "I don't ever want to talk about it."

———

"AH, LATTERBY," SAID BLOODY JOE MANNION ROUGHLY a day later.

He sat Red's back and stared down at the dead old man, whose brains had been blown across the caboose's rear vestibule. Someone had obviously put him out of his misery. Mannion had seen enough wounds to know that the knife wound in the man's belly had been inflicted earlier than the gunshot to his head. Besides, there was a trail of dark-red blood leading out from the caboose to the vestibule. He hadn't made that crawl with his brains blown out.

Henry, most likely.

"Poor kid."

Mannion rode forward to spy more carnage through the windows of both passenger cars. Up front, in the big, black locomotive, the engineer and fireman lay dead, as well, both with bullets to the head. When he'd gotten back to town with Rio, Jane, and Vangie, he'd been told about the Gatling gun the gang had used to kill all the Wells Fargo men and to shoot up the town on their way out. That was gone. So the killers had absconded with roughly eighty thousand dollars in mine payroll money and one Gatling gun.

Mannion hoped like hell Henry, the young man calling himself Quentin Ferguson but who was really Quentin Campbell, Norm Davis—or whoever *he* in hell was, for that matter—and the taciturn odd-job man, Shep Thompson, didn't run into that gun. The gang hadn't taken it because they wanted to take target practice with it. They wanted it to clear their back trail.

Mannion cut the posse's trail, which was overlying the trail of at least a dozen other riders and likely three large pack mules—the mules' prints were larger and deeper than those of the horses—not far from the train. They were heading due west through the high, rough country along the San Juan Range's southern edge.

Mannion had rested Red overnight after he'd gotten back to town with Rio, Jane, and Vangie, but early the next morning he'd rented the fastest livery horse he could find so he could switch horses and make better time. He'd needed an extra night's rest himself, for his ticker was grieving him, but if he'd taken that extra night, he might as well have turned in his badge. Sometimes there was just no time in a lawman's life for extra rest. If he couldn't keep pushing beyond the limits of most people, he needed to retire and go live in an Odd Fellows House of Christian Charity, secretly swilling hooch in his room and playing checkers on the stoop.

He pushed hard, swallowing nitro tablets and occasionally taking modest pulls off a whiskey bottle. It did help, after all, and now was not the time to be discreet; if it killed him, it killed him. He knew he was making up for lost time because the tracks of Henry's four-man posse as well as those of the gang they were trailing got fresher by the hour. The outlaw gang was likely slowed by the heavily burdened pack mules.

He was riding the spare horse and leading Red late in the day, and he and the horses were climbing to the top of a high pass when the crab in his chest closed its claw with special vigor around his heart. Gritting his teeth and hunkered low in the saddle, Joe jerked back on the reins with one hand and reached into his shirt pocket for the nitro tablets with the other hand. Somehow, his right foot slipped out of that stirrup, and he found himself sliding down the side of his saddle. Panicked, he grabbed for the horn, but missed it. That startled the white-socked black; it reared, and Joe went tumbling down and forward, striking the ground on his left shoulder and hip. He'd managed to pull his left foot free of the stirrup, or he might have broken that leg or ankle or been dragged to kingdom come.

Damn fool way for a veteran lawman's life to end— falling from his damn hoss and getting the Dutch ride over rocks and sage until he didn't have a stitch of clothing left on his body. If that were to happen, he hoped no one would ever find him.

He'd dropped Red's reins but the bay stood where he was, eyeing his rider skeptically. Whickering nervously, the black shuffled away, deeply discomfited by its rider's odd behavior.

"Oh, you damn cayuse," Mannion said, feeling the need to lash out at anyone and anything at the predicament he found himself in, thrashing on the ground, practically helpless.

He gained his knees, crawled over to a rock, and sat back against it. He dug the small tin out of his shirt pocket and swallowed one of the tablets. He wanted a pull from the bottle, but the bottle was in a saddlebag pouch on the black's back. The black stood about fifteen feet away, eyeing him dubiously, tail arched. He looked like he might bolt so Mannion decided to stay where he was for the time being.

Hoof thuds sounded to Joe's left.

Two men were talking.

Ah, shit. Someone was coming up the other side of the pass.

A moment later they appeared—two big men in skins and furs. One wore a dirty red knit cap; the other wore a coonskin. When they saw Mannion they reined in their stout, spotted Indian ponies and stood gazing down at Mannion blandly. Their faces were so dark they could have been Mexicans or Apaches but they were white men. Mountain men. Thick-bearded, pale eyed. Their skins and furs were stained from grease of many suppers and the smoke of many fires. They were like wild animals. No, they *were* wild animals. The human kind.

Their gazes brightened when they took in the two fine horses in Mannion's company—Red and the sleek black.

The bigger of the two, as well as the younger of the two, wearing the red knit cap, turned to Mannion, studied him closely then spat a wad of chocolate-colored chaw onto a rock, leaving a good bit in his beard. "Mister, you ain't lookin' so good."

Mannion saw that each man had a Sharps Big Fifty rifle in his saddle boot, and big, old model but deadly

Colt pistols in saddle holsters. Each had two knives strapped on big belts around their waists, on the outside of their coats. Each man had an air of danger about him, the same way a grizzly did. They'd kill a man as easily as any game animal.

Especially one with two fines horses...

CHAPTER 32

JOE SAID, "I GOTTA ADMIT I BEEN BETTER. A LITTLE off my feed's all. I'll be fine in a minute."

The older of the two by a good ten years, with a liberal amount of gray in his dark-brown beard, squinted his deep-set eyes and said, "Say, ain't you Bloody Joe Mannion?"

Mannion didn't know who they were. He'd seen them in town a few times from a distance. They were conspicuous, clad as they were, like two ghosts from thirty years ago in these Rocky Mountains. They were probably market hunters for the saloons, restaurants, and grocery stores in Del Norte and elsewhere. Those Big Fifties could take down a bull griz with a single bullet. They'd blow a man in two.

Inwardly, Mannion winced at the thought.

"I been called worse," he said. "Ride on, will ya, fellas? You're makin' me uncomfortable, me not feelin' so well."

The two mountain men shared an indignant look.

The young one shoved his knit cap up a little higher on his forehead and scowled. "You ain't very polite, fer a man off his feed."

"Say," said the older man, eyeing the horses as though he'd seen them for the first time, "those sure are some mighty fine lookin' hosses."

Bloody Joe was not one to beat around the bush, or mince words.

"They are, aren't they? You want 'em?"

Now the two shared an incredulous look.

The young one spread his cinnamon beard in a broad, oily smile. "Why, sure, sure we do."

Mannion raised the big, silver-chased Russian he'd pulled out from under his wool-lined canvas coat and set down beside him when he'd heard these two human bull buffs approach. He cocked the hammer back and raised it. "Go ahead and try to take 'em, you big, ugly, smelly sons o' bitches!"

"Say now, say now," said the older man, raising his big hands shoulder-high, palms out. "You ain't friendly atall. Not atall."

"Mister," said the younger man, "you asked if we wanted your horses and we just said we did. That's all. Who wouldn't? That's some fine horseflesh there!"

Mannion gestured with the Russian. "Ride on out of here, both of you, before I shoot you for bein' ugly."

"Whoa," said the older man in exasperation "I'll tell you, LeRoy—Bloody Joe sure lives up to his reputation, I'll give him that!"

"Sure as hell does." LeRoy booted his pony forward, causing the black to sidle a little farther away in agitation. "Come on, Zeke. There must be more polite company to be found somewhere."

"Anywhere'd be better than the company here," Zeke agreed, booting his own pony forward, causing Red to whicker and sidestep, too.

Mannion depressed the Colt's hammer and holstered the piece.

"Well," he said with a grunt, placing his hands heel down on the ground to either side of him, "here we go!"

He heaved himself to his feet. He had a little trouble getting both feet set but after he did he walked slowly toward the black, who continued eyeing him warily.

"It's all right, boy. Everything's gonna be all right. I'm back on my feed." The liveryman he'd rented the gelding from had told him that if the black got skittish, to offer him some sugar. He loved sugar. So Mannion filled his coat pocket. He held some out now and that's all it took to get the curl out of the black's tail.

Mannion walked up to the horse and gave him a handful of sugar. He grabbed the reins then, just to be fair, gave Red a handful of the sweets, as well.

Then Joe offered himself a treat. Several pulls from his bottle.

That with the nitro made him feel fine.

Just fine.

He swung up into the leather like a man twenty years younger and booted the black on up and over the pass.

———

MANNION CAMPED THAT NIGHT IN A GROVE OF TREES near a quiet creek.

Joe never camped by a loud creek. A loud creek would cover the sound of ill-spirited interlopers who might want to beat a man over the head with a rock and steal his horses. He wasn't thinking only about LeRoy and Zeke. There were plenty of bad men in these mountains. In the entire frontier west, in fact. Hell, the whole world.

It was just his habit, probably one of the many reasons he'd lived long enough to likely die by a heart attack rather than a badman's bullet. Now, thinking about it as he drifted off in his bedroll, head on his saddle, hearing the horses crop grass, he wasn't sure which would be worse.

One way or another, he was going to die. Soon. He knew that for sure in his brain and it was corroborated by his heavy breathing and the ache in his chest. Annihilation. How odd. He'd been too busy chasing owlhoots in the past to give his death much consideration. But he considered it now. And truth be told—though he'd never tell it to anyone—it scared the bejesus out of him.

His past, his future, all he'd been, would have become, possible grandchildren he'd have bounced on his knee, gone for the ages.

One of the horses whickered, blew.

Instinctively, he reached for one of the big Russians in its holster around which the shell belt was coiled on the ground beside him. He sat up, rocking the hammer back.

Had Zeke and LeRoy come to get their pride back... and to take his horses?

Nah, it was only Red staring at him from the edge of the firelight.

Red stood sideways to him, looking at him, the long white streak in the shape of Florida running down his snout glowing in the dying firelight. The bay gazed at him curiously. Incredulously. Maybe concernedly. As though the horse had read his thoughts. Sensed his mood. Had plugged into his darkness. Horses could do that. People who didn't know horses would scoff at the notion. But they could do all that. And they could take on their rider's mood, as well.

"You gonna miss me, Red?" Mannion said.

Keeping his brown-eyed gaze on his rider, the big bay gave his tail a switch.

Mannion depressed the Russian's hammer, returned the piece to its holster, and lay back against his saddle. "I'm gonna miss you, too."

Stop whimpering and go to sleep, you damn fool.

He did.

———

BOOM-BA-DA-BOOM-BOOM-BOOM!!   BOOM-BA-DA-BOOM-BOOM-BOOM!!

The rocketing reports came suddenly out of the blue the next day around one o'clock in the afternoon, causing a din like the world's ending, issuing from straight ahead along the rocky canyon Mannion was following deeper into the heart of the San Juans—a land of mountain lions, grizzly bears, bighorn sheep, and the ghosts of men consumed by these climes and so long forgotten it was as though they'd never existed at all.

Red stopped suddenly, lifting his head, bunching his muscles beneath the saddle.

BOOM-BA-DA-BOOM-BOOM-BOOM!!   BOOM-BA-DA-BOOM-BOOM-BOOM!!

"Gatling gun!"

Mannion booted the reluctant Red on ahead, tugging the bridle reins of the equally reluctant black trailing behind him. They climbed the sloping canyon that was a raging river during the spring melt and along both sides of which stood tall pines, firs, and spruces, shading the deep cut all day except around noon. They rounded a bend in the canyon and Mannion reined up suddenly as four horses came galloping toward him, wide-eyed and tails curled, bridle reins bouncing along the rocks to either side of them. The lead horse, which Joe recognized as Henry's coyote dun, shook its head as though it had heard something it just couldn't believe.

Both Red and the black shied as the four horses ran past on either side of Mannion, and were gone as fast as they'd appeared, leaving only the smell of their fear sweat behind them on the wind of their passing.

Mannion had to pull back tightly on Red's reins to keep the bay from bolting, as well. When he'd got the bay as settled as he was going to get him, he released the black's reins and swung down from the saddle. He shucked his Yellowboy then dropped Red's reins, as well, and the bay wasted no time in following the black and the other horses back down the canyon, shaking his head at his own dismay at the continuing cacophony.

Mannion racked a live round in the Winchester's action and made his way up canyon, holding the rifle up high and ready, sort of crouching over it, muscles tensing at the prospect of running right into the hail of hot lead that machine was spewing. He dreaded what he'd find just ahead, maybe another fifty yards away, around another bend in the deep cut.

Four riders, including Henry McCallister blown out of their saddles and lying in bloody heaps along the canyon floor?

He rounded a leftward curve in the canyon and stopped suddenly, pulling back as two bullets hammered the bulge in the canyon wall before him, spraying rock shards along the rocks to his right. In that single second he'd peered up canyon before him, he had, indeed, seen a man lying unmoving on the canyon floor, belly down in a pool of his own blood. He'd recognized the man as the odd-job man, Shep Thompson—one of the only three posse members from town, including young Quentin

"Ferguson" and Norm Davis, being led by Mannion's junior deputy. Ferguson was hunkered behind a bulge in the canyon's right wall just up from Mannion's position while Henry was crouched behind a large, square rock to the right of where Shep Thompson lay, likely dead. Davis, hatless and looking uncustomarily disheveled and holding only a pistol, was crouching behind a bulge in the canyon's right wall a little ahead of Ferguson's position.

Henry, sitting with his back to the rock, also hatless, had, in that second Mannion had edged a look up canyon, spied his boss and had widened his eyes in recognition. He sat holding his Winchester across his thighs, wincing and dipping his chin at each blast of the Gatling gun, which now suddenly fell silent.

"Yep, they'd ridden into it, all right," Joe muttered under his breath.

A heavy silence closed down over the cut.

"Henry?" he called.

"Joinin' the dance, are ya, Marshal?"

"You all right?"

"Just took a blue whistler across my leg's all. Been bit by a dog worse. They got us pinned down good, though. Sorry—I shoulda been more careful, scouted ahead of the others, hightailed it, and regrouped when I saw the danger."

"Yes, you should have."

"Am I fired?"

"I'll let you know if we live through it."

"I got a feelin' I'll die with my badge on."

Mannion chuckled. "At least, you've kept your sense of humor."

"That's about all I got right now."

"We have to get out of this canyon. There's enough of

them they can come and shoot us like ducks on a millpond."

"Hold on!"

Bloody Joe started to say, "Wha—?" when the Gatling gun thundered once more. He pressed his back taut against the bulge in the canyon wall and then saw what had prompted the machine to start belching hot lead and cold death again. Henry whipped around the corner of the bulge and shot past Mannion like a human bullet himself, breathing hard and pressing his own back taut against the bulge to Mannion's right.

The deputy was sweating and breathing hard, and his sandy hair hung in his eyes.

"Didn't think I was gonna make it there for a second!"

The Gatling gun fell silent.

"You nearly didn't! Where is that damnable gun, anyway?"

Still raking air in and out of his lungs, young McCallister said, "I think it's in a little nook in an escarpment just ahead and on the left side of the wash, maybe fifty, sixty yards up canyon. It's up high enough that whoever's manning it has a good view of this cut. That's why he's got us pinned down so well."

"Any idea how many men are up there with it?"

Henry shook his head. "Not sure. One, two, maybe. If there were more, I think we'd have seen 'em by now. The gang must have left a man or two here with the nasty weapon to cover their back trail while the others continued to their hideout."

Mannion gritted his teeth and slammed the end of his fist against the stone wall flanking him. "I was afraid of that!"

He studied the canyon's wall to his right as he gazed back in the direction from which he'd come. He saw what he thought might be a way up the steep wall—a gravelly depression cutting back into it at a lesser angle than the rest of the wall and webbed with roots of trees from the dense forest above.

"Come on," he said.

Henry on his heels, he headed back toward what looked like a path deer and elk took to make their own way out of the canyon, for the gravel was peppered with deer and elk beans and the soft sand showing amid the gravel was scored with the prints of cloven hooves as well as the print of a large, clawed paw, likely that of a mountain lion.

With a grunt, Mannion tossed his rifle up onto the floor of the forest above. He drew a deep breath then leaped up to grab a stout root angling out from the gravelly wall and used it to pull himself up, walking up the path, boots slipping on the loose gravel. When he'd taken several steps, he grabbed another root, then another and then, with a great, last pull, heaved himself over the lip of the canyon and onto the forest floor, rolling over the Yellowboy and away from the cut, losing his hat in the process, feeling that damnable crab stubbornly squeeze his heart, as though it took umbrage to his exerting himself at all. To his living long enough to draw another breath.

"Damn you!" Mannion groused, breathing hard, grabbing his hat, reshaping it, and setting it on his head.

He sat up just as Henry emerged from the cut, making the maneuver appear much easier than Mannion had. The younger man did not roll up onto the forest floor but crawled on all fours, casting a cautious look ahead, in the direction of the Gatling gun, then turned back to his boss, eyes cast with concern.

"You all right, Marshal?"

"Damn youth, anyway!" Mannion raked out.

"What's that?"

"Nothing." Mannion drew a deep breath against the crab claw, wishing he had his bottle. "I'll make it. I'll be damned if I won't."

"You don't look so good."

"Oh, shut up!"

"Sorry."

Mannion turned to his right, staring up along the steeply sloping floor of the forest. Through the pines, firs, and spruce trees, he could make out the top of the gray rock of the escarpment sixty yards away. He couldn't see the niche the gun was in. It was probably too low down on the escarpment for him to see it from this vantage, which meant the gunner couldn't see him, either. He and Henry might be able to approach it without being seen if they could work their way around behind it.

Joe picked up his rifle, racked a round into the action, and off cocked the hammer.

"All right," he said. "One last dance, one last dance."

"What's that marshal?"

"Nothin'. Follow me!"

CHAPTER 33

CROUCHING, STAYING LOW, MANNION MADE HIS WAY along the shoulder of the slope, moving away from the canyon in which Quentin and Norm Davis were still pinned down. The escarpment lay uphill on his right, the steep slope offering only brief glimpses of the top of the stony, castle-like dike.

Henry followed about ten feet behind Mannion, both men looking around warily, not knowing how many of the outlaws the main group might have left behind. They might very well be walking into a trap. All that Mannion knew was that he had to try to take out that Gatling gun and free the two men he and Henry had left in the canyon and clear the way so he could continue after the train robbers.

He needed many more men than he had. He needed a good ten, twenty. But sometimes you just had to play the cards you were dealt. He'd gone up against tall odds before. This was nothing new. Well, maybe the odds had never been this tall, and he hadn't had a logy ticker to compound his problem. Still, he wasn't going to turn tail.

Most lawmen would go on home, try to gather a larger posse, or call in the deputy U.S. marshals.

That wasn't Bloody Joe's way.

When he and Henry had walked a good hundred yards, they turned and headed upslope. The climb made Mannion's ticker ache more severely, and his breath grew short. That was due not only to his ailing heart but to the altitude. His lungs felt half their normal size. He'd grown up in the mountains, had spent most of his life in them aside from the years he'd town tamed from Kansas to Texas; he'd never felt the altitude before. Henry followed easily and Joe knew he could more quickly climb the slope but held back out of advertence to his ailing boss.

They gained the rear of the escarpment and Joe pressed his back against the gray rock, breathing hard, loosening his red neckerchief, drawing deep drafts of the thin, cool air. Or tried to. He couldn't seem able to draw a complete, satisfying breath. He was wheezing like an old man confined to a wheelchair in that Odd Fellows House of Christian Charity he so feared. He'd rather die out here than there. If he was going to die, he'd rather die in these mountains, but only after he'd taken down the gang of killers who'd stolen the mine payroll and shot up his town with that damnable Gatling gun.

The gang of killers who'd first sent two men to kidnap his wife and daughter and hold them in a remote cabin with five men to guard them and wait for Mannion, whom they'd known would come.

Well, they hadn't gotten him, by god. He's sprung Jane and Vangie and taken down the five scum but only after Jane and Vangie had taken down two themselves. Tough women. Mannion women.

If only Joe could still be so strong, worthy of such a pair of females in his life.

"One last dance," he muttered, trying with all his might to draw a last, deep breath. "One last dance..."

"I wish you'd stop sayin' that, Marshal," Henry said, standing to his left, holding his rifle between his legs and checking the loads in his old Colt. "You still got many more fights to go."

"Do I?" Joe said, trying not to pant like a damn dog. "Here's hoping so, son..."

Holding his rifle down low in his right hand, Mannion began making his way along the side of the scarp toward the front, Henry dogging his heels. The side of the scarp was uneven and so was the crest, which dipped down in places almost even with the top of Mannion's hat. When they'd walked maybe fifty feet, Joe heard footsteps ahead of him. The smell of tobacco smoke touched his nostrils.

He stopped suddenly, glanced back at Henry.

They both stepped into a niche in the side of the scarp to their left.

Hunkered close to his deputy in the tight slot, Mannion waited. Slowly, he turned his rifle around, taking it by the barrel, holding the rear stock up like a club.

The footsteps grew louder.

The smell of the tobacco smoke grew stronger.

Another crackling footstep and then the man appeared, stepping out from behind a bulge in the escarpment wall. He held a rifle up high across his chest. A quirley drooped from the left corner of his mouth. The man's eyes snapped wide beneath the brim of his black Stetson banded with a diamondback skin and ornamented with silver conchos. He opened his mouth to call out but before any air could rake across his vocal cords, Mannion slammed his rifle's rear stock resolutely against the man's face, making his nose explode like a ripe tomato.

The man dropped his rifle and stumbled backward, bringing his gloved hands to his face.

Mannion hammered him again, harder, and he dropped.

He glared up at Mannion and again opened his mouth to call out.

Joe silenced him with two more savage blows to his head, with the Yellowboy's brass butt plate, crushing his skull. The man's hands dropped to each side of his inert body.

"That's one way to skin a cat, Marshal," Henry said under his breath.

"One way to kill a gutless killer," Mannion corrected his junior deputy.

Mannion looked up along the side of the scarp, glad to see no more men were making their way along it.

He looked down at the dead killer, wondering if he was the only one out here.

He must have suspected Mannion's ploy and left the Gatling gun to investigate.

Joe got his answer when a man's voice shouted, "Come out, come out, wherever you are! How many down there? Why don't you do like men do an' show yourselves?"

He was shouting to the men in the canyon.

Mannion glanced back at Henry, whose eyes were wide, cheeks flushed with anxiousness.

"There's two out here, at least, we know now." Joe dropped his gaze to the dead man. "Were, I mean."

"Were," Henry said, nodding.

Mannion surveyed the side of the scarp.

He and Henry were roughly a hundred feet from

where the front end overlooked the canyon in which Quentin and Norm Davis remained. Only ten feet ahead of Mannion was an alcove gouged into the rocks—a stairway of sorts littered with pine needles and gravel leading to the top of the scarp only about twenty feet above. Mannion's heart quickened. By taking that route to the crest, he and Henry might be able to flank the son of a bitch with the Gatling gun.

Mannion glanced at Henry, then at the stairway of sorts.

"You want I should go first, Marshal?" Henry asked as delicately as possible.

"Like hell!"

Joe handed Henry his rifle. Then he moved up into the notch and began climbing, using his hands as well as his feet, pushing off the wall to either side of him. It was not a steep climb, and Joe made good time, following the slight leftward curve then placing one foot on a rock that appeared before him, then another, and lunging up and forward.

He'd gained the very uneven crest of the scarp!

He glanced back the way he'd come. Henry was already halfway up, just rounding the curve. The deputy paused, tossed Mannion his rifle, and then continued, using one hand and his feet, sort of balancing himself with his rifle. He gained the crest grinning, looking as fresh as a daisy, gallblast him!

"Stop smiling," Joe groused, turning toward the front of the scarp, which he could not see because there was a jumble of large, pale rock between him and the niche in which the Gatling gun resided.

"Come on, you hoopleheads!" the SOB manning the machine gun shouted into the canyon away from Mannion, his voice echoing around the scarp. "Fish or cut bait. Show yourselves or ride on home with your legs between your legs. You know what I think? I think you're all—however many you are—are just a bunch of little *girls*!"

He cackled a wicked laugh.

Mannion took his Winchester in both gloved hands and looked at Henry, the bandage around the top of the younger man's head spotted with blood where he'd taken a graze when the outlaws had struck the train in town. "Time to show that scurvy dog who gets the last laugh. Then we'd best change that bandage of yours."

"Oh, don't worry about me. I'm so riled up by that dang fool I don't feel nothin' but the mad I got on!"

"Sounds like you're ready to dance. Good."

"Oh, I'm ready," Henry said, following his boss toward the rocks. "I'm more than ready, Marshal!"

Mannion threaded his way through the rocks, crossed a fat place littered with pinecones and needles where pine boughs overhung the scarp, then made his way through yet another field of rocks. He came to the front of the scarp opening before him and there, at long last, was the man with the Gatling gun, the back of his black leather jacket facing Mannion.

He was crouched over the savage, brass-canistered weapon before him.

Smoke wafted around his head topped with a funnel-brimmed cream hat. A stag-butted Colt was holstered on his right hip. A pair of saddlebags and an uncorked brown bottle lay on the ground to his right. He was positioned at the very lip of the scarp, the canyon yawning before him.

Mannion stepped forward slowly, holding his Yellowboy straight out from his right hip. Henry followed close behind.

Joe was so intent on the back of the killer before him he didn't see the pinecone until his right foot came down on it, making a dry crackling sound as he crushed it.

The killer swung around in a blur of fast motion.

Suddenly, that stag-butted .45 was in his hand, and was crouched over it, ratcheting the hammer back.

He'd moved faster than Mannion had seen any man move before, until Joe found himself staring into that .45's large, round, black maw.

Suddenly, Joe was in that damned death dream again, pounding at the coffin's nailed down lid.

His sharp-faced, narrowed adversary pulled the .45's trigger.

Joe steeled himself for the bullet.

None came. There was only a weak *pshttt* sound and a muted flash around the firing pin.

The sharp-faced outlaw stared down at the .45 in shock. The fancy gun had betrayed him.

Misfire!

Mannion's and Henry's rifles thundered at the same time, both men firing once, twice, three times, blowing the sharp-faced killer back over the Gatling gun and over the edge of the scarp to the ground below. There was a crunching, resolute thud as he landed out of sight.

Mannion turned to Henry, peering through their own wafting powder smoke, his logy ticker drumming a war rhythm against his breastbone.

"Whew!" the young deputy said, running his arm across his forehead. "That was close."

"Way closer than it needed to be," Mannion said.

Looking around for more possible cutthroats, spying none, he walked around the big, steel and brass mosquito of the deadly Gatling gun and peered over the edge of the scarp. The killer lay in a twisted heap, his .45 lying near his hat. He seemed to be staring at one arm bent before him.

Mannion shouldered his rifle and gazed into the draw yawning before him. "All clear, fellas," he shouted to Quentin and Norman Davis. "Fetch the horses!"

"As for me," he said to himself, turning and picking up the bottle the outlaw had been good enough to leave him. "I'm gonna have a drink."

He sat down against a rock and did just that.

———

QUENTIN WAS RELIEVED TO HEAR THE MARSHAL'S voice.

He'd been sitting tight in the canyon, having only his .45 since he'd had no time to grab his Winchester when that Gatling gun had begun spitting lead at him and the others, punching Shep Thompson out of his saddle first. Quentin's pitching horse had thrown Quentin just as the frightened horses of Henry McCallister and Mr. Davis had unseated them before they could grab their rifles. Like greased lighting, all three horses had wheeled and galloped back down the canyon, bullets tearing up gravel and sand to both sides of their scissoring hooves.

In the aftermath of that unseating, Davis had been sitting tight as well, just ahead of Quentin and on the canyon's opposite side.

Now, as Mannion's voice still echoed, Davis turned to Quentin. He had his own Colt in his hand. Quentin held his hogleg down low against his right leg. Davis was aiming his own sort of negligently at Quentin, from close to his right side. Quentin looked at the cocked piece.

Was the man intending to aim his gun at Quentin, or,

after the shock of their miserable situation, was he not fully conscious of the piece in his hand?

Quentin raised his gaze to the store owner's eyes.

They had a dark, flat, ominous cast.

Quentin flashed back to the eyes of the Union-sympathizing gang leader staring up at him from between those two open barn doors.

Were they the same eyes as those of the man pointing his gun at him now?

Quentin's heart picked up its beat.

Was Davis going to shoot him?

Then the shop owner's eyes seemed to clarify, widening slightly. Davis looked down at the gun in his hand, depressed the hammer, and holstered the piece. "Uh...sorry. 'Fraid my nerves are a little jangled." Chuckling dryly, he started walking down canyon toward Quentin. "Best fetch those horses."

He passed Quentin's position. Quentin turned to watch him tramp off down canyon.

Are you him, you son of a bitch? He wanted so desperately to know. *Are you the man who led those killers against my family?*

CHAPTER 34

Big Fritz Fitzpatrick, proprietor and sole barman of the Rocky Bend Road Ranch sitting in a broad horseshoe bend of the San Juan River, ten thousand feet above sea level in the southern San Juans, leaned forward against the pine planks laid across three stout beer barrels composing his makeshift bar, and silently fumed until his heavy jowls turned crimson.

The infamous Ray Racine Gang was stomping with their tails up, drinking beer and whiskey, guffawing till the rafters shook, dancing with Fitzpatrick's girls while drunkenly playing the piano as well as doing various other things with his girls in the back rooms of the long, low log cabin. Fitzpatrick flinched every time he heard the crack of a hand on flesh and heard the girls scream back there behind the blanket-curtain doorways.

Racine's bunch was notoriously hard on Fitzpatrick's girls.

Now, Fitzpatrick wouldn't have minded the abuse his girls took; after all, women of the line had to expect a certain amount of mistreatment. He wouldn't have minded all the whiskey- and beer-swilling and the dancing and tooth-gnashingly bad piano playing and singing nor even the breaking of his chairs and tables during the general foofaraw as long as Racine paid up before he and the rest of his gang lit a shuck—usually for Mexico where they'd let their heels cool until their next big job north of the border.

But Ray Racine and his first lieutenant, the bearlike Bull Price, were notorious, at least here at the Rocky Bend Road Ranch, for not paying their bills before they left.

What's more, they drove out Fitzpatrick's paying clientele—namely, the miners from the Santiago and Fancy Lady Mines farther up the mountain, as well as the prospectors and mountain men who've called this neck of the San Juans home, even through the long mountain winters, for the past twenty, thirty years, as Fitzpatrick had himself. When the Racine Gang had ridden up to the road ranch just before sunset two hours ago, Fitzpatrick had been doing a lucrative business, for his regulars— miners, nearly twenty of them—had been here enjoying his beer, whiskey, and carne asada, as well as his girls. Nary a single scream had issued from the back rooms. A freight team had pulled in, as well, adding another six big, bearded, hungry mule skinners to the fray.

As soon as Racine and his men had filed through the batwings, however, every man jack of Fitzpatrick's paying crowd had skedaddled like church mice when the preacher lit the candles early on Christmas morning. Then it was only Racine and his uncouth horde taking over the place, demanding food and whiskey and Fitz- patrick's six girls. And what really got Fitzpatrick's goat was that these men could obviously afford to pay.

Two big, iron-banded strongboxes lay open on two tables, and each box was overflowing with nearly minted gold coins. Fitzpatrick didn't know how much money was in those boxes, but there had to be close to fifty, sixty thousand dollars there! Fitzpatrick had been eyeing that loot, glistening in the lantern light, and fairly drooling into his gray-brown bib beard.

Fitzpatrick's only satisfaction lay in the fact that Racine must have lost quite a few men during his last job. Usually there was a good twenty of the rabble-rousers. Now there was maybe thirteen, fourteen at the most. Yessir, Ray Racine must have taken the tiger by the tail during his recent holdup. Judging by what bits and pieces Fitzpatrick had been able to follow amid the celebratory din, they'd struck a train. One carrying mine payroll money. A lot of it.

Racine was just now hooking his arm around the big bull neck of the shaggy-headed Bull Price and yelling, "We done did it this time, Bull, you big ugly bear! Robbed the train right smack in downtown Del Norte, Bloody Joe Mannion's town no less! Now, that's a fact ol' Bloody Joe's gonna have to take to the grave kickin' an' screamin'!"

The two outlaws had a good, long laugh at that, clinking whiskey bottles together in salute and taking several long pulls.

"I wonder how Mannion's women made out!" yelled one of the other drunk outlaws, who was dancing, if you could call it dancing, with one of the half-naked girls near the banging piano.

"Not well—I guarantee you that," intoned Racine, then frowning suddenly. "I just wonder why those fellas who took 'em ain't caught up to us yet..."

His reverie was stopped short by a girl's particularly loud scream.

Then the girl came flying through the blanket curtain

of one of the back rooms, clad in only pantaloons. A pretty, heart-shaped brunette, she landed belly down on a table at which three of Racine's men were playing stud poker, her bare, pink bottom exposed. One of the card players, a thick stogie protruding from his mustached mouth, took the opportunity to swat the girl's irresistible bottom with his bare hand.

The sharp *crack!* sounded like a pistol shout vaulting above the din.

The girl lifted her head and screamed, squeezing her eyes shut against the misery.

A half-naked man pushed through the same blanket door the girl had flown through, staggering drunkenly, a bottle in his hand, long hair dancing in his eyes as he said, "Boss, this here little tart called us nothin' more than a pack of wild, unwashed coyotes who don't pay their bills!"

Racine turned to the man and the girl writhing on the table, unable to rise because two of the card players held her down, on her back now, bare breasts exposed.

"Unwashed?" Racine said with mock indignance. He lifted his arm and sniffed a pit. "Why, I had a bath over Christmas!"

The rest of the room erupted in laughter.

Then the room fell silent as Racine, a wolfish glow in his dung-brown eyes, walked slowly over to where the half-naked girl lay writhing on the table, held down by two of the poker players. The gang leader—tall and slender with long, sandy hair falling down his back and clad in a tan duster and battered bowler hat with a hawk feather protruding from the silk band—stopped at the table and glared down at the girl. He had three long scars running down from just below his right eye to his thin-bearded jawline, compliments of a puta in Old Mexico who didn't cotton to his rough "lovin'" and had ended up with her throat cut and tossed in a shallow ravine outside Durango.

Fear shone brightly in this girl's gray-blue eyes.

"No," she said. "Please...I'm sorry. He made me drink whiskey, and I..."

"Can't hold your whiskey?" Racine asked.

"Yes. Please..."

"Well, maybe you better learn, sweetheart."

Racine swept his nearly empty beer bottle down against the edge of the table, shattering it, sending whiskey and glass spraying in all directions, including into the whore's eyes, burning them. She moaned, blinked, writhed.

"I'm gonna show you what happens to doxies who can't hold their tongue...can't show a little respect..."

The rapacious Racine lowered the jagged edge of the broken bottle in his hands to the girl's neck.

"No!" she screamed. "Please, don't cut me, Racine!"

Racine laughed with vicious joy then, gritting his teeth and hardening his jaws, pressed the broken edge of the glass against the girl's tender flesh. He was about to sweep it sideways, cutting her throat, when a man outside called, "Boss! You best come see this!"

Annoyed by the interruption, Racine turned to the batwings, scowling. "What the hell is it?"

"Best come out here, boss!"

"Oh, fer chrissakes!" Racine threw the broken bottle in his hand against the wall then glanced at his lieutenant, Bull Price, and jerked his chin toward the batwings.

With the hulking Price following, Racine strode a little unsteadily across the room and out the doors. The others in the room all looked at each other then, in various states of dishevelment and undress, followed the gang leaders outside under a sky aglitter with starlight. Two horses stood before the road ranch cabin, hang-headed, starlight glistening in their eyes.

"What the hell...?" Racine said.

The man who'd been on watch stood near the two horses, a rifle held in his crossed arms. He looked at the two leaders standing side by side before the rest of the gang forming a half circle around them. Two men, obviously dead, had been slung across the backs of the two horses, legs and booted feet sticking stiffly out to one side.

"It's Buck Jones and Hal McCaffrey," the man on watch said fatefully.

Racine stepped forward, scowling incredulously. "We left them with the Gatling—"

He stopped abruptly when there was a loud scraping sound and an equally loud squawk of rusty hinges. Racine turned in dread to see the two loft doors in the log barn on the opposite side of the yard swing open, revealing the glistening brass canister mounted on its tripod, the savage maw of the machine gun swinging toward him.

Racine could see a man's silhouette looming over the deadly weapon from behind it.

"It's Bloody Joe, you sons o' bitches, an' I'm here to turn you all toe down with a cold shovel and take your loot back to Del Norte! YeeeeHAWWWWW!"

The wild coyote-like yell was followed by the thunder of the Gatling gun as none other than Bloody Joe himself began turning the crank. The machine gun's round maw spat smoke and stabbed orange flames as the hot lead tore into the gang leader first and then into his lieu-tenant. They yipped like gutshot dogs and then did a bizarre two-step together as more bullets tore into them and then into the rest of the gang that had just started to spread out and flee, some running back toward the batwings only to be cut down midstride.

The horses hauling the two dead men whinnied and fled, buck kicking their dismay at the cacophony.

As the Gatling gun kept up its savage RAT-A-TAT-TAT-TAT!!, three men wielding rifles surfaced from the barn, dropped to knees, and began cocking and firing, cocking and firing, making sure none of the gang managed to flee the hot-lead storm that had been fated to them ever since they'd kidnapped Bloody Joe's wife and daughter and struck the train on the main street of his town.

Several of the dying gang managed to return fire on their executioners but their shots flew wide as more bullets cut into them and sent them screaming into the void of certain death.

On one knee in front of the barn, Quentin finished off one man who'd been trying to crawl behind a stock trough then held his fire. All the killers were down and dying, wailing, or already dead.

All the killers except one, however.

To Quentin's right, he saw the flash of starlight on steel as Norman Davis, having apparently decided to take advantage of the chaos of the lead storm, swung his rifle toward Quentin. Quentin saw the man grit his teeth in the darkness. In the starlight, he saw the flat darkness of the man's gaze beneath his bowler hat, felt the curl of the man's bullet just off his left ear as Quentin drove to his right, rolled, brought up his own rifle, and shot Davis twice in the chest.

Davis grunted and stumbled backward.

He dropped his rifle, tripped over his feet, and fell to his butt.

Hatless, he sat staring, round-eyed and hang jawed.

Quentin gained his feet and walked over to the man.

"It *was* you," Quentin said, rage a wildfire blazing inside him.

Stiffly, Davis nodded.

Woodenly, he said, "Another time, another place. I was a different man...my land taken over by ex-Confederates when I couldn't pay my taxes..."

"You're the same man, Captain Dalton. You just tried to kill me."

"You would have killed me."

"I had reason." In his mind, seeing the killer pull Danny's head up by her hair and cut her throat, Quentin levered another round into his Winchester's breech and shot the cold-blooded Yankee killer through the dead center of his forehead.

Dalton slammed back down against the ground, writhed for nearly a minute, and then lay still.

Quentin turned to see Henry McCallister standing beside him.

Quentin lowered his smoking Winchester. "I...he..."

Henry nodded. "I saw."

"We finished here?"

Henry turned to see the marshal step out from between the barn doors. He moved slowly, woodenly, nearly dragging his boot toes.

"I reckon, Marshal. The killers are all dead. Includin' Mr. Davis...er, Captain Dalton."

Mannion nodded.

"Been a long day," he said.

He stood staring at the dead men heaped in front of the roadhouse.

Already, Fitzpatrick and his girls were going through the bodies, stripping them of valuables. Fitzpatrick himself was just then pulling off the gang leader's boots.

Mannion chuckled. "Well, don't that beat a hen a-flyin'."

He chuckled again then staggered over to sit down against the barn wall, to the left of the doors.

Henry stood before him. "How you doin'?"

"I been better."

"We'll spend the night here. Let you get a good night's sleep, Marshal. Then we'll head back to Del Norte first thing in the mornin'."

Slowly, Bloody Joe Mannion wagged his head. "I don't reckon."

Henry dropped to a knee before him. "You don't reckon what?"

"I'll be ridin' back to Del Norte." Mannion smiled. "Leastways, not upright."

"Don't talk foolishness, Marshal."

Mannion winced and lifted his head till the cords stood out in his neck.

He heaved a long, ragged, sigh. "Oh, Christ, son...I come to the end of the trail."

"Don't say that."

Mannion pressed his thumb to his chest. "My ticker... plum wore out."

"We'll get you to Dr. Ellison. He'll fix you up."

"I love you, Henry."

"What?" Rage burned through the deputy. "Don't tell me that!"

Mannion chuckled.

Henry stared down at him, feeling as helpless as he'd ever felt in his life. He leaned forward, grabbed the marshal by his shirt collar and pulled his head up close to his. "Don't you say that. Don't you even think it. You got two women waiting for you back in Del Norte. You got

Rio. You got me! You're gonna make it, you understand me, Bloody Joe?"

Mannion looked at him, a wry, sad cast to his gaze.

"Joe!" Henry yelled. "Joe, you listen to me for a change!"

Tears oozed from the deputy's eyes, dribbled down his cheeks.

Fumblingly, Mannion removed the badge from his shirt. He pinned it to Henry's.

"Rio won't want it. You deserve it."

"Goddamnit, Marshal Mannion. I don't want it! You're the marshal of Del Norte!"

"Oh, I had a good run, I admit." Mannion gave a crooked, wolfish smile. "Now, it's your turn."

Henry released the lawman's shirt collar. "Please," he sobbed. *"Please!"*

"Son, you tell those two women down there...well, you know what to tell 'em. Hell, they already know. Life never woulda been the same without 'em. *I* never woulda been worth a damn without 'em. But now...I gotta go. They'll understand."

"Please!"

Bloody Joe Mannion jerked with a pain spasm. A last breath ratted in his throat. He gave one final ironic chuckle then slid sideways down against the barn wall to the ground and lay unmoving, wolfish gray eyes staring at the ground that would soon accept him at long last and forevermore.

Marshal Henry McCallister threw his head back and gave one last, bellowing plea to the stars guttering indifferently above him then turned back to Mannion, sobbing. "You always were the most contrary son of a bitch I ever knew!"

RIDE THE ROUGH, LAWLESS TRAILS OF THE WESTERN FRONTIER!

Deputy U.S. Marshal Gideon Hawk is respected throughout the Territory as a lawman of principle—until Three Fingers Ned Meade throws him a curve.

When Meade kills Hawk's ten-year-old boy, the grisly act drives Hawk's grief-stricken wife to hang herself. Now, robbed of kin, he sets out on a brutal quest to find the man responsible—no matter the cost.

Saddle up and read along as one lawman goes rogue and ventures into the heart of vengeance across the unforgiving landscapes of the Western frontier.

AVAILABLE NOW

Peter Brandvold grew up in the great state of North Dakota in the 1960's and '70s, when television westerns were as popular as shows about hoarders and shark tanks are now, and western paperbacks were as popular as *Game of Thrones*.

Brandvold watched every western series on television at the time. He grew up riding horses and herding cows on the farms of his grandfather and many friends who owned livestock.

Brandvold's imagination has always lived and will always live in the West. He is the author of over a hundred lightning-fast action westerns under his own name and his pen name, Frank Leslie.

Made in United States
North Haven, CT
24 March 2024

50425362R00195